ACCIDENT OR MURDER?

"We've got a major pro[...] [...]anda gestured toward the prone bod[...] [...]ick pumpkin vines.

Nick Thor[...] [...]w sagged. "Oh, damn!"

"I'm sure N[...] [...]nts," Amanda said grimly.

Thorn put on hi[...] [...]op face and squatted down on his haunches to check for a pulse. "Damn."

"I believe you already covered that, Thorn."

Thorn ignored his wife's sarcasm and critically surveyed the scene. "From the look of things Nettie's breathing apparatus hose got wrapped around her cane, and the leafy vines entangled her ankle. The oxygen hose came loose from her nose and she couldn't breathe. She suffocated herself."

"That's how it looks. But I don't think that's the way it actually happened." Amanda braced herself for Thorn's anticipated reaction.

Thorn's thick black brows flattened over his narrowed gaze. "Hazard," he said warningly, "this is no time for one of your crazed investigations. You're nine months pregnant!"

Amanda tilted her face to a challenging angle. "Wrong time or not, I believe Nettie had help getting to that Great Pumpkin Patch in the Sky."

Amanda could tell by Thorn's stance that he was summoning patience, so as not to upset her in her "fragile condition."

"Okay, Haz," he said too calmly. "What makes you think someone gave Nettie the deep six?"

Amanda's lips curled at his patronizing tone. "Nettie is wearing house shoes, not her Nikes!"

Thorn muttered something obscene. Amanda didn't ask him to repeat it. "You're crying murder based on a pair of house slippers?" he asked incredulously. "You have no evidence, no probable motive."

Thorn was nothing if not predictable. "I will have motive and evidence when I conclude this investigation," she assured him. "Just you wait and see!"

Published by Kensington Books

DEAD
IN THE
PUMPKIN
PATCH

An Amanda Hazard Mystery

Connie Feddersen

KENSINGTON BOOKS
Kensington Publishing Corp.

http://www.kensingtonbooks.com

KENSINGTON BOOKS are published by

Kensington Publishing Corp.
850 Third Avenue
New York, NY 10022

First Kensington Printing: October, 2000
10 9 8 7 6 5 4 3 2 1

Printed in the United States of America

DEAD IN THE MELON PATCH

"The characters are genuine small-town folk, with the talk, attitude, and dress of rural living. The description is vivid, and the humor priceless. DEAD IN THE MELON PATCH grabbed me from the first page and didn't let go until the last word. Wonderful!" —*Rendezvous*

DEAD IN THE DIRT

"A disastrous trip to Velma's salon and a surprise for Amanda at the end of the story are only two of the highlights of this fun, pleasant read. Fans of the series will be delighted with the depth of plot."

—*Romantic Times*

DEAD IN THE MUD

"DEAD IN THE MUD is a sparkling story that is bound to tickle your fancy. Ms. Feddersen mixes a nice blend of humor and drama here, coming up with a most compelling story." —*Romantic Times*

DEAD IN THE DRIVER'S SEAT

"If you like witty, humorous mysteries, you'll love DEAD IN THE DRIVER'S SEAT."—*Romantic Times*

DEAD IN THE HAY

"Connie Feddersen, aka Carol Finch, has given us a most delectable treat in DEAD IN THE HAY. Best of all, catching up with Nick and Amanda is like visiting with old, beloved friends." —*Romantic Times*

This book is dedicated to my husband, Ed, and our children—Christie, Jill, Kurt, Jeff, and Jon—with much love. And to our grandchildren, Brooklynn, Kennedy, and Blake. Hugs and kisses!

ONE

"You'd better get your act together, because you're running out of time," Amanda Hazard-Thorn, CPA, said to her reflection in the rearview mirror.

With the baby's due date only a couple of weeks away, Amanda knew she had to get things squared away at her accounting office, decorate for the annual Festival of the Pumpkin in Vamoose, Oklahoma, and participate in the upcoming community activities.

Mentally clicking off the list of errands she had to run, Amanda drove down Main Street, waving to friendly motorists who passed by. It was a crispy, hazy October morning. The temperature was in the mid-fifties and a stiff north wind provided a wake-up call for slow risers—which Amanda wasn't, until prospective motherhood made it difficult for her to drag herself out of bed.

Amanda glanced down at her tummy as she cruised past Thatcher's Oil and Gas Station. She looked as if she had swallowed a pumpkin, and these days she couldn't find a comfortable position for sitting, sleeping, or standing.

That adage about pregnant women positively glowing was a crock of malarkey, Amanda mused as she reassessed her appearance in the rearview mirror. She had enough bags under her eyes to pack for a two-week vacation. Her hair had turned completely unmanageable. Her face was so puffy she looked like Miss Piggy!

Amanda hung a left and turned her shiny new fire-engine-red extended-cab Chevy four-by-four truck into her office parking lot. Clamping a puffy hand on the steering wheel to steady herself, she slid off the seat and landed on her feet with all the grace of a hippopotamus.

Grabbing her briefcase, Amanda waddled—yes, damn it! waddled like a duck—past the square hay bales stacked on either side of the office door. Her hubby, chief of the Vamoose police and part-time rancher Nick Thorn, had delivered the bales the previous evening. Amanda reminded herself to purchase pumpkins to decorate for the festivities.

"Hi, boss," Jenny Long-Zinkerman greeted as Amanda galumphed toward her desk. "You're looking exceptionally radiant this morning."

Amanda's reply was a grouchy snort.

"Well, you are," Jenny contended.

"I look like an elephant in this gray preggo dress," Amanda groused. "And how an elephant can survive a gestation period of two years is totally beyond me. God must really have it in for female elephants. Nine months is driving me batty. I would never make it for two years without going stark, raving mad. . . . Oh, hell, I'll be back in a minute."

Jenny giggled when Amanda lumbered heavily toward the rest room. Amanda spent more time bowing to, and sitting on, the porcelain throne than she cared to—another inconvenience of her expanded condition.

When Amanda returned to the main office, Jenny—who looked annoyingly attractive in her crisp hunter green business suit, with her hourglass figure and *un*swollen face—was still grinning.

"Oh, shut up!" Amanda snapped crankily.

"Did I say anything?" Jenny asked innocently.

"You don't have to say anything," Amanda muttered as she levered her barrel-shaped body into her chair. "I can read your mind. You're silently poking fun at me because I look like the Goodyear blimp."

"I have been there and done that, boss. Believe me, I know what you're going through," Jenny commiserated. "How is Nicky holding up? Is he still giving you grief because of his overprotectiveness?"

Amanda blew her flyaway bangs from her eyes. "He hovers over me like a mother hen. He constantly tries to tell me what I should do and shouldn't do in my 'fragile condition.' "

"He's suffering from Expectant Father Syndrome," Jenny said, then chuckled.

"You certainly have that right." Amanda snorted. "He has read every prenatal-care pamphlet and child-rearing manual he can get his hands on, and he spouts his newly acquired knowledge at me nightly. He has bought out the nation's supply of ice cream and pickles, and there is no room in the fridge or freezer for the basic food groups."

Jenny shook her head. "I still can't believe the chief has gone so far overboard."

Neither could Amanda. Mr. Tough and Capable had turned into an absolute putz, a sentimental sap. Who would have thought it?

Amanda couldn't wait until Thorn was able to turn all his gushing concern on his offspring and give her a break. Her strong, independent nature was crying out for relief.

"Is Nicky still adamant about not wanting to know the baby's sex until the time of delivery?" Jenny questioned.

Amanda nodded her scraggly blond head. "He insists that he wants it to be a surprise. I, of course, don't like surprises. Never have, never will."

Jenny leaned forward. "So tell me, boss. Will it be a boy or a girl? I promise I won't tell another living soul. Cross my heart, swear on a stack of Bibles."

"I know you won't, but Thorn made me swear not to tell anyone, so don't try to twist my arm and make me break my solemn vow of silence. Thorn wants this to be a surprise for everyone in Vamoose."

Jenny slumped, disappointed. "Well, fine. Don't give me the advantage in the baby pool—"

"Baby pool? What baby pool?" Amanda cut in.

Jenny grinned. "The one at Thatcher's Gas and Oil. Everybody in town has selected the arrival date and sex of your bundle of joy."

Amanda groaned. Thorn and the whole damn town had turned this event into a circus.

Turning her attention to business, she levered herself upright in her chair. "Since I'm going to be away from the office for a few weeks, I want to be sure everything is in proper working order. With all these new clients—"

"It's your own fault," Jenny inserted. "You've gained so much notoriety from solving murder cases that everybody wants you as an accountant. Must be nice to be a household name, boss. I'm sure Nicky is holding his breath, hoping another case doesn't spring up before your delivery date."

"You've got that right," Amanda admitted, squirming uncomfortably when kicked from inside out. "Thorn cringes at the prospect of my opening an unofficial investigation before D day. Preparing for the October festival will be enough to deal with. . . . Which reminds me, I have the orange decorative lights in my truck. Would you mind getting them for me? The office has to be completely decorated before the judges can pick this year's winners. The decoration deadline is staring us in the face."

Jenny bounded up and headed for the door. Amanda sighed enviously. She couldn't remember the last time she had vaulted quickly, gracefully, from a chair. If she grew much larger she would have to hire a crane to hoist her to her feet.

Jenny whizzed through the door, her arms laden with boxes of miniature orange lights. "Don't worry about putting these up, boss. I'll have my husband and son help me string these around the office after work tonight."

"I can't let you—"

"Nonsense. You know I'm glad to help out," Jenny broke in. "If not for you I wouldn't have this new lease on life, this new career opportunity. I've gained all sorts of respectability by association. I can't thank you enough for that. I love this job!"

Amanda wished she shared Jen's enthusiasm, but carrying extra weight was draining her energy and exuberance.

"This office will place in the Halloween decoration contest," Jenny said confidently. "Dave volunteered to set up the floodlights and design the scarecrow. Once we have pumpkins placed on the hay bales we'll be in business."

"I'd better call Nettie Jarvis about purchasing the pumpkins," Amanda said, mentally calculating how to fit the trip into her busy schedule.

"No one grows pumpkins bigger or better than Nettie. I honestly don't know how she does it, considering her health problems. Yet she has won the Biggest Pumpkin contest five years running."

Amanda didn't know Nettie's secret, but the spinster, despite her declining health, was indeed the pumpkin queen of Vamoose County. Some folks said "Nutty" Nettie talked to her pumpkins. Amanda believed the old woman simply had the gift of a green thumb. Indoor and outdoor vegetation flourished on Nettie's farm. Ferns, philodendrons, azaleas—you name it and it grew profusely for Nettie.

"Dave and Timmy and I went out last night to pick up some pumpkins so I can bake pies and breads for the bazaar,'' Jenny said as her perfectly manicured nails clicked against the computer keyboard. ''Nettie was staggering around in her Nike tennis shoes—which my son Timmy thought was so cool. He loves that brand of shoes.

''Nettie was pointing her cane at the best baking varieties in her pumpkin patch. She was huffing and puffing a lot, but she enjoys being outside. If not for her portable breathing apparatus I don't think she would have enough breath to walk from her house to the garden. Then when her asthma and allergies kick in, she has to stop and rest about every twenty steps.''

Amanda was well aware of Nettie's health problems. The woman complained constantly about the inconveniences that slowed her down. Amanda could relate to that. Pregnancy made her cranky at times.

''Oh, before I forget,'' Jenny said, plucking up three phone messages. ''Gertrude Thatcher and Cleatus Watts called and asked if you could stop by at your earliest possible convenience. Gertie is having fits over the state's new tax forms for gasoline. Cleatus and Cecil Watts can't figure out where they screwed up on the monthly accounts at the mechanic shop. I told them I would be happy to help, but they insist that you are more familiar with their accounting systems.''

''They're just dragging their feet,'' Amanda declared when Jenny's smile faded. ''When I am out of commission for a few weeks, they'll have to rely on you to solve their financial problems. Then they will realize how efficient and knowledgeable you are.''

Jenny squared her shoulders and sat up a little straighter in her chair. ''I'm up for the job, boss.''

''I know you are,'' Amanda said with perfect confidence.

''All these night classes at the vo-tech are really helping me get a firm handle on the ins and outs of the accounting profession.''

"I am well aware of that and I have never doubted you."

"Thanks, boss." Jenny beamed at her. "Your approval means a lot to me."

"Now that we have that settled and out of the way, I'd better call Nettie before I get sidetracked with other duties."

Amanda picked up the phone, looked up Nettie's number, then dialed. The phone rang six times before the spinster answered.

"Huh-lo . . ." Nettie panted.

"Nettie? This is Amanda Hazard-Thorn—"

"You must have ESP, girl." *Gasp, pant.* "I was getting ready to call you."

Amanda decided to state the reason for her call, so she could give the old woman time to catch her breath. "I was wondering if I could purchase some of your prizewinning pumpkins to decorate my office and the Halloween haunted house."

"Take as many as you want," Nettie said in a wheezy voice. "In fact, you can have all you can haul off if we can trade favors."

Amanda frowned curiously, then grimaced when she received another unexpected kick in the rib. Damn, she felt like a punching bag. "Favors?" she repeated.

"I need some financial consultation," Nettie rasped. "And I have something I want you to take for safekeeping. Something that certain folks around here would love to get their itchy fingers on, but I won't let them. *You,* I can trust."

"What is it?"

"A ticking time bomb, that's what," Nettie muttered in annoyance. "Try as they might, no one is going to get their hands on my little black book. You'll know how to handle the situation, and you can advise me on what I should do."

"Exactly what is in this little black book, Nettie?"

Amanda frowned at the desperate, staccato tone of the woman's voice. Something had definitely upset Nettie.

"We can't discuss something like this over the phone," Nettie muttered. "You need to get out here, now. I've got some arrangements to make, and I need you to tell me how to handle this situation. Something isn't right."

Situation? What situation? "Nettie, are you feeling all right?"

"Hell no, girl. I'm seventy-three years old, going on ninety. My equilibrium went out of whack about the time President Johnson left office. This confounded asthma is ruining my disposition. It's high time I made a move, and I'm damn sick and tired of everybody pussyfooting around!"

Amanda yanked the phone from her ear when Nettie's voice hit an ear-cracking pitch. "Who is everybody, Nettie?"

"Just hightail it out to my farm, girl. I'll meet you down at the pumpkin patch. I am counting on you to help me, because no one else will be honest and fair."

"I have a couple of—"

The phone went dead.

"Something wrong, boss?" Jenny asked as she watched Amanda stare pensively at the phone.

"Nettie is in a tizzy." Amanda replaced the receiver. "She demands immediate financial advice, but she refuses to discuss it on the phone. I wonder if she has become paranoid in her old age."

"Now that you mention it, Nettie seemed a little annoyed and impatient last night. She kept tapping her cane in the dirt, and she seemed distracted while I was talking to her. I had to repeat myself a few times."

The phone jingled and Jenny answered it quickly. "Hazard Accounting," she said in her most professional voice. "Yes, ma'am. Certainly." She directed Amanda's attention to the phone on her desk. "Line two. It's your mother."

Amanda sighed inwardly. Between Thorn and Mother, she was getting no peace. "Hello, Mother."

"How are things going in Dog Patch, Daisy Mae?" Mother singsonged.

"It's *Vamoose,* Mother," Amanda managed to say in a civil tone. Mother constantly poked fun at this small rural community that was a hop, skip, and jump from the bustling metropolis of Oklahoma City.

"Dog Patch, the boondocks, Nowhereville . . . whatever." Mother cleared her throat and changed topics. "So . . . how are you feeling, doll?"

"Marvelous," Amanda lied.

If she voiced a complaint Mother would rattle off a dozen quick cures—none of which would work. Amanda knew that for a fact, because she had tried one or two in the past.

"I think it's time you told me if my grandchild will be a boy or a girl. I'm trying to buy supplies, you know."

"Stick to unisex colors," Amanda suggested flippantly.

"Darn it, doll! Just because that country bumpkin of a cop you married has this stupid fetish about surprises is no reason to keep the rest of us in suspense!"

Amanda jerked the phone away before Mother's loud yowling blew out an eardrum.

"And don't you dare let your hick of a husband stick with those hideous names he has picked out for that baby!" Mother yipped.

Amanda smiled devilishly. "You don't like Thea Rose Thorn or Thane Edward Thorn?" Amanda couldn't resist annoying Mother. She usually had it coming.

"Thea Thorn? Thane Thorn?" Mother howled like a wounded wolf. "Lord save me from the hillbillies of this world!"

"Thorn has wonderful taste in names," Amanda defended her verbally abused husband.

"The man is named after a *sticker,* for heaven's sake,"

Mother said in a hoot. "And you are *stuck* with him. At least give my grandchild a break!"

"How's Daddy?" Amanda asked abruptly.

"Your daddy is just like he always is during the month of October. When the major-league play-offs and the World Series are in progress he is glued to the tube. I can't get him out of the house," Mother grumbled. "Now, back to the gender of this baby."

"It is classified information, Mother," Amanda insisted. "Thorn wants this to be a surprise, and that is how it is going to be. I am the only one around here who knows and I am going to keep it that way."

"You won't even tell your own mother?" Mother whined. "Ungrateful, that's what you are. I suffered through your delivery—oh, how I suffered! Nearly died a couple of times before you arrived. And this is how you repay me for my pain and discomfort? You don't care about all those years that I nursed you through fevers, flu, and childhood diseases?"

Amanda refused to hitch a ride on Mother's Guilt-Trip Express. "Sorry, Mother, you will find out at the same time everyone else does. Gotta go now," Amanda hurried on. "I've got to get my accounting business in order before *labor* day. 'Bye."

"But—"

Amanda hung up the phone, smiling triumphantly. Finally the time had come for *Amanda* to drive *Mother* crazy. She was loving every minute of it.

Jenny waved another phone message to gain Amanda's attention. "Velma Hertzog called to double-check on Saturday's baby shower. I wonder if she and Beverly Hill can top the decorations they created for your wedding shower and reception."

Amanda winced. Second-guessing the gum-chewing beautician's prenatal decor didn't bear thinking about!

"Call Velma and tell her I'm still on for Saturday afternoon, barring an early delivery," Amanda said.

When Jen completed the call, Amanda grabbed the phone to call Janie-Ethel, the police dispatcher.

"Vamoose police."

"Janie-Ethel, it's Amanda."

"Good. You saved me a call. The chief told me to find out how you're feeling."

"I'm perfectly fine, same as I was when we left the house together about an hour ago." Damn it, if Thorn didn't stop asking how she felt, every hour on the hour, she was going to have to strangle him! "Is Thorn at the station?"

"Negative. He's investigating a traffic accident," Janie-Ethel informed her. "Somebody practically blew Elvina Keef off the road a couple of minutes ago. The woman is ninety years old and she should not be behind the wheel. She can barely see over the dashboard. Nonetheless, she was driving into Vamoose and swerved into the ditch. Good thing she has a cell phone. This is the third problem she's had in the last three months. Thorn drove out to check on her."

"I'm headed out to Nettie Jarvis's place," Amanda reported. "Ask Thorn to stop by Pumpkin Hollow when he has a chance so he can help me load the pumpkins."

"Ten-four, Amanda, but don't you dare load those pumpkins by yourself. Thorn will have a conniption fit, you know."

"Tell me about it," Amanda mumbled.

"Pardon?"

"Nothing, Janie-Ethel."

"Er . . . Amanda? Is it a boy or girl?"

"You know I can't answer that without upsetting Thorn."

"I would never breathe a word to the chief," Janie-Ethel insisted.

"You're right. You won't, because you won't know."

The dispatcher sighed dramatically. "I don't know what the big deal is. People have kids every day. Hardly anybody waits until the baby arrives to find out what it is these days.''

Amanda smiled to herself. "That is why I married Thorn. He doesn't do anything the way anybody else does. Makes him unique.''

"Well, I agree that he's unique. This morning he was actually reading the directions so he could set up the baby crib tonight after work. He never reads directions before assembling anything.''

"Gotta run, Janie-Ethel.'' Amanda rang off, then braced her hands on the armrest to hoist herself to her feet—feet she hadn't seen in months! Ah, she yearned for the good ol' days, when standing up was practically an involuntary action.

Jenny frowned as she appraised Amanda's profile. "Are you sure D day is still a couple of weeks away? You look like you're about to pop.''

"Thanks,'' Amanda muttered as she scooped up her briefcase.

"Sorry, boss.'' Jenny blushed in embarrassment. "But before Timmy was born I—''

"Never looked this bad?'' Amanda frowned darkly. "Keep talking and you will find yourself demoted to the position of janitor.''

When Jenny's face turned the color of cornstarch, Amanda shook her head and sighed. "I'm not serious. I told you that you are the best secretary I could ever have. Now hold the fort until I get back, will you?''

Jenny bolted to her feet to give Amanda a snappy salute. "Yes, ma'am, boss! The fort will most definitely be held, boss ma'am!''

Amanda walked away, rolling her eyes. Jenny was so determined to be taken seriously in her chosen profession that she had gone as far overboard as Thorn had on this baby business!

*   *   *

Chief of the Vamoose police Nick Thorn shoved the prenatal pamphlets into a neat pile beside him on the car seat, then headed to the scene of Elvina Keef's most recent accident. The old woman, who wore glasses as thick as ice cubes, had no business on the road. Three weeks earlier she had backed into a corner post by her rural driveway. A month before that she forgot to put her car in park and it rolled across the street from the grocery store and crashed into a fire hydrant. Her old car had so many dents and dings that it would cost more than the value of the vehicle to repair them. If the old woman wanted to drive she needed to buy an army tank!

As Nick sped down the gravel road he mentally listed the tasks he planned to tackle after he got off police duty. He would feed the sheep and cattle and make sure all the livestock had fresh drinking water. Then he would assemble the baby crib. If he had time left, he would pack Hazard's hospital bag. If he left the chore to her, she would put it off until the last minute. In Nick's opinion, the woman simply wasn't taking her condition seriously enough!

Hell, she even refused to attend the Lamaze classes. According to Hazard she could wing it. Nick shook his head in dismay. Hazard's confidence and independence were going to leave her ill-prepared for this delivery, sure as shooting.

Three months earlier Nick had assumed most of the cooking duties so that Hazard and the baby would receive proper nourishment. He also handled cleaning chores, because the prenatal pamphlets said she shouldn't breathe the harmful fumes of cleaning supplies. He saw to it that she got plenty of rest, whether she thought she needed it or not.

Nick had also requested that Hazard cut back to a four-hour workday, but the suggestion had nearly instigated a domestic war. Hazard intensely disliked being pampered and coddled, even for her own good.

She was much too feisty and independent, he thought to himself.

And her disposition . . . Nick rolled his eyes, remembering Hazard's radical mood swings. One minute she was whining about being elbowed and kicked in a dozen different places. The next minute she was crying for no reason. And when she lost her temper, claiming he was babying her, smothering her? Whew! Being at ground zero when Hazard blew up was no picnic!

Still, Nick tried to be supportive and understanding, just as the prenatal pamphlets said he should be.

"Two more weeks, Thorn. You can do it," he told himself.

"Chief?" The two-way radio crackled to life. "Your wife called and asked you to meet her at Nettie Jarvis's place to load pumpkins after you rescue Elvina Keef."

"Oh, hell," Nick muttered into the mike. "You *did* tell Hazard that she was not to lift a single pumpkin until I got there, didn't you?"

"Of course I did," Janie-Ethel said defensively.

"Did you wring a promise out of her?"

"Well . . ."

"Well, hell." Nick put the pedal to the metal. He had to pull Elvina's car from the ditch, write up the report, and make tracks. If Hazard got impatient and strained herself Nick would never forgive himself!

Sipping on the chocolate malt she picked up at Toot 'N' Tell 'Em, Amanda sped east. An odd tingle assailed her as she cruised into Pumpkin Hollow and veered into Nettie's driveway. Amanda shrugged it off. She'd been having these twinges at irregular intervals all week. As much as she anticipated D day, she preferred to wait until after the Festival of the Pumpkin.

There were simply too many community activities to miss. Amanda had visions of gorging herself on the mouthwatering pumpkin pies piled high with whipped cream, iced pumpkin bread, and chilled pumpkin delight desserts that her secretary was famous for.

Amanda salivated like Pavlov's dog, just thinking of all the goodies she was going to wrap her gums around to appease her ravenous cravings.

Applying the brake, Amanda put the big red Chevy truck in reverse, then eased back to the gigantic pumpkin patch that sat beside a monolithic wooden barn that had been built at the turn of the twentieth century. Colorful orange pumpkins gleamed in the frothy vegetation. North of the garden, square hay bales formed a tall pyramid decorated with perfectly shaped melons. A fierce-looking scarecrow stood vigil to keep birds and varmints from invading the patch. An oversize black cat was perched on top of the straw pyramid, licking its paws, as if washing up after feasting on a juicy mouse. . . .

The thought caused Amanda's stomach to pitch.

Climbing down from the truck, Amanda waddled toward the pumpkin patch, wondering where Nettie was.

"Yoo-hoo, Nettie! It's Amanda. Where are you?"

She glanced toward the barn, then at the run-down house. "Nettie?"

Amanda lumbered toward the pyramid of hay bales, then stopped dead in her tracks. There, partially concealed by oversize pumpkins and thick vines, lay Nettie Jarvis. Her floral-print day dress and faded green house slippers blended into the pumpkin patch like camouflage. Amanda hadn't noticed the old woman until she practically trampled her.

Leafy vines entangled Nettie's left ankle. The hose attached to her portable breathing apparatus was wrapped around the discarded cane.

"Damn, this doesn't look good," Amanda mumbled as she stepped carefully toward the downed woman. The last thing Amanda needed was to trip and fall. Then she and Nettie would both be in a predicament.

Cautious where she stepped, Amanda inched toward Nettie, then squatted down to note that the breathing device had been jerked from her nostrils, preventing her from receiving much-needed oxygen.

Nettie's wrinkled face was blue.

That was not a good sign.

Amanda reached out to check for a pulse in Nettie's neck.

Nettie didn't have a pulse.

"Damn, double damn, triple damn!"

Amanda struggled to her feet to retrace her footsteps. The poor old spinster had flitted off to that Great Pumpkin Patch in the Sky. She wasn't going to participate in the upcoming festivities, wouldn't receive the award for the best pumpkin farmer in the county. . . .

Her grim thoughts trailed off when she noticed Nettie's faded green house slippers. Her eyes widened in surprise.

"Uh-oh," Amanda murmured.

Unless she missed her guess, and she rarely did, this was no accident. Somebody had launched Nettie Jarvis into a higher sphere.

D day or no D day, Amanda was going to uncover the whys and wherefores of this case.

Thorn was going to throw a ring-tailed fit.

"Well, that can't be helped," Amanda said to herself as she hiked off to make use of Nettie's bathroom.

TWO

Nick skidded the squad car to a halt in the loose gravel, then backed toward the old Chrysler that sat at a forty-five-degree angle in a ditch. He bounded out to check on Elvina.

"Blew me right off the road!" Elvina Keef said after she cranked down the window. "Young whippersnappers drive too fast!"

Clearly Elvina had been shaken by the incident. Her liver-spotted hands were clenched on the steering wheel and her knuckles were white. Impatient though Nick was to meet Hazard, he smiled reassuringly at Elvina.

"I'll hook up the chain and have you back on level ground in two shakes. Just put your car in drive when I give you the signal."

Elvina nodded her frizzy gray head, but she was still muttering something about road rage when Nick walked away.

With the chain hitched beneath each bumper, Nick returned to the black-and-white, then waved his arm in an expansive gesture. Although he could barely see Elvina's head above the steering wheel, she did raise her arm to notify him that she had the Chrysler in gear. Nick eased forward, careful not to give the old woman whiplash when the chain became taut.

Once the old car had all four wheels on the road, Nick unhooked the chain and returned it to his trunk.

"Now then, Elvina," Nick said. "I'll need a description of the vehicle that blew past you."

"A description?" Elvina echoed. "There is fog in the air, and I didn't see the dadblamed thing coming for all the dust I kicked up. I just heard the roaring engine before I was covered by a bigger cloud of dust."

Nick jotted down notes.

"I was afraid of being sideswiped, so I veered toward the ditch. Thank goodness Commissioner Harjo keeps these roads and ditches in good condition or I might have flipped my car!"

"Yes, ma'am." Nick agreed. "Harjo is the best commissioner we've had in years."

"I think the person who ran me off the road might have been driving a pickup," Elvina went on to say. "But I'm not absolutely certain. I was too busy trying to steer my car out of the way, and the dust was rolling like you wouldn't believe. We sure could use a rain."

"Sure could," Nick concurred.

He smiled into Elvina's wrinkled face. Her turned-down mouth sported bright red lipstick, and two blotches of powdered blush stained her cheeks. In her day Elvina had been a looker who was never seen without a fresh coat of makeup. Nowadays she looked pale and frail behind those splotches of colorful makeup and thick eyeglasses.

"Sometimes, after a traffic scare like this, a person reflects on what happened and begins to remember a few details," Nick told her. "If you recall more about the vehicle I would appreciate it if you would call headquarters. Will you do that for me, Elvina?''

"Darn tootin' I will,'' Elvina affirmed. "I always think well while I'm baking. I'm on my way to the grocery store to get some ingredients for my pumpkin bread and pies for the baazar. When I get home I'll think real hard about what happened.''

Nick patted her bony shoulder. "Thanks, Elvina. Now you try to have a good day, even if the morning had a shaky start. Make sure you take the back roads to town so you don't have to contend with highway traffic.'' *And highway traffic doesn't have to contend with you!*

She bobbed her Brillo-pad head. "You let me know when that new baby arrives. I'm crocheting a receiving blanket for the little tyke.''

Nick watched Elvina cruise off a little faster than a ninety-year-old person needed to be driving. When she veered from one side of the road to the other, Nick shook his head. Elvina's driving was well known in Vamoose. Most folks drove defensively when she was within crashing distance. The feisty old lady was a traffic accident waiting to happen.

Plunking onto the seat of the squad car, Nick grabbed the mike and checked in with the dispatcher. Then he scattered gravel in his haste to reach Pumpkin Hollow, which was only a couple of miles northeast of his present location.

Damn it, Hazard had better not have started lugging pumpkins to her pickup. According to the prenatal pamphlets he'd read—memorized, actually—mothers-to-be were not to lift excessive weight while carrying the additional weight of a child. But Hazard thumbed her nose at several no-nos—stubborn, self-reliant woman that she was.

"Just a couple more weeks,'' Nick chanted as he made tracks to Jarvis Farm.

* * *

Amanda watched Thorn hang a left and sail down the driveway. She noticed that she had been able to see the squad car coming for three-quarters of a mile. Problem was, Jarvis Farm was in an isolated area, with dozens of access roads to pastures and oil-well sites. There was an abundance of trees along the winding creeks to block the view from the road.

Whoever had done Nettie in—and Amanda was convinced the spinster's death was not an accident—could easily make an undetected getaway.

"How are you feeling?" Thorn asked as he unfolded his masculine hunk of a body from the car.

"I am fine," Amanda said irritably. "I have been fine for almost nine months. I will let you know when I am not fine."

Thorn, apparently oblivious to her annoyance with his repetitive question, glanced toward the bed of the red Chevy truck. "Glad to see you didn't start loading pumpkins without me. I don't want you to strain yourself."

"I got sidetracked," she said as she motioned for him to follow her. "We've got a major problem here, Thorn." She gestured her hand toward the prone body that was partially concealed by thick pumpkin vines.

Thorn's cocoa-brown eyes widened. His jaw sagged. "Oh, damn!"

"I'm sure Nettie shares your sentiments," Amanda said grimly.

Thorn put on his serious cop face and stepped carefully over the pumpkins and vines. He squatted down on his haunches to check for a pulse.

"Damn," he muttered.

"I believe you already covered that, Thorn."

Thorn ignored Amanda's sarcasm and critically surveyed the scene. After several pensive moments he arrived at his conclusion. "From the look of things Nettie's breathing apparatus hose got wrapped around her cane, and the leafy vines entangled her ankle. She must have tripped over the vines and the plastic hose, then fell. The oxygen hose was jerked loose from her nose, making it impossible for her to breathe. She obviously suffocated herself.''

"That's how it looks. But I don't think that is the way it actually happened." Amanda braced herself for Thorn's anticipated reaction.

Thorn swiveled his head around. His thick black brows flattened over his narrowed gaze. "Hazard," he said warningly, "this is no time for one of your crazed investigations. Must I remind you that you are nine months pregnant?"

"Believe me, Thorn, I am painfully aware of that." Amanda tilted her puffy face to a challenging angle. "But wrong time or not, I think Nettie Jarvis had help getting to that Great Pumpkin Patch in the Sky. This was not an accident."

Thorn rose to his full stature. Amanda could tell by his stance that he was summoning patience so as not to upset her in her "fragile condition." He had the look of a man who had already convinced himself that whatever explanation she was about to offer was based on pure fiction and wild imagination.

"Okay, Haz," he said too calmly. "What makes you think someone did Nettie bodily harm?"

Amanda's lips curled at his patronizing tone. "Look at Nettie's shoes."

He did, then arched a quizzical brow. "Yeah, so what about them?"

"They are *house* slippers," she snapped.

Again Thorn summoned his hidden reserve of patience and smiled indulgently—Amanda really hated it when he did that. "Which is why Nettie got tripped up. Those floppy slippers didn't provide stability for the old woman."

"Darn it, Thorn, don't you get it? Nettie was killed in the house!" Amanda exploded. "Then she was hauled out here to make her suffocation look like an accident. Somebody jerked her breathing apparatus loose!"

Thorn muttered something obscene. Amanda didn't ask him to repeat it. "You are crying murder based on a pair of house slippers?" he asked incredulously. "You are going to have a hard time convincing me that someone gave Nettie the deep six so they could make off with her prizewinning pumpkins. You have no evidence, no probable motive to support your theory."

Amanda knew Thorn would kick up a fuss. He was nothing if not predictable. "But I will have a suspect, motive, and evidence when I conclude this investigation."

And she would have, Amanda told herself confidently. Damn the man, would the day ever come when he took her feminine instincts and intuition seriously?

Thorn flung up his hand like a cop directing a traffic jam. "Hold it right there, Hazard. No. Absolutely, positively not. No way. No chance. We are having a baby very soon. For all we know it could be tonight or tomorrow. After I carefully examine the facts in this case"— he paused when Amanda let loose with a sardonic snort— "I will handle this investigation."

"No, you won't. You will be too busy reading prenatal pamphlets to focus on this case," she accused harshly.

"I've already memorized them," he snapped, finally losing his temper with her—which was okay with Amanda, because she preferred his temper to his infuriating male indulgence. "Damn it, I have enough memory banks left to handle an investigation! You know what your problem is, Hazard? You don't have enough faith in my abilities to let me handle these cases! How do you think that makes me feel? Huh? You think you are the only one around here who has enough brains to do it!"

Amanda felt the sting of tears, prompted by his harsh, booming voice and damning remarks. Well, so much for preferring his temper to indulgence, she thought on a sob. These days she could cry at the drop of a hat. She, who rarely cried, began to blubber. But just once she wanted Thorn to recognize her ability to spot trouble at a glance, then act accordingly. She wanted him to put faith in her instincts.

The anger drained from Thorn's face like water swirling down a toilet. "Aw, honey, don't cry. I'm sorry I yelled at you. It was a rotten, unforgivable thing to do," Thorn cooed as he stepped carefully from the pumpkin patch to cuddle her close—as close as he could with her rounded tummy between them. "Now tell me what alerted you to suspicions of foul play, sweetheart. I'm all ears."

Amanda was no fool, at least not today. It suddenly dawned on her that she could turn Thorn's aggravating, overprotective tendencies toward a positive direction here. She could play on his Expectant Father Syndrome and ensure that he listened to her suspicions.

Okay, so maybe using this flood of tears to her advantage was a teensy-weensy bit manipulative, but she was working on a short clock and she needed Thorn's cooperation.

Amanda let the tears flow unhindered as she looped her arms around Thorn's neck. "N-Nettie was upset when I sp-spoke to her on the phone this m-morning," she blubbered. "She w-wanted immediate consultation, w-wanted me to take her little black book for s-safekeeping. She said she was d-depending on me to straighten out her s-situation."

"Of course she was," Thorn murmured as he patted her quaking shoulder sympathetically. "Everyone in Vamoose County knows how reliable, responsible, and efficient you are, sweetums. That's it now, just let those pent-up emotions flood out. I'll make everything better, sugar."

"You're so wonderful, Thorn. The best."

Might as well butter him up, she decided. Plus, she

could compensate for all the times her physical discomfort and roiling hormones had made her crabby and she took it out on him. Well, not crabby, she amended; she had been downright *bitchy* a few times. . . . Several times . . . Oh, hell, a lot.

He grazed her forehead with a kiss and gave her another comforting hug. "Now, is there anything else about this case that's bothering you?"

She nodded against Thorn's broad, muscular chest. "Jenny was out here yesterday to gather pumpkins and she mentioned Nettie had on her Nike tennis shoes for stability." Amanda sniffed loudly and swiped at the dribbles of tears. "While I was waiting for you to show up I went to the bathroom in the house. Nettie's Nike tennis shoes are sitting beside the front door. Her bifocals are lying on the end table beside the phone."

"So something doesn't *ring* true for you, huh?"

Amanda managed a slight smile in response to his pun. "We need to find that little black book Nettie planned to give to me. I have the uneasy feeling that whatever is in it is tied to her death. And Thorn?"

"What, sugarplum?" he murmured.

"I need to use the bathroom again. Somebody just drop-kicked my bladder."

He gently set her an arm's length away and used the hem of his shirt to mop her splotchy face. "Feeling better now, hon?"

She bobbed her head.

"Go up to the house while I call the medical examiner. Take all the time you want to check over the house to support your theory. Just don't leave any fingerprints. Okay, sugar?"

"I know the drill, dear," she muttered, her mood taking another nosedive.

"Of course you do, darlin'," he cooed. "Old cop habits made me say that. I didn't mean a thing by it."

Amanda turned away. He didn't see the wry smile

pursing her lips. All these months—almost nine of them—Amanda had gotten huffy and bent out of shape when Thorn babied her, smothered her with concern. What an idiot she had been. Why, the man gushed cooperation when she allowed him to portray the doting husband and expectant father. He *was* going to help with this case from its onset. Good for him. Two heads were always better than one, even if one of those heads was male.

Nick watched Hazard toddle toward the house. The stiff autumn breeze swirled her skirt, providing him with a sneak peak at her fantastic fanny. Things were looking up, he mused as he grabbed the mike to the two-way radio. Hazard was finally leaning on the shoulder he was willing and eager to provide when she got upset. They had shared a touching bonding moment and he'd let her get her suspicions off her chest—weak suspicions though they were.

While Nick was on the horn with the medical examiner, he glanced back at the body. Hazard was wary because the spinster wore house slippers to the garden? Geez, talk about grasping at straws!

Oh, well, Nick would cater to Hazard's squirrelly suspicions, and when the baby arrived she would be too busy to realize he had wrapped up this open-and-shut case. A crying baby who needed food and a diaper change would provide Hazard with plenty of distraction.

Amanda made a thorough search of the house while Thorn and Clint Pine, the medical examiner, did their thing. First off, she checked the trash can under the sink for names and addresses of people who had been in contact with Nettie recently. Amanda found the discarded envelopes from a phone bill, electric bill and water bill, but no personal letters. *Damn.*

Second, she opened the refrigerator. She adhered to the theory that you could tell a great deal about people by checking the contents and tidiness of their fridge. People were what they ate, and if they cleaned the appliance regularly, they lived a reasonably tidy life.

Sure enough, Nettie was organized and neat. Food was stored in sanitary containers. Amanda opened the drawer labeled MEATS to find ham and bologna, but no little black book. Amanda's shoulders slumped, wishing that book had turned up the first place she looked.

There was always the possibility that whoever gave Nettie the deep six had confiscated the book. Yet Amanda figured that if that book held important information—the kind that could get a person killed—Nettie wouldn't leave it lying around in plain sight. . . . Unless she was expecting Amanda's arrival and somebody else showed up first. . . .

Using the kitchen towel to prevent leaving prints, she opened cabinet doors, hoping to find the book wedged between boxes of Wheaties, Rice Chex, and Grape-Nuts.

No such luck.

When she rummaged through the antique oak secretary, with its curved glass door, she found Nettie's bank statements and canceled checks for the past three months. Amanda immediately tucked them in the elastic panel on her maternity skirt.

Kitchen towel in hand, she lumbered down the hall to Nettie's bedroom. A twitchy sensation dribbled down her backbone. Bad vibes? Amanda wasn't sure what caused her reaction. She didn't consider herself psychic, but there was a sinister, oppressive aura hovering around this room.

Amanda appraised the bed that boasted a handmade quilt. Then her gaze settled magnetically on the lacy pillow shams.

Another odd sensation assailed her—one that was too strong to ignore.

How could an old woman, who walked with a cane and portable breathing apparatus, manage to keep her bed looking as if an army private had tidied it up for inspection? *Hmm.* Talk about something not ringing true.

Shaking off the gooseflesh at the back of her neck, Amanda retraced her steps to the living room. A frown knitted her brow when she noticed the brochure on the coffee table.

Amanda plopped down to take a load off her swollen feet.

The advertising brochure boasted high praise for New Horizon Retirement Village. Amanda had heard about the newly completed facility that had been built near Adios— the laid-back hamlet located near Buffalo Lake.

Amanda used the kitchen towel to thumb through the brochure a second time, then studied the pricey down payments and monthly service fees for the exclusive condos.

Good heavens, was Nettie considering selling her homestead in Pumpkin Hollow and moving to the ritzy retirement village? Amanda needed to check Nettie's bank statements and tax files to determine whether the old woman could afford the luxury of continual health care and elite housing accommodations.

It occurred to her that Nettie might have used her mysterious little black book to blackmail someone. Had Nettie intended for someone—whose name might be in the black book—to pay her down payment and monthly fees?

Amanda definitely had to get her paws on that book!

Hurriedly, she reached for the phone, then dialed. She needed background information on Nettie Jarvis. There was one surefire place to get it—Velma's Beauty Boutique. Velma had her finger on the pulse of this small-town American community.

"Beauty shop." *Smack, chomp.* "Do we have a 'do for you! Velma speaking." *Crack, pop.*

"Velma, this is Amanda."

"Hi, hon! Is the baby here already?"

"No, I just need a pick-me-up hairdo to compensate

for feeling bloated and insecure about my appearance," Amanda replied.

"Well, how about if I get you all dolled up and ready for your baby shower, hon. Nothing like a new 'do and facial makeover to lift your drooping spirits." *Pop, pop.* "If you can come in around two this afternoon, I'll work you in."

"I'm there," Amanda confirmed, smiling in satisfaction.

Velma and the patrons of the beauty shop might save her considerable legwork on this case. Right now Amanda didn't have the legs for it. The load she was carrying around was getting her down.

"Hazard? Are you ready to go to lunch?" Thorn called as he strode across the wooden porch.

"Come in here a sec, Thorn," she called back. "There is something I want you to see."

Thorn, still wearing latex gloves, opened the door. "What's up?"

"Please pick up that brochure and address book on the coffee table," she requested. "I want to study them at length."

Thorn opened his mouth to object, forced a smile, then complied. "Sure, Haz. Anything else?"

"Are you going to dust this place for prints?" When he hesitated she plunged on. "I doubt that whoever bumped off Nettie was careless, but you never know. We might get lucky."

"I'll call the county sheriff and have one of his detectives take care of it after lunch," he said.

"Good." Amanda held out the plastic bag she had scrounged from the kitchen. Thorn dropped the address book and brochure inside. "What did the medical examiner have to say?"

Thorn opened the door for her. "Suffocation, lack of oxygen. Asthmatic attack. I asked him to check for particle samples under the fingernails, just in case."

"Good work, Thorn," she complimented.

"Thanks, Hazard," he said as he took her arm to assist her down the rickety steps.

Amanda bit back the reflexive comment that she could make her own way down the steps. If she wanted Thorn's investigative cooperation she would have to stroke his protective male instincts.

A fair trade, she decided as she waddled toward her pickup truck.

THREE

Amanda cast a withering glance at the squad car that pulled in directly behind her at Velma's Beauty Boutique. She saw Thorn stab his forefinger toward the protective dust-and-particle mask he had insisted she wear during her visit to the beauty salon.

"This is so ridiculous," Amanda muttered as she slipped the lightweight mask over her nose and mouth.

According to Thorn, mothers-to-be should be careful about inhaling the harmful fumes of hair spray and peroxide. Next thing Amanda knew Thorn would probably have her wearing a portable respirator like the one Nettie used.

The instant Thorn was out of sight, Amanda jerked off the stupid mask and crammed it in her purse. She held open the door a moment longer than necessary to let the lingering fumes escape before she entered the salon.

"Hi, hon." *Crackle, chomp.* "My, but you have blossomed since the last time I saw you!"

Amanda smiled past the awkwardness of having everyone in the beauty shop stare at her Santa Claus-size belly. Velma, Amanda noticed right away, had dropped a few pounds from her Amazon physique and had applied a heavy hand to the copper-red dye that tinted her cropped hairdo.

"You're looking chipper, Velma," Amanda observed.

"Think so?" Velma chewed her gum vigorously and preened in front of the mirror. "I decided to get down to my fighting weight before the eating frenzy of the upcoming holiday season." She winked her fake lashes. "I've been surviving on celery, pickles, and chicken and anticipating the eating extravaganza at the Festival of the Pumpkin."

"Like, Aunt Velma looks great, doesn't she?" Beverly Hill spoke up. "She even has me on her celery-pickle diet."

Amanda noticed that Bev had shed a few pounds also. In addition, Bev had been experimenting with incandescent eye shadow. Today she was sporting glittering eye shadow that matched her pale green frock. Bev looked like an oversize lime.

"Velma rocks," Amanda agreed. "Both of you look terrific."

The patrons of the salon, in varying degrees of cosmetic improvement, nodded in unanimous agreement. Velma did look better now that she had begun her weight-reduction program.

"So is it gonna be a boy or a girl?" Velma asked as she snipped the split ends off Jonella Figgins's frizzy hair.

"You know perfectly well that I can't divulge that information. Thorn would have a hissy," Amanda assured Velma.

The phone rang and Velma clamped the receiver in her meaty fist. "Well, hi there, handsome. Uh-huh, yeah, uh-huh."

Amanda tensed when Velma's thick-lashed gaze landed on her. "Thorn?" Amanda murmured.

Velma bobbed her copper-red head. "Of course

Amanda has her mask on, just like you told her. No, no, we wouldn't want her breathing harmful fumes, either. . . . Uh-huh, sure, right . . . Well, you have a good day, too, Nicky."

Velma hung up, then pointed her scissors at Amanda. "Put on your mask, hon. I do not want it said that I lied to the chief of police. And don't make these poor women lie, either. Knowing how protective Nicky is of you, he is bound to interrogate the whole bunch of us."

Amanda snatched the damned mask from her purse and secured it to the lower portion of her face. "This is the dumbest mandate Thorn has come up with yet!"

"Like, I think it's so sweet the way Nicky takes care of you," Bev put in as she scooped up the cuticle remover.

Sweet enough to cause nausea, thought Amanda.

"After you called"—*smack, pop*—"Bev and I put our heads together to exchange ideas so we could give you a new look." *Snip, whack.* "You're going to walk out of here feeling like a brand-new woman, hon."

Amanda didn't want to be a new woman; she just wanted to scare up some facts that would put her on the right investigative track.

"There you go, Jonella," Velma said as she spun her customer toward the mirror. "Perky! Doesn't she look perky, girls?"

The "girls," ranging from ages fifty to eighty, nodded agreeably.

When Jonella stood up, Velma motioned Amanda to The Chair. Amanda promised herself that, no matter what upcoming cosmetic disaster awaited her, she could waddle away with scads of beneficial information about her case.

"Bev, hon, round up some of that new dye and bring me the picture we selected from the fashion magazine," Velma instructed her niece.

"You bet!" Bev enthused as she scurried to the store-room.

"We decided lots of curls and a little dye would brighten you up." *Chomp, chomp.*

"Actually, I was thinking of just a trim—"

"Nonsense. We are looking for *dramatic* here. I want you to appear *spectacular* for the baby shower this weekend."

"But—"

"Here you go, Aunt Velma. All mixed and ready to pour. Here's the picture of the hairdo we selected." Bev's Shirley Temple Black curls bounced around her full jowls as she breezed across the salon. "Amanda is, like, going to look *sooo* cool!"

Amanda took one glance at the photo from the magazine and cringed. The model looked like an older version of Little Orphan Annie. *Oh, God!*

Before Amanda could object, Velma cranked The Chair backward. Amanda's head thumped against the faucet. Meaty fists vigorously scrubbed her scalp. Water and orange-scented shampoo bubbles landed on her eyelashes and forehead.

While Velma washed and rinsed, Bev unclamped Amanda's left hand from the armrest. "Like, you aren't going to believe the eye-catching color of nail polish I have created for you. It is, like, *sooo* flashy!"

Amanda was already drawing unwanted attention to herself because she looked like a beached whale. She did not need flashy.

"This baby shower is going to be lots of fun," Velma said as she slapped a towel around Amanda's soggy head, then hauled her upright. "And wait till you see the cake Maggie Whittlemeyer is making for the occasion. It's going to be darling."

But would it be edible? Amanda wondered. Maggie had created the cakes for her wedding and reception. They crumbled to pieces and fell on the floor. Amanda sighed inwardly, certain that another catastrophe loomed on the horizon.

"Like, has everybody here heard that Vamoose has two candidates campaigning for mayor?" Bev asked while she scrubbed Amanda's nails.

"You bet," Myrna Thomas spoke up. "Claude Padden and Phil Darnell have been kissing up to the city council, trying to win support."

"Either one of them should make good mayor material," Velma said as she squeezed the moisture from Amanda's hair. "One's a retired doctor and the other is a lawyer. I think it's a toss-up. Personally, I don't care which one wins."

All the patrons dipped their heads, agreeing with Velma. As for Amanda, she wasn't acquainted with either man. She couldn't say who was the better mayoral candidate.

"Aunt Velma, did you try that new recipe Millicent Patch gave you yesterday?" Bev questioned, head bowed in concentration over Amanda's fingernails.

"You mean that to-die-for chocolate cake?" *Pop, snap.* "No, I didn't. It's not on my diet."

The comment prompted a flurry of conversation about low-calorie recipes. Amanda didn't pay much attention, just sat there breathing through her ridiculous-looking mask. Cooking was not among her talents, or interests, she was sorry to say.

If you can't nuke it, then don't cook it. That was Amanda's motto.

Amanda allowed the patrons to swap recipes for casseroles and desserts for ten minutes before she made the announcement that was sure to provide her with information for her investigation. "I guess y'all heard the bad news about Nettie Jarvis."

"Nettie?" *Chomp, crunch.*

Heads thrust out from under the humming hair dryers. All eyes focused on Amanda.

"What about Nettie?" the patrons chorused.

"I went by to see her this morning and found her collapsed in the pumpkin patch."

Everybody gasped in unison.

"It looked as though Nettie tripped over the thick vines, fell, and jerked her breathing apparatus loose. I arrived too late to revive her."

Velma shook her head sadly. "Poor Nettie. Her health hasn't been good lately, and her allergies were really acting up this fall. She claimed her previous profession was responsible for that."

"Her previous profession?" Amanda asked as Velma spun The Chair around.

Myrna Thomas, the thick-chested, heavyset woman who sat beneath the corner dryer, leaned forward. "She used to be Vamoose's barber and beautician, before Velma got her license."

A sinking feeling settled in the pit of Amanda's stomach. The news indicated that Nettie once had her finger on the pulse of this rural community. There was no telling what kind of damaging information about the citizens of Vamoose had been written down in Nettie's little black book!

"Course, Nettie wasn't one to pass along gossip," Sally Strump put in. She touched her steel wool-colored head, which was adorned with pink plastic rollers. "Somebody told me that Nettie didn't pass news around, but wrote it in a journal. Ah, the stories that woman could have told if she'd wanted to!"

Amanda was pretty sure that journal had been the death of Nettie. But why now? she kept asking herself. Why after all these years?

"Mama says, like, all that aerosol hair spray and peroxide fumes aggravated Nettie's asthmatic condition," Bev Hill said as she labored over Amanda's fingernails. "Like, Mama is always harping at me and Aunt Velma to wear masks like Amanda has on. But those masks look so silly—" Bev smiled apologetically as she glanced up at Amanda. "But not on you, of course."

Amanda smirked behind her protective particle-and-dust mask.

"Anyway," Bev rushed on, "after Nettie began to suffer relapses from her childhood condition she decided to retire, and she rented out the building she owns here in town."

"Which building is that?" Amanda asked.

"The mom-and-pop grocery store." *Snap, crackle.*

Velma squeezed the plastic bottle over Amanda's head. Strong fumes permeated the room. Amanda tried to breathe only when absolutely necessary.

"Ginger and Melvin Rumley have rented that building space for years. I wonder who the new owner will be now that Nettie's gone?" Velma mused aloud.

"Maybe her brother," Myrna Thomas inserted. "And he'd better not sell that property or Nettie will roll over in her grave. She had a hissy when Odell sold the town property he inherited when their daddy passed on."

"And what property would that be?" Amanda questioned curiously.

"The Jarvis family once owned the land that Vamoose Bank sits on," Sally Strump reported as she resettled beneath the dryer. "Odell decided to take the cash and play the stock market. Nettie called him ten kinds of fool, the way I heard it. Odell lost his shirt—pants, too. Now all Odell has is the farmland he inherited. He never was much of a financial manager. His younger sister, Faye, isn't much better. Nettie was the brains in that Jarvis outfit."

"Is that why Nettie never married? Too busy holding the family and the inheritance together?" Amanda asked, then winced when Velma jerked up strands of hair to apply more perm solution.

Several faces in the shop broke into wry grins.

"What?" Amanda demanded. "Come on, girls, spill it. I'm in charge of settling Nettie's estate. I need to know as much about her as I can find out."

"Suffice it to say that just because Nettie never married doesn't mean she wasn't what the young folks these days refer to as a *fox*. She had plenty of male admirers," Sally declared.

"And not all of them were bachelors," Velma imparted. "She was a barber as well as a beautician. Men lined up for haircuts and . . . whatever." *Chomp, pop.*

Holy kamoley! Nettie's black book might contain a complete listing of the men she'd fooled around with on the sly. The men involved might have become desperate to keep that information quiet.

"But Nettie was nothing if not discreet," Myrna insisted.

"Discreet?" Sally snorted. "Seemed to me that Nettie enjoyed keeping us all in suspense, wondering if it was one of *our* husbands she had been fooling around with."

"Wasn't there a single man in her past who tempted her to marry?" Amanda questioned.

"Two, as I heard it told. But that's all hearsay," Velma said as she squeezed the last of the perm solution on Amanda's head. "Jim Foster is long gone. Died in a traffic accident while he and Nettie were dating in high school. I heard that it took a long time for her to get over losing her first love. As for the other love of her life . . ." Velma shrugged her linebacker shoulders. "That mystery man has been one of Vamoose's best-kept secrets. Nettie mentioned the man of her dreams often, but never by name."

"Yeah," Sally grumbled. "That's the one who had us all wondering if he might be one of *our* husbands."

Amanda recalled that her own impression of Nettie was that of a feisty, spirited individual. In her day, Nettie must have been a male magnet.

"Like, do you remember that day last spring when Nettie came in to have her hair done and Pansy Quinn was in here at the same time?" Bev piped up.

Velma groaned. "How could I forget!" *Chomp.* "I had to call the fire chief to revive Nettie."

"What happened?" Amanda had to know.

"Like, Nettie was violently allergic to cats, and Pansy keeps a houseful of them. Always has cat hair all over her clothes—and she smells like a cat. We put Nettie under the dryer Pansy had used previously. I guess all that cat hair was floating around and wham! Nettie suffered a fierce reaction."

"Nettie's eyes started watering and burning. Welts broke out on her face and neck. She couldn't catch her breath, and she frantically gasped and wheezed," Velma added. "When she started choking and turning blue it scared the pants off me."

"Were there many witnesses on hand?" Amanda questioned.

"Like, the place was packed," Bev reported. "That was the day before the community garage sale, I believe."

In other words, thought Amanda, the incident probably hit the gossip grapevine and everyone in town knew about Nettie's violent reaction to cats and her asthmatic problems. Anyone who felt threatened by what was in that missing black book could have preyed on Nettie's vulnerability. . . .

Amanda frowned, remembering the black cat that had been prowling around the pumpkin patch. Had the cat been there by accident? Or on purpose? And why now? That question had been hounding Amanda since the supposed "accident" had happened.

"Did Nettie mention to anyone that she was thinking of moving into that retirement village near Adios?" Amanda tossed out to the patrons.

The question drew unanimous stunned stares.

"Really? First I have heard about it." Velma smacked her gum as she wrapped a plastic cap around Amanda's head. "Sounds like it would have been a good place for

Nettie, what with all those continual health care options."
Crackle, chomp.

"*If* she could afford it," Myrna piped up. "I would love to move into one of those pricey condos within the next few years. No more lawn mowing and home repairs. A cafeteria within walking distance of a condo. Round-the-clock nursing staff. What could be better, I ask you?"

Most of the patrons agreed that would be swell.

"Did Nettie have any close friends or other relatives I should contact, besides her brother and sister?" Amanda baited.

"Only Mr. Mysterious, whoever he may be," said Sally.

"Like, somebody needs to contact Ginger and Melvin Rumley at the store. They will have to pay rent to the estate," Bev commented.

"And don't forget about Mickey Poag, who rents Nettie's farmland and pastures for his wheat crop and cattle herd," Myrna interjected.

"You also need to call Arthella Carson," Velma said. "She is the home–health care nurse who has been checking in with Nettie three times a week for the past year. Before that, Eileen Franklin took care of Nettie. Eileen still stops by a couple of times a month to drive Nettie into town to run errands."

Amanda made a mental list of everyone she needed to interrogate. Nettie's brother and sister definitely knew about her health problems and could have preyed on her. The home–health care nurse? Certainly. The Rumleys and Mickey Poag? Amanda wasn't sure what they had to gain from Nettie's death, but she was determined to discover whether they had a motive. And what about this Mr. Mysterious? Who the hell was he?

When Velma hoisted Amanda from The Chair, she waddled to the lopsided vinyl couch to wait for the perm solution to set. Conversation turned to the anticipated activities for the Pumpkin Festival. Amanda half listened while the "girls" discussed the baking and decorating contests, the costume street dance, and the haunted house set up to benefit the fire department.

Thirty minutes later Amanda returned to The Chair to have the neutralizer dripped onto her scalp and into her ears. Bev was hard at work putting the finishing touches on Amanda's nails when Velma called for the dye.

"I'm not sure I—" Amanda tried to protest.

"Trust me on this, hon." *Pop, pop.* "This new, revitalizing color will be gorgeous on you."

Dye burned Amanda's sensitive scalp. She was certain the combination of perm and dye would interact to set fire to her head. Sure enough, the two chemicals started fizzing and burning.

"Ouch!" Amanda squawked.

"Oh, rats! Like, I forgot how sensitive Amanda's skin is!" Bev howled.

"Quick! Somebody get a can of Coke to pour over her head!" Velma yelled.

Myrna plowed forward like a defensive linebacker. "Got it! Catch, Bev!"

The aluminum can sailed across the room. Bev reached out to snag the Coke before it thumped Amanda on the forehead. Amanda hissed and sputtered in pain, until the Coke dribbled onto her head, putting out the chemical fire—the latest in a long line of cosmetic disasters she had suffered in her quest for investigative information.

God, the sacrifices Amanda made for these unofficial investigations!

Silence reigned in the salon. All eyes were on Amanda's scorched scalp. Judging from the reactions, the result was catastrophic.

Oh, God. Oh, God! thought Amanda.

"Oops," Velma wheezed. "Er . . . hon, how . . . um . . . do you feel about the color orange?"

"Orange?" Amanda parroted.

Damn it to hell, Thorn was going to blow his stack when he saw her hair!

"Wait a sec." Bev's fake Marilyn Monroe mole disappeared into the thick rolls of skin beside her mouth. "Like, I've got a terrific idea! Aunt Velma, remember that giant pumpkin costume you wore to the festival last fall?"

Velma nodded, her uneasy gaze fixed on Amanda's head.

"You could let Amanda borrow it, since it matches her . . . um . . . new hair color. She will be color coordinated for the festival."

"Great idea," Myrna and Sally chimed in.

"We'll tell everybody that Amanda is showing her support for the festivities by really getting into the swing of things with her pumpkin-colored hair," Bev continued.

"Since all the monetary proceeds are going to the volunteer fire department for protective gear, Amanda will be a natural for Pumpkin Queen," Myrna added.

Amanda sank a little deeper into The Chair. She was hyperventilating behind this stupid mask Thorn made her wear, and she was afraid to face the mirror to determine just how bad this latest hair calamity looked.

"Bev, get on the horn, PDQ, and call Delmar Sparks, the fire chief." *Snap, crackle, crunch.* "Tell him we've got our honorary queen for the festivities."

The "girls" nodded in absolute agreement.

When Bev scuttled off, Amanda looked down at her hands, which were clamped on the armrest of The Chair. She groaned in dismay. Bev had painted Amanda's fingernails fluorescent orange, with black triangles. For heaven's sake, her nails boasted jack-o'-lantern faces!

"Just hold on, hon. I'll have this dye rinsed out in a jiffy; then we will blow-dry your hair," Velma said.

Amanda noted that no one left the salon. They were waiting to see the end results of Amanda's perm and dye.

Fifteen minutes later Velma spun The Chair to face the mirror. Amanda bit back a horrified wail of dismay. Her hair was definitely, positively orange! Velma had used a pageboy style, which made Amanda's head resemble a pumpkin.

Well, shit. She had no dignity left.

"There we go. May I present the reigning Pumpkin Queen of Vamoose," Velma announced.

In the mirror, Amanda watched the "girls" bite back snickers.

"No charge today, hon," Velma said generously.

As if Amanda would pay to be victimized!

Amanda took a deep breath when Velma swooped down with a can of hair spray. The room fogged up. Sticky particles settled on Amanda's head and shoulders. Though she was wearing the protective mask, she could smell the choking fumes.

The "girls" coughed simultaneously.

"See ya at the school cafeteria at two o'clock Saturday for your baby shower," Velma called as Amanda staggered out the door.

Amanda made a neutral sound. The price of information was always steep here at Velma's Beauty Boutique. It seemed Velma's best intentions became Amanda's worst calamities. This latest disaster really took the cake, Amanda decided. The prospect of facing Thorn made her cringe.

Thorn's least favorite color in the whole wide world was *orange!*

FOUR

Amanda hung a left and whipped into the service station to fuel up her truck. Thaddeus Thatcher, dressed in his brown uniform, hiked up his droopy breeches as he moseyed outside to wait on her.

"Hey there, li'l girl . . ."

Amanda knew the exact instant Thaddeus became aware of her pumpkin-colored hair. His eyes widened and his jaw sagged. But to his credit, he recovered quickly and pasted on a smile.

"How is it going, Amanda?" Thaddeus leaned his forearms on the side of the truck and stared at her through her open window. He was careful not to lift his gaze to her outrageous hairdo.

"Things are going fine, Thaddeus. Could you fill up my truck and clean the windshield, please?"

"You bet, li'l girl."

"I come bearing bad news today," Amanda said as Thaddeus pushed away from the truck. "Nettie Jarvis passed on this morning."

"Aw, you don't say. I'm sorry to hear it. I always liked old Nettie. She was full of spunk."

"Yes, she was," Amanda was quick to agree. "Since I'm in charge of handling Nettie's estate, you can send any outstanding bills to me and I will make sure they are paid."

Thaddeus crammed the nozzle into the gas tank of Amanda's truck. "You better take that up with Gertie. She takes care of office accounts and mailings. She has been in a tizzy all morning because of the government's new regulations and changing gasoline forms."

"So I hear. Gertie called my office to see if I could help her figure out the new forms." Amanda grabbed the steering wheel and slid off the seat. "I'll go see if I can't get things straightened out while I'm here."

"Thanks, li'l girl. We sure appreciate that."

Amanda lumbered into the station, then veered down the hall to the office. Gertie, with her gray hair pulled back in a severe bun, sat at her desk with her head bowed over the stack of papers in front of her.

"Hi, Gertie," Amanda greeted.

Gertie glanced up to note Amanda's orange hair. Like her husband, Gertie recovered rapidly, then smiled. "Boy, I'm sure glad to see you. These tax forms are making me crazy. I swear the government purposely flip-flops these forms to confuse people. Then they send out those auditors to catch us screwing up so they can slap a few fines on us. I have made it my ambition to come back to haunt the IRS when I'm gone! The agency has certainly haunted me the whole time Thaddeus and I have been in the service station and fuel business."

Amanda glanced over Gertie's thin-bladed shoulders to appraise the complicated form. "It looks as if the new form has reversed the order of reported income from farm fuel and road fuel." Amanda pointed a jack-o'-lantern-tipped finger at the paper—in triplicate. "Put your two subtotals in these spaces." She indicated the correct spot to report the information. "Then calculate your discount for fuel delivered to farms and ranches in this slot. Then place the total for all gallons of fuel sold over here in this space."

Gertrude nodded pensively. "Okay, now I think I see what they've done. I can't say that this form is better than the last one. Neither do I understand why they had to go and change the wording on the form."

"The government calls it progress when they come up with new technical terms to place on their forms," Amanda said, then snorted. "Nowadays every form is supposed to be precise and ensure that no one is cheating on Uncle Sam. He wants his cut. You know what they say: there is no escaping death or taxes."

"Well, I still think all this new jargon is idiotic babble," Gertrude muttered sourly.

"I couldn't agree with you more. . . ." Amanda's voice faded away when she noticed the stack of checks written to Thatcher Oil and Gas. Apparently Gertie was on her way to the bank to collect the station's due. The check sitting on top of the stack was from Nettie Jarvis.

Amanda reached out to pluck up the check. "Nettie passed away this morning," she reported bleakly.

"Oh, dear, I'm sorry to hear that. Poor Nettie was really suffering from her health condition."

"I'm sure this check will clear," Amanda said. "But I suggest that you send all future bills to me, since I'm handling the estate. . . ." Amanda frowned at the amount on the check. "My goodness, Nettie sure used a lot of fuel the past two months, didn't she?"

"Actually that isn't Nettie's bill. She paid her brother's for him, because it was delinquent," Gertie explained. "Nettie was all the time doing things like that for her brother and sister. It embarrassed her when Odell let his bills pile up. She insisted on taking care of them after they dragged out for more than two months."

"Did she do that sort of thing often?" Amanda asked.

"About three times a year," Gertie replied.

"Well, I want you to make certain that Odell pays his own bills this month," Amanda instructed. "Nettie's estate will only cover her outstanding debts."

"I kept telling Nettie that she wasn't responsible for Odell's failings, but she always insisted on paying. She even paid a few of her sister's bills over the years. Nettie always took care of her family and tried to keep the family reputation intact."

The comment caused Amanda to frown ponderously. When she lurched around to leave, Gertie grabbed her hand.

"Girl, are you sure you aren't due for another couple of weeks? You sure have filled out a lot lately."

So everybody kept telling her. Amanda smiled wryly at Gertie. "Are you thinking of changing your bet for the baby pool, after you got a good look at me?"

Gertie blushed profusely. "So you heard about the baby pool, did you?"

"Yes, I heard." Amanda waved as she lumbered toward the door.

"You aren't mad, are you?" Gertie called after her.

"Nope. I'll just be glad when D day arrives." Amanda halted, then pivoted to face Gertie. "I want you to give my secretary the chance to prove she can solve any problems that might arise while I am on maternity leave next month. Jenny knows the business, Gertie. She is itching to have my clients realize that she knows exactly what she is doing."

Gertie smiled guiltily. "Okay, Amanda."

"Good. Jenny thanks you and I thank you," Amanda said before she lurched around and toddled from the office.

Amanda piled into her truck and stared through the clean windshield. "Thanks, Thaddeus. Now I can see where I'm going."

"Anytime, li'l girl." He pulled off his brown ball cap

and raked his fingers through his silver-blond hair. "Now you take good care of yourself, hear?"

Amanda nodded, then drove off to solve Cecil and Cleatus Watts's accounting glitch at the mechanic shop.

Amanda wheeled into the parking lot of Watts Mechanic Shop. Cecil and Cleatus moseyed outside to appraise her shiny new four-by-four truck.

"Whoa, man, some powerful truck you've got here," Cecil said as he puffed on his cigarette.

"What he said," Cleatus agreed.

Amanda eased clumsily from her truck while the Watts brothers closely examined the interior, then checked under the hood.

"Three-fifty engine, huh?" Cleatus said, raising his bushy head to glance in her direction. "Really cool, man."

Amanda watched in amusement while the Watts brothers, dressed in faded T-shirts and jeans that were permanently stained with paint and grease and aerated by holes caused by dripping battery acid, rattled on about the luxurious accessories found on her "country limousine." The men were so busy salivating over the truck that they barely noticed Amanda's hideous hairdo. When they did notice, they swallowed their grins and politely refrained from commenting.

"I stopped by to straighten out your problem with your accounting ledger," Amanda announced as she strode toward the cubbyhole office located at the rear of the mechanic shop. "While I'm out of commission for the upcoming month you can call Jenny to help you pinpoint errors."

"Yeah, but—" Cleatus tried to object.

"But nothing, boys," Amanda cut in sternly, determined in her campaign to see that Jenny received the credit she deserved. "Jen has come a long way in the accounting business. She takes her job and responsibilities very seriously. You boys need to cut her some slack. Okay?''

"Okay, 'Manda, we get the picture,'' Cecil mumbled as he and Cleatus followed in her wake.

"Thanks.'' Amanda waddled into the office to appraise the untidy stacks of invoices and bills that were scattered across the metal desk. Her sense of order and organization took offense at the sloppy mess.

Amanda glanced over to see an ashtray, heaping with butts, sitting on top of the file cabinet. A girlie calendar hung on the wall. Miss October wore only the skimpy bottom half of a bright orange bikini. The bleached-blond model strategically held two pumpkins in front of her silicone-endowed chest.

Amanda raised a brow, then shot the Watts brothers a glance. "My, Miss October is sporting some nice pumpkins, isn't she?''

Cleatus and Cecil both shifted awkwardly from one booted foot to the other. Then Cleatus scuttled meekly across the office to remove the offensive calendar and place it on the file cabinet.

"Let me see your ledger, boys,'' Amanda requested.

Cecil hurriedly scooped up the stack of invoices that were piled on the chair so Amanda could sit down at the desk.

Within five minutes Amanda noticed the mistake and pointed it out with a jack-o'-lantern-tipped forefinger. "Invoice seventeen-twelve is listed as a billing account,'' she said.

"Is it?'' Cleatus scratched his head as he leaned over Amanda's shoulder to study the ledger. "Well, hell, it is. What's the date on that invoice?''

"Last Friday,'' Amanda replied.

"Well, damn,'' Cecil muttered. "I must've screwed that up because I was in a hurry. Nettie Jarvis brought her car in for repairs and I must've switched the bill with the invoice for that new starter I put on her car.''

"Nettie drove herself into town?" Amanda asked, glancing up.

"Naw, that Franklin woman chauffeured her," Cleatus explained. "Nettie pays the lady to help her tend errands; then Nettie buys her lunch at the Last Chance Café. We did a hurry-up job while they had lunch so Nettie wouldn't have to hang around here longer than necessary. Those car fumes really get to her, ya know?"

Amanda wondered about Eileen Franklin's reasons for doing odd jobs for Nettie. *Hmmm.* Was Eileen chauffeuring Nettie out of kindness and friendship? Or did the part-time nurse have an underlying motive?

Once Amanda made the correction in the ledger, she grabbed the solar-powered calculator and refigured the totals. "Now you are squared away and your books are balanced," she declared.

"Thanks, 'Manda. Me and Cecil may have magical hands when it comes to mechanical work and auto-body repair, but we don't have the best heads for business."

Amanda smiled wryly at them. "You probably got distracted while filling in your ledger because your eyes strayed to Miss October and her pumpkins. I certainly hope Miss *November* is wearing enough clothes to keep herself warm. You might get distracted again."

Both men grinned, then chuckled good-naturedly.

Amanda's smile faded. "I'm afraid I have some bad news. Nettie Jarvis will no longer be coming here for auto repairs. She passed away this morning," she reported as she hoisted herself from the folding chair.

"Oh, damn. Her asthma got to her?" Cleatus questioned.

Amanda didn't reply, just shrugged noncommittally.

"That sure is a shame," Cecil murmured as he reached for a cigarette, then refrained from lighting up in the small office, as a courtesy to Amanda. "Nettie was a spirited old gal. Used to cut our hair when we were kids."

"Was Eileen Franklin good with Nettie?" Amanda wanted to know.

Cleatus shrugged his bulky shoulders. "She never had much to say. Nettie did most of the talking."

Amanda glanced at her watch, then waddled toward the door. "I need to get back to my office."

"Thanks for stopping by, 'Manda," Cecil called.

"Yeah, thanks for finding our mistake," Cleatus seconded.

"No problem." Amanda glanced over her shoulder. "One more question. Did Nettie ever pay outstanding bills for her brother or sister?"

The Watts brothers nodded simultaneously.

"Recently?" Amanda questioned.

"Been about six months ago," Cleatus replied. "She paid Faye's bill for a new fuel pump and filter. Faye let the bill go for three months."

Amanda muttered under her breath as she zigzagged around the car parts that were strewn on the floor of the mechanic shop. Nettie seemed to think she was the family's keeper. Her siblings were nothing but a couple of leeches.

Amanda clambered into her pickup and switched on the ignition. The country limousine growled to life. Checking both directions before pulling onto Main Street, Amanda cruised back to her office.

"Ohmigod! What have Velma and Bev done to you this time?" Jenny yelped when Amanda toddled clumsily into the accounting office.

"Great news," Amanda said with feigned enthusiasm. "I've been named honorary Pumpkin Queen. So . . . do you think my new hair color and style make me resemble a pumpkin?"

"Absolutely . . . I mean . . ." Jenny's voice dried up; she was unsure what her response should be.

Amanda sank down at her desk. "Don't worry about it, Jen. At this point in my life"—she glanced down at her protruding tummy—"physical appearance is the least of my concerns. Now then, is there anything I need to take care of before I call it a day? I stopped by Thatcher Oil and Gas and Watts Mechanic Shop to solve their accounting glitches on my way back to the office."

Jenny picked up a phone message. "This will be something you will want to handle personally, considering the events of the day."

Amanda frowned curiously.

"Odell Jarvis called shortly after you left the office. He wanted to know how long it would take you to finalize Nettie's estate."

Amanda's brows shot up like exclamation marks. "I wonder why Odell is in such a flaming rush to have his older sister's estate settled?"

"Rumor has it that Odell lives on borrowed money. Maybe he is hoping to inherit," said Jenny.

"I'm sure he is," Amanda murmured pensively.

Her suspicions fluttered to life and she hoisted herself from her chair. "I think I'll stop by Odell's to offer my condolences on my way home. Will you call the home–health care service and inform them that Nettie has passed on? Just to satisfy my curiosity, find out what days Arthella Carson visited Nettie. I would like to know if the nurse noticed anything odd about Nettie's behavior or an increase in health complications."

"Sure thing, boss." Jenny glanced up as she reached for the phone. "Is Nicky going to bring the load of pumpkins by the office after he gets off duty this evening? Don't forget that Dave, Timmy, and I are going to decorate the place tonight."

Amanda nodded her pumpkin-colored head. "He'll be here."

"Good, we'll have the lights and decorations in place before dark."

Waving a hand that boasted jack-o'-lantern-decorated nails, Amanda exited her office. She swung by Toot 'N' Tell 'Em to grab a vanilla malt to curb a sudden craving. Geez, if she didn't deliver soon she was going to weigh five hundred pounds!

Amanda applied the brake and stared thoughtfully at the ritzy home, gigantic metal barn, expensive tractor, machinery, and shiny new pickup truck at Odell's farm. The place reeked of money—borrowed money, if the rumors were to be believed. While Nettie muddled by without collecting status symbols of wealth, her younger brother advertised the fact that money flowed freely from his pockets.

Amanda approached the house and rang the doorbell. Odell appeared immediately. Judging by his appearance, Odell was half a dozen years younger than Nettie. His egg-shaped face broke into an eager smile as he greeted her.

She took a moment to size up Odell, who was dressed in expensive Western clothes. Thick brown hair capped his head. Straight brows lay across his broad forehead like caterpillars. There were pouches under his deep-set eyes and another pouch around his midsection. His starched blue jeans creased over a pair of Mercedes boots. Yep, Odell was dressed as if he had money to burn. Self-image was obviously important to him.

Odell stepped aside, his arm sweeping in an expansive gesture. "Come on in. I was hoping you would stop by."

Of course he was, thought Amanda. She held the purse strings to Nettie's estate, and Odell wanted his cut of the dough.

"Nice place you have here," Amanda said as she appraised the sprawling living room with its matching sofa, love seat, and recliners.

"Thanks." Odell closed the door and gestured for her

to take a seat. "Thorn came by to give me the news. He said you were the one who found Nettie."

It greatly disturbed Amanda that Odell hadn't shown the slightest grief for his departed sister. Now why was that?

"I was exceptionally fond of Nettie," she said.

"Were you?"

Not, "So was I," Amanda noted. Odell didn't seem all that broken up about the loss of his older sister. There was no reason for her to console Odell, she decided. She might as well get down and dirty and forget the chitchat.

"No money is going to change hands until I see Nettie's journal." She paused for emphasis. Sure enough, Odell's eyes bugged out and his jaw scraped his chest. He definitely knew about the journal, and perhaps knew of its contents. "Furthermore," she continued, "I haven't seen Nettie's will. When I do, you will be notified. . . ."

Amanda's voice trailed off when she noticed a taffy colored, declawed tomcat entering the room and making itself at home on the sofa. "You keep a cat?" she asked, surprised.

Odell, who had yet to recover from Amanda's statement about the journal, merely nodded.

"Even though your sister was violently allergic to them, you kept a cat in the house?"

He shrugged his bulky shoulders. "She didn't stop by very often."

"Did you stop by to see her often?" Amanda quizzed him.

"On holidays or on matters of business," he replied.

"Now why was that?"

Odell blinked, then recoiled warily. "Why was what?"

Amanda made note of his defensive posture. Odell was suddenly aware of her reputation as an amateur hacksaw. He was being *too* careful about what he said.

"Why didn't you visit your ailing sister? Were there

ill feelings between you? Was she still irritated because you sold your inherited property in town to the bank?"

Odell's eyes popped. "Well, hell, how did you know about that?"

"As executor of the estate I make it my business to know the wheretos and what-fors associated with my departed clients," she informed him.

He glowered at her, then stared pointedly at her pumpkin-colored 'do. "You've been at Velma's gathering gossip, is my guess. Those old hens just love to cluck and spread rumors. Fact is, Nettie didn't give a rip what I did with my property."

Liar! "We'll see about that when her journal turns up."

Odell gnashed his teeth. "Journal or no journal, I need to know what Nettie left me."

"Need to know?" Amanda repeated emphatically. "Why? Outstanding bills to be paid? Like the one Nettie paid at the service station for you? Mortgages due?"

"Look, Hazard—"

"Hazard-Thorn," she corrected tersely.

"What's going on in my life is none of your damn business," he snapped. "I called your office for information. I have a right to know how long it will take to settle Nettie's affairs and divvy up the inheritance. And don't lay your interrogation routine on me. I know how you operate. So does everybody else in Vamoose. When somebody kicks the bucket you're Johnny-on-the-spot, asking suspicious questions, sniffing out possible suspects. Well, for your information, Nettie had health problems for years, nearly bought the farm a couple of times because of her asthma attacks. She was seventy-three years old, after all. Things happen."

"Were those attacks brought on by stress caused by dealing with her brother?" Amanda fired the question at him.

"I never gave Nettie grief!" he all but shouted.

"Where were you at ten-thirty this morning?" she shot back.

"Hauling hay to my cattle," he said, and scowled.

"Why did you confiscate the little black book Nettie intended to entrust to me?"

His doughy face turned white. "I never touched the damned thing!"

Amanda wasn't prepared to believe a word he said. "If my brother was as indifferent to my unexpected departure from this world as you are about Nettie's, I would come back to haunt him," she said for shock value.

Odell slumped back in his recliner, stared at the ceiling, then sighed audibly. "Fine, you want the truth, then here it is. Nettie and I didn't get along all that well. Never did."

"Why is that?"

"That's none of your business, either. Suffice it to say that she tried to run my life because she was the oldest. I wouldn't have it. I told her I didn't particularly care for the way she lived her life, either. But you don't get to pick your family, only your friends, so Nettie and Faye and I were pretty much stuck with one another. Nettie was a lot like Dad."

"Was that good or bad?" Amanda wanted to know.

"Bad. He tried to run everybody's life as if we were an extension of his own."

"So you and Faye rebelled against Nettie," Amanda speculated.

"We ventured out on our own early in life," Odell admitted. "Nettie stayed in the original homestead with Dad. She never married."

"Was that because she was grieving the loss of Jim Foster, who was killed in the auto accident?"

When Odell squirmed uneasily, then stared out the window, Amanda sensed there was more to the story than she had heard told. Efficient gumshoe that she was, she started digging for the rest of the story.

"So . . . who was it who did not approve of Jim Foster as Nettie's boyfriend? You or your dad?"

"Everybody liked Jim just fine," he said shortly.

Amanda watched Odell fidget in his chair for a few more moments; then she stared very deliberately at him. She had the unshakable feeling that Odell might have been involved in that incident.

"You were in the car when Jim was killed, weren't you? Were you driving?"

Odell's back went up, his hands clenched on the armrests. "Certainly not. What in the hell made you ask that? I was six years younger than Jim. Why would I be driving?"

"Maybe because you talked him into letting you drive, because Jim was sweet on Nettie." She noticed the scar near Odell's left eye and she had a pretty good idea how and when he had received the injury. "You lost control of the car, didn't you? Was Jim thrown from the car when you received the cut on your face?"

His face blanched and his thin mouth puckered unattractively.

"You may as well admit it, Odell. I can go back and check newspaper reports and police records to find out for certain."

He clamped his lips together, stuck out his square chin, and refused to speak.

Amanda was nothing if not relentless. "What did you do, Odell? Inform the police that Jim was driving, not you? Was booze involved? Did you cover up the story? No wonder you and Nettie had a conflict. She probably was a long time forgiving you for your part in taking the first love of her life away from her."

"I am not answering any more questions on this subject. The accident happened years ago. The case is closed. It's over and done and forgotten."

Over and done for Odell, but it was probably never over for Nettie, Amanda suspected. That incident was just one more thing that caused dissension between Nettie and her younger brother.

"Nettie wanted to live on the farm and take care of the finances when Dad became too feebleminded to do it himself," Odell said in a rush, anxious to change the topic of conversation.

"How often did you borrow money from Nettie?" Amanda asked abruptly.

"Never!" he roared.

"No?" Amanda didn't believe him. His denial was a little too loud for her tastes.

"Certainly not. I could take care of my own family without Nettie's help."

Amanda stared at the bookshelves that boasted family pictures of two egg-shaped-faced children . . . and no wife.

"Are you married, Odell?"

"Divorced," he responded tartly.

"For how long?"

Odell shifted awkwardly on his recliner. Amanda's probing questions made it difficult for him to sit still. "The divorce was final twenty-four years ago."

When Amanda opened her mouth to pose another question, Odell flung up a beefy hand. "It's none of your business why the marriage broke up. My ex-wife moved out of state and remarried. The kids went with her. I only see them on holidays, if I'm lucky."

From the sound of things, Odell had isolated himself from his older sister, his ex-wife, and his children. There was definitely more to the story than Odell wanted to tell. Damn, if only she could get her hands on Nettie's journal. The answers to her questions were probably there, in black and white.

Odell surged from his chair, then glanced at his Rolex

watch. "I have a meeting to attend tonight, so you will have to excuse me. I'll expect a call from you the minute the estate is settled."

Amanda took her cue to leave. She decided, on her way down the sidewalk, that Odell Jarvis was suspect numero uno. There was no love lost between him and Nettie. Because of Odell's reckless foolishness, Nettie lost her first love. Yet despite the bitterness and tragedy, the Jarvis family had closed in to protect one of their own.

Odell behaved as if he had something else to hide besides his involvement in the traffic accident. Amanda couldn't help but wonder what it was that made Odell defensive. Amanda was also curious to know what had broken up Odell's marriage almost a quarter of a century ago.

No doubt the divorce had been expensive. Rumor had it that Odell had lost money in the stock market, trying to make fast cash with risky investments. He had sold his town property to keep up appearances and make ends meet. He had very expensive tastes in clothes, home furnishings, and vehicles. There was no telling how much money Odell had gone through in his life.

Nettie probably knew, right down to the penny.

But Nettie wasn't around to divulge that information. How convenient.

Amanda had the unmistakable feeling that Nettie had died because she knew too much.

During the drive home Amanda recounted the bits of information she had gathered about Nettie Jarvis and her family. Not much had been said about sister Faye. Amanda wondered how the woman fit into the family dynamics, wondered if Faye would be as reluctant to spill her guts as Odell was.

Amanda turned into the gravel driveway, serenaded by mooing cattle, clucking chickens, and baa-ing sheep. She smiled to herself, knowing that Thorn's family farm would be a grand place to raise kids. There were plenty of wide-open spaces and lots of fresh air. She could only hope their children didn't turn out to be as alienated from one another as the Jarvises appeared to be.

FIVE

By the time Nick reached the farm it was nearly dark. He still had hay to feed to the cattle and sheep. The amount of time needed to haul the pumpkins from Nettie's homestead to Hazard's accounting office left Nick scrambling to complete his farm chores. Hurriedly he broke apart chunks of alfalfa hay bales and tossed them to the sheep. He climbed on the Allis-Chalmers tractor to feed a round bale of wheat hay to the cattle. Between his police duties and farm chores he was meeting himself coming and going. But no matter how busy he was, he fully intended to make time when the baby arrived. He was going to be a doting father and husband. He had seen too many kids go bad because of lack of parental involvement and guidance.

His kids were *not* going to go bad, not if he could help it!

"Thorn!" Hazard's loud voice rang through the still evening air. "Thorn, come here!"

Nick bounded from the tractor and hit the ground running. *Oh, my God!* Hazard had gone into labor! This was the big moment, he thought, frantic. It was time! Was he prepared? Would he make a good labor coach? He had read the manuals from cover to cover, though Hazard hadn't bothered. He had to be good enough to get both of them through this delivery.

Nick tore off his work gloves and sprinted toward the front steps. He saw Hazard resting her arms on her distended tummy. *Oh, God, oh, God!* He hadn't packed her suitcase yet. He was ill-prepared for one of the most important moments of his life!

"Supper's ready," Hazard said as he bounded onto the porch.

Nick skidded to a halt, his eyes wide as silver dollars. "Supper?" he repeated stupidly.

"Yeah, you know, the meal we eat about this time every evening." Hazard stared curiously at him while his chest rose and fell in panted breaths. "Are you okay, Thorn? You look a little peaked."

"Fine," he wheezed. "I'm just fine." He willed his pounding pulse to return to normal.

"Then why did you come charging up here as if your pants were on fire?" she asked.

Nick curled his arm around Hazard's waist to escort her into the house. "I thought you had gone into labor."

Hazard lifted a brow and grinned in amusement. Nick looked down at her, then realized that he had been so frantic that he hadn't noticed that her silky blond hair was a nauseating shade of orange.

"What the hell did you do to your hair?" he chirped.

Her face fell, and Nick mentally kicked himself for upsetting her. These days it didn't take much effort to upset Hazard. Her emotions swung like a clock pendulum.

"Sorry, sweetheart," he cooed as he shepherded her into the dining room. "I presume this new 'do is the direct result of your fact-finding mission."

She bobbed her orange-tinted head. He noticed her fluorescent, jack-o'-lantern fingernails and he inwardly groaned. Those blasted beauticians had turned Hazard into something akin to a circus freak.

"Well, I guess your pumpkin hair is the perfect color for the Halloween season, isn't it?" he said in a feeble attempt at humor.

The comment had the reverse effect on Hazard. She was upset, not amused. Fat tears rolled down her cheeks.

"Oh, Thorn!" she wailed. "I look positively hideous. Orange hair and nails, belly like a blimp. Face like rising dough and swollen feet that I can't see when I'm standing up!"

"There, there, sugarplum," he murmured, giving her a compassionate hug. "You still look gorgeous to me."

"You're just saying that," she sniveled.

"Haz, haven't I been there for you during seven previous cosmetic disasters?"

Sniffing, Hazard bobbed her orange-tinted head.

"Wasn't I there when you had purple hair? Pink hair? A bad case of frizz head? And how about the time Velma nearly scalped you? Or the time she used such strong peroxide that your hair broke off? My feelings for you didn't change, did they?"

"No, but"—*hiccup, sob*—"you almost didn't marry me," she reminded him in a quavering voice.

"That's because I was so jealous of Sam Harjo that I couldn't think straight. I thought you preferred the county commish to me. I was out of my mind, scared spitless that I was going to lose you."

"Oh, Thorn!" She flung her arms around his neck and hugged the stuffing out of him.

Nick smiled grimly. Hazard's abrupt mood swings weren't easy to handle, but he would make it through these last few weeks. Somehow.

Then he would have to deal with postdelivery depression. *Gawd!*

"Feeling better now, honey-bunch?" he asked hopefully.

"No."

"Maybe after you eat . . ." His voice dried up when he glanced over her orange-colored head to see the entrée. Shit on a shingle. His stomach flipped over. "You cooked. You really shouldn't have, Hazard."

Hazard's culinary skills were limited to creamed tuna on toast and a variety of microwavable dinners, most of which were barely edible.

"Well, doesn't this look yummy," Nick lied through his cheery smile. "Sit down, Haz. I'll grab a couple of glasses of iced tea."

"We don't have iced tea." Hazard plunked ungracefully into her chair. "I had a wild craving for cranberry juice."

Nick absolutely hated cranberry juice. "Sounds great. I'll get us a glass."

When he returned to the table Hazard was chowing down on the unappetizing food. Nick made himself eat, promising his stomach that a tasty midnight snack was forthcoming.

"Did you deliver the pumpkins to my office?" Hazard asked between sips of juice.

"Yes. Jenny, Dave, and little Timmy are doing a fantastic job of decorating the place. But Thaddeus Thatcher is going to be tough to beat in the decoration contest this year. He has glow-in-the-dark spooks circling around his service station. He rigged up some kind of mechanical device to keep the ghosts parading overhead."

"Velma also went all-out this year. She had all her relatives swarming around the beauty shop, putting up decorations. She has enough orange and purple lights on the roof and eaves to land an aircraft," she added.

"Cecil and Cleatus Watts are stringing lights all over a pickup truck that sits in front of their automotive shop. The truck bed is loaded with lighted jack-o'-lanterns, and chaser lights are wrapped around all four wheels to make it look as if the truck is in motion. Pretty impressive,'' Nick commented.

"I would like for you to call the medical examiner and ask him to check to see if Nettie had any scratches or welts on her face and neck."

Nick nearly choked on his god-awful cranberry juice when Hazard blurted her demand, right out of the blue. "Why?" he peeped, after he caught his breath.

"Because I found out at the beauty shop that, besides Nettie's asthmatic condition, she suffered a severe allergic reaction to cats last spring. It nearly did her in. There was a black cat near the pumpkin patch when I found Nettie this morning. She didn't keep cats, because of her health condition."

"Hazard—" Nick said warningly.

"We don't have much time to solve this case, Thorn," she cut in, then gave him a pleading look.

Nick had always been a sucker for those hypnotic eyes. "Okay," he heard himself say.

"Thanks, honey."

When she smiled gratefully at him, his shit on a shingle went down much easier.

"I talked to Odell Jarvis today. Doubt he'll lose much sleep over Nettie's passing," Nick commented.

"Probably not. I also stopped by to see him on my way home. As I heard it told, Odell and Nettie weren't on the friendliest of terms. There were some serious conflicts in their past that made for ill feelings." Hazard chewed her creamed tuna, swallowed, then asked, "Do you have any idea why Odell's wife left him?"

Nick shrugged. "I was just a kid at the time. I was too busy fishing, hunting, and fighting with my older brother to pay much attention to what was going on with the older generations."

"Maybe I'm just extrasensitive right now—"

"That's one way of putting it." Nick slammed his mouth shut when Hazard gave him the evil eye. He smiled good-naturedly, then added, "According to everything I've read, altering moods and supersensitivity come with the territory."

"As I was saying," Hazard went on. "When I asked Odell about his divorce, I swore I saw him wince, saw him try to conceal a pained expression. There is something about the divorce that still causes him discomfort, even after all these years. I think he is hiding something, and I keep wondering if it has something to do with Nettie."

"Don't wear yourself out stewing about this case," Nick said after he forced down a bite of tasteless creamed tuna. "I promised to look into it."

"I'm grateful that you have taken my suspicions seriously, Thorn." She gave him one of those smiles that made his brain go into nuclear meltdown.

"After you check with the coroner I would like for you to talk to Ginger and Melvin Rumley."

"The Rumleys?" he parroted. "How come?"

"They rent the building space from Nettie. Just poke around a bit. See if they get touchy when you question them about their dealings with their landlady."

"Sure thing, Haz, I'll do it tomorrow."

Another blinding smile. Nick marveled at Hazard's startling mood swings. One minute she was bawling like an abandoned baby—which *his* kid never would be!—and the next minute she was giving him those knock-'em-dead grins. It was like being married to two different women. He never knew which one was going to show up.

"You also might check with Mickey Poag, who farms Nettie's farmland. Find out where he was this morning," she suggested.

Although Nick was pretty sure Hazard's roiling hormones and chemical imbalances had affected her suspicions, he didn't protest questioning the Rumleys and Poag. A man had to do what a man had to do when dealing with his pregnant wife.

Nick wiped his mouth with the napkin, then picked up the empty plates. "Thanks for supper. It was good." *Yeah, right!* "I'm going to set up the crib this evening."

"Thorn, there is something I need to—"

"Just go put your feet up and relax," Nick cut in. "You've had a hectic day, and the prenatal manuals insist that you should have plenty of rest."

"Fine, I'll look over Nettie's tax files, but we still need—"

The phone rang, interrupting her.

"I'll get it, Haz. Go relax," he ordered in a no-nonsense tone.

Nick snatched up the phone on the second ring. "Thorn here."

"Hi, Nicky, it's Mom. Is everything all right with you?"

Nick grimaced. Between his mom and Hazard's mother there was no peace to be had around here. Mom made it plain that she thought Nick and Hazard had jumped the gun with this baby business. According to Mom, the newlyweds should have waited a couple of years—to make certain this ill-advised marriage would stick— before starting a family. Mom still wasn't convinced that a mixed marriage between a city girl and a country boy could work. In addition, Mom didn't think Hazard was good enough for her darling son. Then there was Mother Hazard, who was positively certain that Nick was nothing but a rock-stupid bumpkin who didn't deserve a woman like Amanda.

"Everything is dandy fine here in Vamoose, Mom. How are things down in Texas?"

"The weather has been great down here in Retirement Valley. Your dad is still playing golf two times a week. Of course, he is no better at the game than he was when he retired and took up the sport, but it does get your dad out of the house and out from under my feet.

"Now, enough of this small talk, Nicky," Mom said.

"I called to see how things are going between you and that *Hazard* you married."

"Things couldn't be better," Nick said enthusiastically. "She fixed a delicious supper for me this evening, and she had it ready when I came in from doing my farm chores."

"Delicious?" Mom sniffed sarcastically. "Please, Nicky. I am not stupid, you know. I am aware that Hazard can't cook a lick. Are you getting enough to eat? You haven't lost weight, have you? I don't want her piling on the pounds while you slough them off from lack of proper nutrition."

"Not to worry, Mom," Nick said, gritting his teeth to prevent himself from yelling at his meddling mom. "I am nutritiously fit and healthy as a horse. Hazard is taking great care of me and I'm taking great care of her."

"I don't think you would tell me even if you weren't in perfect health. I don't know why you try to defend that *Hazard* to me. You know how I feel about this marriage you rushed into without thinking things out clearly. Just look what happened to your big brother when he married that idiotic woman who up and left him and broke his heart. I don't want that to happen to you."

"It won't," Nick assured Mom. "This marriage is forever."

"Well, I guess I will find out for myself how things are going between the two of you when Dad and I drive up to see the new baby. And speaking of the new baby, you should seriously consider hiring a responsible nanny to look after your little tyke. I'm not sure Hazard knows any more about child rearing than she does about cooking, cleaning, and caring for her busy husband. I assume she still hasn't quit her job to stay home and become a model farm wife."

"No, Mom," Nick said through his teeth. "Hazard has entirely too many clients depending on her for financial advice to even consider shutting down her accounting office. She is still in great demand around here.''

"Well, I suppose it's good that she is efficient at something, though cooking, cleaning, and providing a contented home for her husband is not high on the list.''

"Mom,'' Nick snapped, at the end of his patience, ''I am perfectly satisfied with the woman I married. I would appreciate it if you would cut Hazard a little slack.''

"I will when and if I discover that things are truly good between you and that woman you married in a flaming rush.''

"We did not marry in a flaming rush,'' Nick gritted out. ''We dated for a couple of years.''

"Years, decades, whatever,'' Mom said. ''The problem is that you come from entirely different backgrounds. Then, of course, there is the problem of Hazard's obnoxious mother.''

"Ah, yes.'' Nick grinned for the first time in several minutes. ''I recall how the two of you came to blows at the wedding. Pardon me for saying so, Mom, but at the time, it was hard to tell who was being obnoxious.''

Mom howled at the insult. ''What a horrible thing to say to your own mother!''

"Sorry, Mom, I don't know what came over me.''

"Now tell me the truth, Nicky. Are you and Hazard getting along all right?'' Mom persisted.

"Hazard and I are happy,'' Nick said firmly. ''Incredibly, deliriously happy.''

"You wouldn't lie to me, would you, Nicky? This marriage isn't headed for divorce already, is it?''

When Nick assured his mom—for the forty-seventh time—that there was no trouble whatsoever in paradise, she finally gave up and said good-bye.

Nick hurried off to assemble the crib and arrange the other furniture in the nursery. He returned to the living room an hour later to see Hazard sprawled in her La-Z-

Boy recliner. Nettie's open file lay on her rounded tummy and she was fast asleep.

Nick set aside the file, scooped up Hazard, and carried her to bed. She mumbled something indecipherable, then snuggled against his chest.

"Eat your heart out, Sam Harjo," Nick said as he tucked Hazard in their king-size bed.

Nick shook his head in self-deprecation. He thought he had overcome his insecurities where Sam Harjo was concerned. Apparently not, if he was still making smart-ass comments like that one.

"Just get over it, Thorn," Nick told himself as he crawled into bed beside Hazard. "You are the one who took home the grand prize. So don't rub it in Harjo's face."

On that noble thought, Nick faded off to sleep.

SIX

Amanda yawned as she pulled her truck to a stop in front of Nettie Jarvis's house. After spending the evening poring over the spinster's tax files, Amanda realized that the rent income received from Mickey Poag and the Rumleys, plus the social security checks, would not cover the monthly fees and down payment for the New Horizon Retirement Village. Where had the money come from?

When the numbers didn't add up Amanda's mathematical mind immediately turned suspicious. She wondered if Nettie's interest in moving into New Horizon had something to do with the events leading up to her death.

But since Nettie couldn't afford the steep down payment, had she planned to sell her farm? To Mickey Poag, perhaps? To her brother Odell? To her sister Faye Jarvis-Mithlo?

Yet Nettie had been annoyed at her brother for his involvement in her high school sweetheart's tragic death and for selling his city property. Would her long-harbored resentment prompt her to sell the land passed down from one Jarvis generation to the next so Odell couldn't have it?

Amanda made a mental note to call Jenny at the office and ask her to check out Odell's and Faye's tax files for average annual income. Amanda didn't think either of Nettie's siblings could afford to buy a one-hundred-sixty-acre farm. Same for Mickey Poag. She didn't know how much financial backing he had behind him. Agricultural profits were down, and Amanda suspected that Mickey was barely getting by.

The moment before Amanda shuffled into Nettie's house, she put on her latex gloves to keep from leaving fingerprints, then grabbed the phone and dialed.

"Hazard Accounting. Jenny speaking."

"Jen, it's Amanda."

"Are you okay, boss? Are you in labor?" Jenny asked excitedly.

Amanda smiled to herself, recalling how Thorn had dropped what he was doing the previous evening to come racing to the house. The false alarms would only grow worse these next couple of weeks, she predicted.

"I am perfectly fine," Amanda assured her. "I want you to check some files for me. I need to know the average annual income for the past five years for Odell Jarvis, Faye Jarvis-Mithlo, Mickey Poag . . . and why don't you give me the net income for the Rumleys while you're at it."

"Are we looking for evidence of foul play, boss? You don't think Nettie died by accident, do you?"

"As my loyal employee, I am swearing you to secrecy," Amanda said gravely. "I do not want word to get out that I have suspicions. You can't even tell your husband. Got it?"

"Got it, boss. Mum's the word. Promise. I have always wanted to help with one of your unofficial investigations."

Amanda noted the excitement in Jenny's voice. She was eating this stuff up. "Okay, between you, me, and

Thorn, we are going to find out if anyone had reason to want Nettie dead. I need to know if the people I mentioned are sucking air, financially speaking.''

''I'll have the info for you, PDQ. Where are you, boss?''

''At Pumpkin Hollow. I'm going to sniff around and see what turns up. Call me here at Nettie's when you've got the figures.''

''Right, boss.''

Amanda hung up the phone and took a moment to survey the old farmhouse. Now where—if Amanda were Nettie—would she stash that journal? Nettie walked unsteadily with a cane and wore a portable breathing device. Nettie would not have been climbing or crawling around to conceal that little black book. It had to be hidden within easy reach.

Okay, Amanda told herself as she wandered down the hall. She checked the medicine cabinet and linen closet in the bathroom, after making use of the facilities.

Still no little black book.

Amanda veered into Nettie's bedroom, then stared at the quilted bedspread. Very interesting, Amanda thought as she bent forward to pluck up a long, straight black hair. Cat hair, as in the black cat she had seen in the pumpkin patch.

That sinister sensation that had assailed her the first time she entered the room yesterday bombarded her again. Something had happened in this room. Unless she missed her guess—and she seriously doubted she had—this was where the murderer had done his/her dastardly deed.

The evidence of black cat hair on the bed—and there were a good many of them, Amanda noticed—suggested Nettie had had a cat stuffed in her face and someone jerked her breathing respirator loose. It was here that Nettie had gasped for breath, just as she had last spring at the beauty shop.

Nettie had been wearing house shoes when she died,

because she had been in her house, on this bed. *Not* in the pumpkin patch.

The killer was familiar with Nettie's habits and health problems, Amanda assured herself. He/she had done the dirty deed, then staged the accident in the garden to ward off suspicion. But the killer had neglected one minute detail—the house shoes.

Either that or Amanda had arrived before the killer could exchange Nettie's house shoes for her Nikes.

Amanda frowned. Her guess was that the killer simply overlooked the telling detail, because there wasn't a vehicle parked in the driveway when Amanda had arrived. That suggested the killer had fled the crime scene minutes before Amanda appeared.

Damn, if only she had been a quarter of an hour earlier she might have prevented the crime—or got caught up in it. . . .

The uneasy thought gave her the willies.

Wheeling around, Amanda strode back to the kitchen to find some plastic bags. She had every intention of having both pillow shams tested. One of them could have been used to suffocate Nettie while she was reacting violently to close contact with the black cat.

Definitely a clever killer, Amanda mused as she sacked the pillows. He/she had preyed on Nettie's health condition, committed the crime, then moved the body.

Clever or not, Amanda was determined to see justice served before her D day.

The phone jingled. Amanda plucked up the receiver from the nightstand. "Yes?"

"It's me, boss. I've got the info you wanted."

"Good. What's the bottom line?" Amanda asked.

"Mickey Poag operates in the red. He owes more than he earns in annual income. Odell Jarvis's tax file tells the same story. He hasn't made money in three years. Interest on his loans is sucking up his farm income. Faye and Willis Mithlo show an average yearly income of twelve thousand dollars. I'm not surprised about that, though. I knew the Mithlos weren't financially affluent. But they gave most of what they had to one of their two children.''

"And their children are . . . ?'' Amanda waited for Jenny to fill in the blank.

"Roy and Delilah.''

Roy Mithlo's name was familiar to Amanda. She re-recalled that Roy worked at the nearby town of Pronto as a grease monkey at the tractor supply and repair service. She had often heard Thorn grouse about the ridiculous amount of time it took Roy to make repairs. He was slow and ineffective and pure-dee lazy, according to Thorn.

"Do I know Delilah?'' Amanda asked belatedly.

"Sure you do. That's Sis.''

Sis? Delilah is Sis Hix? Bubba's wife? Bubba Junior and little Sissy's mother? Good gad! Sis was Nettie's niece? Odell's niece?

"Boss? Are you still there?''

"Yes, I am mentally processing information. Sis's maiden name is Mithlo, huh?''

"Yep,'' Jenny confirmed. "I always felt sorry for Sis, because Roy got most of the attention. Sis was just left to grow up, away from the family limelight. Her aunt Nettie was the only one who ever paid much attention to her.''

While Jenny rattled on about how Roy had pocket money handed to him and Sis was left to clean houses and baby-sit to make spending money as a teenager, Amanda's thoughts ran rampant.

Sis was ignored, except by her aunt Nettie? Nettie the spinster? Was it possible that Nettie might have been Sis's real mother and Faye had raised the child to avoid family scandal?

Amanda knew that older generations took a dim view of unwed mothers. Many were shipped off to distant relatives until their children were born, then given up for adoption or raised by married siblings. These days unplanned pregnancy wasn't hushed up. In fact, there were signs posted all over the state that read: PREGNANT? NEED HELP? CALL 1-800 . . . yada, yada, yada.

Had Nettie and Mr. Mysterious created a child named Delilah whom Faye had reluctantly raised as her own? That would explain why Sis was treated like a stepchild at home.

Poor Bubba and Sis Hix, thought Amanda. Neither of them had had an easy life. Money was scarce and the struggling couple had two young children to raise.

"Anything else you want me to check on, boss?" Jenny questioned eagerly.

"Yes, call New Horizon Retirement Village in Adios and see if Nettie had her name on the waiting list for one of the condos. See if you can find out if anyone there spoke to Nettie in person or on the phone. I want to know if Nettie put down a partial down payment."

"What if the retirement center won't give me the information?"

"Tell them our accounting agency is handling the estate and that we need to know if Nettie made a partial payment. Ask if the money can be returned, since Nettie died before she could take up residence."

"Wow, boss, you sure know how to get around all that bureaucratic red tape. I'm impressed."

"If you want to be an amateur sleuth you have to find your way around all sorts of obstacles," Amanda insisted. "After your phone call, trot over to the bank and see if there is a will or black book in Nettie's safe-deposit box. The key is in my briefcase with Nettie's tax file."

"Sure thing, boss."

"And do not explain yourself more than you have to," Amanda instructed. "Let the bank tellers think you're checking on your own safe-deposit box."

"Right, mum is still the word," Jenny said.

When Jenny hung up, Amanda dialed the police dispatcher. "Janie-Ethel? It's Amanda. I need you to contact Thorn."

"Oh, my gosh! Are you in labor?"

Amanda gnashed her teeth. The entire population of Vamoose was collectively holding its breath in anticipation of Amanda's private labor day.

"No," Amanda said calmly. "I just need the information Thorn promised to get for me."

"He went to Elvina Keef's house," Janie-Ethel reported. "She called at nine o'clock to say that she was beginning to recall a few details about her traffic accident."

"What accident?"

"You know, the one she had yesterday."

Amanda suddenly remembered. "Tell Thorn to meet me at the Last Chance Café at eleven-thirty."

"Ten-four, Amanda. Don't overdo it, you hear? You know how much the chief worries about you."

And how! Amanda thought as she hung up. She glanced at her watch. She had an hour to search for that little black book. After reviewing the information Jenny supplied, Amanda mentally added a few more names to her suspect list.

Faye and Willis Mithlo could certainly use the financial boost of an inheritance.

Mickey Poag might have gotten desperate, if Nettie announced to him that she planned to sell the farm so she could make a down payment on a retirement condo. Maybe Mickey couldn't afford to buy the property and he was afraid the new landowner would want to farm the land himself. Mickey would be out in the cold—with all sorts of farm machinery and no plot to plow.

No, on second thought, Mickey would have preferred to keep Nettie alive, rather than see her dead, Amanda reasoned. Better the devil you know, as the adage went.

Amanda was certain Mickey had one hell of a deal going with Nettie. Her farmland was worth considerably more than Mickey paid her in rent. Mickey wouldn't want anyone messing with that arrangement. But now there would be another owner. If Mickey had bumped off Nettie in a burst of impulsive anger, without thinking the matter through, then he had screwed up in reverse, Amanda decided. The man just didn't have that much to gain by disposing of his landlady. Mickey would be better off if Nettie were still alive . . . wouldn't he? Or had Amanda merely scratched the surface of the relationship between Nettie and Mickey Poag? Did she know something about Mickey that he didn't want exposed, same as Odell Jarvis?

Mulling over those questions, Amanda checked under the mattress, inside the nightstand drawers, and on the closet shelf, but there was no sign of that tell-all journal. Damn it, that book had to be here somewhere, and it was definitely linked to this case! Amanda could feel it in her bones.

Amanda checked the mattress in the spare bedroom, then rifled through the bookshelves. She received nothing but a nagging backache for her efforts. Then her hopes soared when she returned to the kitchen for a drink of water and noticed a black notebook tucked between several old cookbooks.

Her shoulders slumped in disappointment when she opened the little black book to find two dozen recipes for pumpkin pie, bread, cake, and pastry. Frustrated, Amanda headed for the barn. Maybe Nettie had stashed her journal outside the house. The spinster certainly made the jaunt from her house to the pumpkin patch often enough. It was not inconceivable that Nettie had found an easily accessible hidey-hole in that gargantuan barn.

Amanda scrounged around in the barn for ten minutes and found nothing but straw and dust that left her sneezing her head off. The roar of an engine interrupted her search. She lumbered outside to see who had arrived in Pumpkin Hollow.

Mickey Poag, driving a beat-up, bucket-of-rust truck,

wearing a pair of patched overalls, stepped down. He was a stout, burly, large-boned brute of a man with a broad head and noticeably large ears.

His mouth turned down at the corners; then he spit tobacco juice and glared at Amanda. "Nice hair, Hazard," he said, then scoffed. "I never dreamed that you got your kicks from looking like a human pumpkin."

Amanda refrained from retaliating by poking fun at his oversize ears. Exchanging insults was beneath her, or so she told herself.

"I guess I have you to thank for siccing Thorn on me," he growled at her.

The man was radiating hostility. She watched Mickey clench his fists at his sides and take a defensive stance. His neck was bowed and he kicked at the ground like a bull preparing to charge.

He wouldn't dare do bodily harm to a pregnant woman, would he?

" 'Just routine questions,' Thorn told me." Mickey snorted. "He asked me where the hell I was yesterday morning. He wanted to know if I had a witness who could verify my whereabouts. You call that routine? Damn it, Hazard, everybody in Vamoose knows you lead the chief around by his dumb handle, especially since he got you pregnant."

Amanda bared her teeth. "Watch your mouth, Mickey. There is nothing dumb about Thorn."

He shut his trap—fast. His gray-eyed gaze leaped from her to the pumpkin patch, then riveted on the black cat that hopped gracefully upon the pyramid of hay bales.

"Is that your cat?" Amanda inquired.

"Nope."

"It certainly doesn't belong to Nettie. She is allergic to them, you know."

"More than likely it's a stray that's mousing in the barn. And don't try to sidetrack me, Hazard. I want to know why you think I bumped off Nettie. And that is what you're thinking, isn't it? You've got Thorn poking around town to substantiate your harebrained suspicions!''

Mickey was getting more belligerent with each passing minute. What did he have to hide?

"Did Nettie announce she was going to raise your rent when you came by here yesterday?" Amanda grilled him. "Did you raise hell with her about it?"

Mickey nearly swallowed his wad of tobacco. "Who said I was here yesterday morning?"

"I did. Ranchers check their cattle and their fences daily. You are a creature of habit. Nettie wasn't stupid. She knew when you would come around, so all she had to do was flag you down."

Mickey shifted uneasily from one tree-stump leg to the other. "Okay, so I was here. That doesn't make me public enemy number one."

"So you admit that you talked to Nettie Monday morning," she pressed.

"On the front porch. I never set foot in the house," he clarified.

Why it seemed important for Mickey to point that out, Amanda wasn't sure. "Was she wearing her house slippers when you saw her?"

Mickey stared blankly at Amanda. "What?"

"House shoes or tennis shoes?" Amanda questioned.

"House shoes, I think," he said, then frowned ponderously. "Yeah, definitely house shoes."

"What time did this conversation take place?"

"Look, I've already been through this with Thorn," he muttered irritably.

"Indulge me. I'm pregnant and emotionally off center." She flashed him a pitiful smile as she rested her arms on her protruding tummy.

"About nine o'clock," Mickey grumbled.

His gaze darted away, which made Amanda wonder

why he couldn't maintain direct eye contact for more than a few seconds at a time. Was guilt eating away at him?

According to Mickey, if he was to be believed—and Amanda wouldn't want to wager money on that—he had communicated with Nettie an hour before Amanda arrived at the farm. *Hmm.* A lot could happen in an hour.

"What did you say when Nettie told you she wanted to raise your rent so she could move into the retirement village?"

Mickey's jaw sagged noticeably. "How did you know she hit me up for money for that?"

She didn't know. It was just a shot in the dark. But Amanda wasn't about to let on that she was shooting blanks. "I make it my business to know everything that goes on in the life of one of my clients who suddenly finds herself deceased."

"Well, hell, she told you, didn't she? All of it, then? Damn."

Amanda frowned, unsure what he meant, but she fully intended to play along with whatever Mickey thought she knew. "You've got that right, Mickey," she said. "I know all about it."

She glanced pensively at the faded brown truck and wondered if she might have seen it racing away from the scene, though she had been entirely too preoccupied to notice. The truck was the same color as rolling dust, so it was conceivable that Mickey had whizzed off while Amanda was distracted by the discovery of the dead body. That sort of thing had a way of preoccupying the most observant individual.

"Until further instruction, you are to send your rent payment to my office," Amanda said. "You will be notified when the will is read."

If there is one, she silently tacked on. Amanda certainly hoped so. Otherwise, good ol' Uncle Sam would get his sticky fingers on a good deal of Nettie's estate. Uncle Sam never missed a trick.

"May I be excused?" Mickey asked sarcastically.

"For your rudeness? No, there is no excuse for it," Amanda said just as sarcastically.

"Your hair really does look ridiculous." He repeated his earlier insult before he whipped around and stamped back to his truck.

"Up yours, asshole," Amanda muttered as the old truck sped away.

So, she thought as she ambled toward the storm cellar to search for the missing black book, Nettie had hit Mickey up for money . . . and something else. Mickey's comment indicated there was something else going on here besides the expected rent. What? Amanda wouldn't have a clue until she got her mitts on that journal!

Amanda wondered if Nettie had also hit the Rumleys up for an increase in rent for the property in Vamoose. How had they reacted? Unfavorably, most likely.

Amanda wrinkled her nose at the musty smell that greeted her on the first step of the stone shelter. She stared into the underground room, then took another tentative step down, bracing both hands on the crumbling walls on either side of her. She squinted at the incongruous shadows lurking below her. Surely Nettie wouldn't have stashed her journal down here. It would have been difficult for the older woman, using a cane, wearing her portable breathing apparatus, to descend the steps to this dank cellar.

When an unidentified sound drew Amanda's attention, she retreated. Rats, she speculated, then shivered. The disgusting rodents were scurrying around this antiquated cellar. *Ugh!*

Amanda hurried back to the house to collect her purse, then checked under the sofa cushions. "Well, darn it, Nettie, where did you put that blasted journal?"

Amanda made another pit stop in the bathroom—her second home nowadays. She pulled back the shower curtain, hoping to see the black book perched on the wire rack that contained shampoo and soap. No such luck.

"Hell." Disgruntled, Amanda returned to her pickup and zoomed off to meet Thorn for lunch.

SEVEN

"Hi, gorgeous."

Amanda pulled a face at Sam Harjo, the handsome county commish who had gone from potential boyfriend to dear friend after she married Thorn. Harjo was playfully ornery and fun-loving, and he delighted in teasing her and Thorn—especially Thorn.

"You can look at my puffy face, ballooned figure, this gawd-awful hairdo and call me gorgeous?" She smirked at him.

"Yeah, I can." Harjo gestured for Amanda to join him in the back booth at the Last Chance Café, where he was dining on a cheeseburger and fries. "Where's the Lone Ranger? I can't imagine that he would let you dine alone. Word around town is that the Heap Big Police Chief has the worst-case scenario of pussy-whipped. And he's overprotective to boot."

Amanda rolled her eyes at the commish, who reminded her of Clint Eastwood during his spaghetti westerns. "Don't you dare tease Thorn when he gets here, or I will have the waitress poison your iced tea," she threatened.

"Me? Tease Lone Ranger?" he said, all feigned innocence and engaging grin.

"Yeah, you. Unmercifully," Amanda affirmed. "Lay off of him, Harjo."

He gave her a playful wink. "Only because you asked, doll face."

"I guess you heard about Nettie Jarvis," Amanda commented as she sipped the water Trudy, the waitress, left for her.

"Yeah, Thaddeus Thatcher told me while I was fueling up my truck at the service station. I was down at Pumpkin Hollow the other day, checking the condition of the gravel roads. I waved when I saw Nettie wandering around outside with her caregiver."

"Was she wearing tennis shoes?" Amanda asked.

"Who? Nettie or the caregiver?"

"Nettie."

Harjo frowned thoughtfully. "Tennies, I think."

The general consensus was that Nettie always wore her tennis shoes when she went outside and her house slippers when she was inside—except the day she died. Amanda was absolutely certain now that her suspicions were correct. The accident had most definitely been staged. The killer had simply overlooked an important detail by not switching Nettie's shoes.

"I swung back by Nettie's house on my way to town and bought a few pumpkins from her to decorate the county machine shop," the commish went on to say. "Nice décor at your accounting office, by the way. You really got into the swing of Halloween festivities."

"You, too, from what I hear," Amanda replied. "According to the news buzzing around the beauty shop, you volunteered to decorate and give tours of the haunted house to raise money for the firefighters."

Harjo stretched his long, muscled legs beneath the table and poked a french fry into his mouth. "I've got a bunch of teenagers helping with the creepy-crawly stuff." He grinned. "With the black strobe lights, swirling artificial fog, and nerve-tingling sound effects, the house should raise a few goose bumps. We've got all your basic thrills and chills—ax murderers prowling the hallways, chain-saw killers looming on the staircase, vampires stalking the basement, and headless phantoms and hideous ghouls pouncing from closets. . . ."

When a long shadow fell over the table Harjo's voice trailed off and he glanced up.

"What are you doing, Harjo? Trying to charm my wife, the mother of my future child, *again?*"

Amanda cast Thorn a withering glance. She had hoped he'd gotten over his unwarranted jealousy of Harjo, but obviously he hadn't.

"Yeah, kemosabe," Harjo said, then chuckled. "I was telling her about the special visual and sound effects and costumes the kids and I have come up with for the haunted house. Really turned her on talking about slimy snakes, gigantic spiders, and stuff."

"Oh," Thorn mumbled as he staked his territory by cozying up beside Amanda, then looping his sinewy arm around her shoulder.

Harjo noted the possessive display and grinned. "I suppose Hazard has you scouting around for clues about Nettie's *supposed* accident. She's already asked if I noticed anything unusual while I was cruising around Pumpkin Hollow."

Thorn shot Amanda a dark look, then focused on the commish. "There is no official investigation. It was an accident."

"Right, so what have you got so far?" Harjo asked.

"I said—"

"I heard what you said," Harjo cut in. "But when somebody turns up dead around Vamoose, Pronto, or Adios, Hazard's suspicious instincts go to point. *She* hasn't been wrong yet, as I recall. *You,* however, have been. Seven times, in fact."

Thorn winced at the gibe. "You're a butthead, Harjo. I don't know why I put up with you."

Harjo's eyes twinkled. "You put up with me because there have been times in the past when I have been able to provide Hazard with information for her unofficial investigations. Furthermore, you know I'm gonna be there for you if you need me, and vice versa. That's what pals are for. 'Helpful' is my middle name."

"Yeah." Thorn grunted. "And 'Not' is your first name."

Harjo ignored that and turned his attention to Amanda. "So what difference does it make if Nettie was wearing tennis shoes when I saw her?"

"Don't answer that, Haz," Thorn commanded in his best cop voice.

"Give it up, Thorn. Harjo is not stupid," Amanda said.

"Thanks for sticking up for me, gorgeous."

"Knock it off, Harjo," Thorn said in a growl.

Amanda sighed audibly. "You boys need to get your high testosterone levels under control here. We are wasting valuable time. In my condition, I don't have a lot of time left before my labor day. Now don't upset me. I don't want to burst into tears and embarrass myself in front of the patrons of the Last Chance Café."

Both men, she noted, came to immediate attention. Good, enough of this silliness. Harjo had become a close friend who contributed to her fact-finding crusades. His job took him through the towns and back roads of the county and he was a valuable, reliable source of information. If Thorn still harbored ill-founded jealousy, then he just needed to get over it.

"Here's the deal, Harjo," Amanda said, leaning forward, lowering her voice. "I need descriptions of vehicles regularly seen around Nettie's farm. I believe Nettie was suffocated in her bedroom, then hauled to the pumpkin patch to make her death look like an accident."

"Damn it!" Thorn howled.

"Sh-sh!" Amanda scolded.

Heads turned in synchronized rhythm toward the corner booth, where the former rivals for Amanda's attention sat. Everybody looked as if they expected a fight to break out any second.

Amanda gouged Thorn in the ribs. "Laugh, Thorn," she ordered. "You, too, Harjo."

The two men burst out in chuckles, as if sharing a joke. The other patrons, assured a brawl wasn't forthcoming, resettled in their seats and resumed eating.

"Where the hell did you come up with that theory, Haz?" Thorn asked, still sporting a fake smile.

"I found black cat hairs on Nettie's bed," she murmured. "I also brought the pillow shams to be tested. I believe Nettie was dead long before she ended up in the garden."

Harjo's eyes bulged. Thorn's jaw scraped his broad chest.

"You figured all that out because of the tennis shoes?" Harjo asked in amazement.

"No, because of the house shoes."

"I don't get it," Harjo grumbled.

"No," Thorn said, grinning smugly. "You sure as hell don't, but *I* do, anytime I want it—Ooof!"

Amanda elbowed Thorn for voicing that sexual innuendo. There was no need to goad Harjo, especially while they were discussing the case.

"I have several suspects who stand to gain from Nettie's demise," Amanda hurried on. "The first two are Odell and Faye, Nettie's younger brother and sister. They are in financial straits. A hefty inheritance could bail out Odell and Faye.

"Mickey Poag, who rents Nettie's farmland, got all bent out of shape when I interrogated him. I swear there is something he isn't telling me, but I don't have a handle on what it might be yet. I do know that Nettie said something to Mickey yesterday about bumping up his rent."

Thorn blinked. "He told you that? He didn't mention it to me when I questioned him."

"Maybe you asked the wrong questions," Amanda offered.

When Thorn puffed up like an offended toad, Harjo chuckled. "Don't get huffy, Lone Ranger. Your wife is a whiz at posing tough questions. I should know. She grilled me unmercifully when she suspected that I was involved in the Dead in the Mud case. After she laid out her theory to me, she almost had me thinking I *did* do it."

Amanda turned her attention back to Thorn. "What did you find out from the medical examiner?"

"Cat scratches on Nettie's arms and wrists. Black cat hair between her fingers. Welts on her neck and puffiness around her eyes. She appeared to have had an allergic reaction," Thorn confirmed.

"What did the Rumleys have to say when you told them about their deceased landlady?" Amanda wanted to know.

Thorn stared dubiously at Harjo. "I don't think he needs to be privy to all this, Haz."

"Of course he does," Amanda contradicted. "Harjo will be working at the Pumpkin Festival. He will be in a perfect position to keep watch on our suspects. He can also report in if he sees any suspicious activity around Nettie's home during the next few days. He makes a perfect undercover detective and you know it, Thorn."

"Yeah, I'm indispensable." Harjo's white teeth gleamed when he grinned. "I'll keep my eyes and ears open and keep tabs on the suspects. If I note anything suspicious I'll call."

"You will call *me*," Thorn insisted, "not Hazard."

Before the two men suffered another attack of machismo and became sidetracked again, Amanda repeated her question to Thorn. "What did the Rumleys have to say?"

"Not much. I mentioned Nettie and the rent due at your office and they clammed up. Melvin's ruddy face paled noticeably. He was butchering pork while I questioned him and he nearly whacked off his forefinger. Ginger kept swallowing nervously, as if she had a rock stuck in her craw. Husband and wife kept glancing uneasily at each other, as if they were concealing something, but I haven't figured out what they don't want me to know."

Amanda was pretty sure it had something to do with money, but she didn't share the thought with Thorn.

"Now, if only I could figure out who Mr. Mysterious is, I could pose a few questions to him," Amanda mused aloud.

"Mr. Mysterious?" the men echoed in unison.

Amanda nodded her orange-tinted head and leaned closer. "Rumor has it that Nettie, in her prime, had at least one affair. According to speculation—"

"If it came from the beauty shop then it is purely speculation," Thorn clarified.

"Mr. Mysterious is most likely a married man. He might even be deceased, for all I know. But here is the thing. . . ." Amanda lowered her voice a few more decibels. "I'm wondering if Sis Hix might actually be Nettie's child, not sister Faye's."

Thorn and Harjo's mouths dropped open.

"Nettie used to be Vamoose's barber and beautician, so she associated with married men and bachelors alike." Amanda turned to Thorn and said, "I want you to contact your brother, Rich, at OSBI and ask him to check with the Bureau of Vital Statistics. I want to know whose names are listed as the parents on Sis Mithlo-Hix's birth certificate. I'm also curious to know if there was another woman who gave birth on the same date, at the same time, to a female child. Chances are that Faye and Willis Mithlo's names are listed on one certificate in an attempt to keep the scandal hush-hush. It could be that someone tampered with the birth certificates.''

''Probably so,'' Thorn agreed.

''Rich should be able to cross-check the information with other children who have the same birth date, time of delivery, and weight. I expect he will find a duplicate if he digs deeply enough.''

Harjo shook his head in amazement. ''Hazard, does this stuff just come to you out of the blue or do you actually sit around trying to figure all the angles?''

''Feminine intuition,'' she replied.

Both men looked at each another, then smirked.

''Here ya go, y'all,'' the waitress said as she plunked down two plates. ''I figured you wanted your usual. Since y'all were jawing so intently over here, I didn't think you wanted to be interrupted.''

''Thanks, Trudy,'' Thorn said as he appraised his wife's plate. ''You did use the low-cholesterol oil for Hazard's french fries, didn't you? She is to have no more than thirty percent of her calories from fat.''

''You bet, Chief,'' Trudy confirmed.

''Lean hamburger meat?'' Thorn questioned. ''She needs an extra ten grams of protein per day.''

''You're looking at the leanest of the lean in hamburger,'' Trudy assured him.

''Skim milk in her malt?''

''Okay, Thorn. Geez!'' Amanda muttered, exasperated. ''You're a walking encyclopedia of prenatal care!''

Harjo snickered in amusement. ''Man, Lone Ranger, you really are a basket case when it comes to Hazard.''

''Tell me about it,'' Amanda grumbled, after Trudy sashayed away. ''Thorn read in the manual that cats, sheep, and cattle can carry parasites and bacteria that might be harmful to an unborn child, so he booted Hank the tomcat out of the house and has banned me from going down to the barn when he feeds the livestock.

''He also read that household chemicals for cleaning

should not be handled, because they can be absorbed through the skin, so I'm not allowed to touch them. If I don't get a full eight hours of rest per day, he orders me to bed, like a convict being locked up for the night.''

Harjo glanced at Thorn's scowling face. ''How does she put up with you?''

''Just shut up and eat your greasy cheeseburger, Harjo,'' Thorn snapped.

''I don't wanna shut up. It is entirely too much fun tormenting you,'' Harjo replied, undaunted.

Thorn gave him a long, meaningful stare. ''You know damned well that you would be just as protective if you were in my boots.''

''You are probably right,'' Harjo admitted as he scooped up his half-eaten burger.

Amanda laid her hand over Harjo's, demanding his attention. ''Please do not spread around the information about this case. This is just among the three of us.''

''Sure. Nobody will know I'm helping with this unofficial investigation. Not a peep from me, doll face.''

Amanda smiled to herself as she sipped her malt. She had her spies and informants—Jenny and Harjo—thinking they held exclusive confidences. Amanda let them both think they were singularly privy to this investigation. And now, with Thorn taking her suspicions seriously, maybe she could resolve this case before D day.

Amanda lumbered into her accounting office to see Jenny beaming in triumph.

''I got the papers from Nettie's safe-deposit box, no sweat,'' she said without preamble.

''Good work,'' Amanda complimented as she dug into the plastic sack on the edge of Jen's desk. Disappointment caused her expectant smile to falter when she realized the little black book wasn't there.

''Something wrong, boss?''

"No journal," Amanda grumbled. "Where could Nettie have put that blasted thing?"

"Maybe the killer made off with it."

"I am beginning to think that might be the case." Amanda slouched in her chair and sorted through the legal documents. "I guess I am going to have to do this the hard way—dig for every blessed clue."

"That has never bothered you before," Jenny reminded her.

"Yeah, but I haven't had to work under the pressure of a deadline." Amanda pointed to her rounded tummy. "I am going to be pretty busy for several weeks."

"Weeks?" Jenny bubbled with laughter. "How about years. But not to worry, with Timmy in school, I will be your safety net at the office."

"Thanks, Jen. I don't know what I would do without you."

While Jen typed tax reports, Amanda turned her attention to the titles and abstracts in the sack. She sincerely hoped there was a will in here somewhere that might offer her some productive leads.

Sure enough, Amanda found a handwritten document—Nettie's holographic will. It was written entirely in Nettie's hand, signed and dated five years prior. Two witnesses, employees of Vamoose Bank, had put their names on the dotted lines and the document had been notarized.

Well, that solved several problems, Amanda thought, relieved.

"Find anything interesting in the sack?" Jenny asked when she stopped typing on the computer keyboard to take a sip of Coke from her Styrofoam cup.

"Yep, Nettie's will is here," Amanda said, distracted. "Nettie left the original homestead her family claimed during the 1889 land run to Faye and Odell, but she stipulates that it is not to be divided or sold. Only the income from farm crops, cattle, and mineral rights from possible oil production can be equally divided between her brother and sister.''

Amanda read on, then erupted with, ''Holy kamoley!''
''What is it?''

Amanda glanced up from the document and stared somberly at her secretary, who was decked out in a plum-colored silk business suit that made Amanda pine for her own lost figure. ''This information is not to leave this office.'' She waited until Jen raised her hand and gave her solemn vow of secrecy. ''When Odell and Faye pass on, the property will be passed down to Sis Hix.''

''No kidding?'' Jenny chirped. ''Why would Nettie single out just one of her nieces and nephews?''

Amanda had a pretty good idea why. She was fairly certain Sis was Nettie's child, who had been raised by sister Faye to avoid public humiliation. Mr. Mysterious probably knew the truth about Sis's biological parentage. The fact was undoubtedly noted in Nettie's journal—wherever the damned thing was.

Maybe Mr. Mysterious had nabbed it, Amanda mused. *If* Nettie's unidentified lover was still alive and kicking, that is. But Amanda wasn't ready to rule out the other suspects who had something to gain by Nettie's death—whether it be money or permanent silence. Unless Amanda missed her guess—and how often did something like that happen?—that little black book was loaded with information that could turn Vamoose wrong-side out.

''It says here that Nettie wants her caregivers to equally divide two thousand dollars from her savings account as a bonus for looking in on her the past five years. Do you know anything about the woman who provided care for Nettie before Arthella Carson took over some of the duties last year?''

Jenny bobbed her head. ''You mean Eileen Franklin? She still works part-time for home-health care services.'' She sniffed and her voice quavered. ''That sure was nice of Nettie to give her nurses a bonus, wasn't it?''

Jenny teared up, sentimental fool that she was. Amanda blinked rapidly. Damn it, she was *not* going to cry, especially when Eileen or Arthella might have bumped off the spinster for a cash bonus.

"The will states that the cash in Nettie's savings and checking accounts, after the two grand is subtracted, is to be equally divided between her four nieces and nephews. According to the last bank statement I saw, that equals about three grand apiece."

"Roy Mithlo will blow his inheritance in one weekend," Jenny predicted. "Don't know about Odell's son and daughter. They moved off with their mother years and years ago, so I don't have a clue how they turned out."

Amanda didn't have a clue either. She had never laid eyes on either of them.

"Sis can really use the cash," Jenny commented. "With two young kids to raise, and Bubba working as a mechanic at Thatcher's Oil and Gas, it has been hard for them to make ends meet."

Amen to that. Having been named Bubba Junior and little Sissy's honorary aunt, Amanda helped the family through financial scrapes whenever she could. Sis Hix deserved this financial break, even if she was unaware that the woman she knew as her aunt might very well have been her mother.

Amanda turned back to the holographic will, noting that Nettie had bequeathed her pumpkin recipe books to her sister Faye, along with an assortment of antique furniture, heirloom quilts, and family memorabilia. Surprisingly, Sis Hix was generously invited to live in the house or to claim any or all of the furniture and appliances as her own. After which Odell could take the leavings.

Those were Nettie's words, verbatim. Amanda got the distinct impression that Odell had been on his older sister's shit list at the time Nettie penned this will.

Small wonder why, Amanda mused. Not only had Odell

sold his town property, against Nettie's wishes, but he had contributed to a traffic accident that cost Jim Foster his life. No doubt the weasel hadn't served time for his negligence. Or had he? Amanda wondered.

"Boss, would you mind if I skipped out a little early today? Dave and I want to take Timmy to the mall to buy new shoes. The kid is growing like a weed and so are his feet."

"Sure," Amanda murmured, her head bowed over the will, locked in profound concentration.

"I won't breathe a word about this case or about the terms of the will," Jenny promised.

Amanda looked up, then flashed Jen a grave stare. "If you did, you would be out of a job and I would lose the best secretary I ever had."

Jenny stood a little straighter. A proud smile pursed her lips as she offered Amanda a snappy salute. "You can count on me, boss."

Jenny plugged in the bright orange lights that were strung around the outside of the office. "Don't forget the decoration contest judges will be here tomorrow night."

"Mmm." Amanda never looked up from the will.

"Aliens just touched down in the parking lot," Jenny added. "They want to beam me up to the mother ship. You don't mind, do you?"

"Mmm."

Jenny exited, knowing Amanda was so deep into her investigative mode that she was paying absolutely no attention to what transpired around her.

EIGHT

Nick paced the floorboards at his farm, then checked his watch for the umpteenth time. "Where the hell is Hazard?" he muttered to the world at large.

All sorts of unpleasant visions danced in his head. Hazard might have gone into labor while driving home. She could be sitting by the side of the road, unable to get out to flag someone down. She could have been involved in a traffic accident.

Nick spewed a few obscenities, glanced out the window—again—then turned back to the stove. Dinner was being kept on warm, drying out with every minute that ticked by.

Hazard's faithful guard dog stood on the porch, staring north. When the Border collie's bobbed tail thumped against the storm door, Nick knew Bruno had Hazard in his sights. *Finally*! Nick was going to have a severe case of ulcers before Hazard delivered his baby!

Humoring Hazard through her unofficial investigation also grated on his nerves. He still wasn't convinced Nettie's death was murder, but Hazard claimed she had found black cat hairs on the bed and insisted that he send the pillow shams to the county crime lab. Nick hoped like hell that Hazard was mistaken. He didn't need a murder to solve on the eve of D day.

The phone blared and Nick snatched up the receiver. "Thorn residence."

"Nick, I have the report you requested on your pillow," the medical examiner announced.

"And?" Nick held his breath.

"I hate to have to tell you this, but your wife was right again. Man, she's got the uncanniest instincts I ever saw. How does she figure this stuff out?"

"Is there a point in here somewhere, Clint?" Nick asked impatiently.

"Yeah," Clint Pine replied. "You married an investigative genius who was absolutely right about the pillow sham being used to suffocate the victim. I found the victim's hair follicles and smears of makeup on the back side of that sham. Looks like you've got a murder, Nick."

"Well, hell," Nick said, then scowled.

"Good talking to you, Nickster." Clint chuckled. "All my best to your little lady."

"Yeah, yeah, yeah," Nick grumbled.

Nick replaced the receiver, only to have the phone blare at him again. He took the call from his brother. During their conversation Nick heard Hazard's powerful four-by-four truck cruising up the driveway.

Hazard came through the door, waddling like a goose. "Hi, honey. I'm home!"

Nick waved as he listened to his brother offer his report. Nick was cool. Hazard would never know that he had worn a path on the carpet, fretting over her tardiness.

"Who was on the phone?" Hazard asked as she poked her orange-colored head in the fridge to retrieve the jar of cranberry juice.

"Brother Rich," he replied.

Hazard glanced up quickly, all ears. "What did he find out from the Bureau of Vital Statistics?"

Nick ambled into the kitchen to grab the plates and silverware. "He found Sis's birth certificate. The document is on file, signed and imprinted with an official seal."

Amanda galumphed to the table, and Nick hurriedly pulled out her chair. "Did Rich cross-check the data for duplication? Did he find the document of live birth for a baby whose mother's name was Nettie Jarvis?"

Nick scooped up the skillet of rice and glazed chicken, then gave Hazard a generous portion. "Negative."

Hazard looked up, surprised.

"Rich found another record of live birth that matched Sis Mithlo-Hix's stats perfectly, but the mother's name was Candice Randolph."

"Do you suppose Nettie used the name as an alias?"

Nick shrugged, then took a seat. "Don't have a clue, Haz. It could be an alias, or the time and date of the other delivery could be a coincidence."

Hazard raised a perfectly sculpted brow. "Same birth weight, length, and exact minute of entrance into this world? Yeah, right, Thorn. Like that happens every day. I think somebody pulled a fast one to ensure Sis had a last name and legitimate family."

"And you are absolutely convinced that Nettie was Sis Hix's mother," he presumed.

"Looks that way to me," Hazard said, then chewed on her chicken. "Wow, Thorn, this stuff is really good."

"Thanks." Nick sampled his culinary efforts. Mmm, not bad for a hurry-up job, he congratulated himself. "I also got a call from Clint Pine, the coroner."

"And?" she asked between bites.

"You . . . um . . . were right," he admitted reluctantly. "The pillow sham shows evidence of being used to suffocate Nettie in her bedroom."

Hazard beamed—gloated was nearer the mark.

Nick really hated it when she did that. She had been right eight times and he had been dead wrong. Damn, that was hard to stomach.

"I found Nettie's will in her safe-deposit box," Hazard informed him. "Nettie sounded very put out with Odell. She was also amazingly generous with Sis Hix. And get this, Thorn. Nettie listed Sis as her one and only beneficiary on her life-insurance policy."

Nick blinked, then choked on his chicken. "You think Sis Hix axed Nettie for the dough? Geez!"

Hazard rolled her eyes. "Of course not. I don't think Sis has a clue about her background. I am going to have the grand pleasure of presenting Sis with a sum total of seventy-five thousand dollars in inheritance money. I can't wait to see the look on Sis's and Bubba's faces when I tell them."

"So who bumped off Nettie?" Nick asked. "Seventy-five grand ain't small potatoes. According to the detective manuals the first thing you do is follow the money trail . . . and this one leads straight to Sis Hix."

"Don't be ridiculous. Sis wouldn't harm a fly." Frowning pensively, Amanda toyed with her food. "I don't know who bumped off Nettie, but I'm digging for motive and clues."

"*We* will be digging," Nick corrected. "We are going to have to double up on interviews to move this case along before you domino."

Hazard chewed hungrily, then nodded her pumpkin-colored head. "Right, and this is going to be one hectic weekend—Ouch!"

Nick froze in midbite. "What's wrong? Labor pains? Is it time?"

Hazard grabbed her stomach and slouched in her chair. The color drained from her face as she took his hand and laid it on her tummy. Nick blinked in surprise when he felt the repetitive thumps.

"Do you have the slightest idea how it feels to have

somebody kick the heck out of you when you least expect it?''

Amazed as always, Nick felt the jabs beneath his splayed hand. "It must be a boy. The kid will probably come out swinging."

"Thorn, I think it's time I told you—"

"Don't tell me!" Nick yelped. "I've waited this long and I can wait a little longer. I want this baby to be a surprise. Come on, Haz, you promised!"

Hazard sighed, then struggled to right herself in the chair. "Fine. You want a surprise, then you've got it." She picked up her fork and continued eating. "Now, as I was saying before I got clobbered a dozen times, this is going to be a wild weekend. Tomorrow night is the decoration contest and grand opening of the haunted house and pumpkin parade. Saturday morning is the pumpkin bazaar. Our baby shower is a come-and-go affair beginning at two P.M."

Nick groaned. Hazard would run herself ragged, he predicted.

"The blue ribbons for largest pumpkin and best baked goods will be announced when the costume street dance begins at seven-thirty. The way I see it, we will have the perfect opportunity to grill our suspects at the community events."

Nick shook his finger in her face. "You *have* to take time out to rest. You *definitely* need to rest. It says so in every prenatal manual I've memorized."

"I'll take it easy tomorrow," she promised.

Hazard take it easy? She never took it easy.

Nick stood up, hoisted Hazard to her feet, then scooped her into his arms.

"Thorn, what are you doing?"

"Taking you to bed."

"At seven-fifteen?"

He waggled his eyebrows suggestively. "You don't have to go to sleep just yet, Haz."

"I love it when you get frisky, Thorn," Hazard purred.

He grinned roguishly on his way to the master bedroom. This was his favorite time of the day.

Amanda timed her visit to the Hixes' rundown trailer house to coincide with Bubba's lunch break from Thatcher's service station. She wanted Bubba and Sis to be on hand to hear the news of their forthcoming inheritance.

The moment Amanda started up the uneven bricks that served as a sidewalk she heard Bubba Junior chattering nonstop while his baby sister wailed at the top of her lungs. Amanda had to pound both fists on the door to be heard over the commotion.

Bubba Hix's broad, bulky frame filled the doorway. He was wearing his official brown uniform that was covered with grease and grime. " 'Mandy! How are ya? C'mon in."

He held open the floppy screen door that had weathered one too many Oklahoma windstorms.

"Sis! Look who's here. One of our favorite people."

Amanda winced when Bubba nearly blew out her eardrum while making himself heard over the racket created by his young children.

Sis appeared from the trailer's narrow hallway, her eyes puffy and red. She offered Amanda a watery smile. "Hi, 'Mandy."

"Sis has been in tears since Aunt Nettie died. They were really close, ya know?" Bubba said confidentially to Amanda.

"Hope you've been feeling okay," Sis said as she entered the living room, looking like a poster model for frazzled motherhood.

The noise level bouncing off the walls of this dilapidated trailer was obviously getting to Sis. Plus, she was upset about the loss of her favorite aunt—or mother, if Amanda's suspicions turned out to be correct.

Little Sissy's wailing stopped abruptly. Apparently it was naptime, and the little tyke finally gave up her squalling and fell asleep in her crib.

" 'Manna!'' Bubba Junior raced down the hall in his training pants and flew at Amanda with his pudgy arms outstretched.

"Whoa, B. J.'' Bubba intercepted his steamrolling son before he plowed into Amanda. "Your honorary aunt is gonna have a baby, remember? Gotta be real careful with her, just like you were with Mama.''

B. J., in his terrible-two phase, would hear none of that logic. He thrust out his grimy hands and leaned away from his dad. Amanda sank down on the spongy couch, then removed the toy tractor that was poking her in the fanny.

"Okay, kiddo, now I can hold you,'' Amanda said.

B. J. jabbered nonstop while his dad lowered him into Amanda's arms. The kid gave her such a tight hug that it was a few moments before Amanda's vocal apparatus functioned properly.

"Good to see you again, too, Beeje. How have you been?''

B. J. responded with more unintelligible jabbers, then snuggled up beside Amanda.

"I'm sorry about Nettie,'' Amanda said as she watched Sis plunk down in the threadbare rocking chair.

Sis sniffed, blotted her nose with a tissue, then nodded her mousy brown head. "Me, too. I'm really gonna miss Aunt Nettie.''

"Your aunt was excessively fond of you,'' Amanda declared. "So fond, in fact, that she named you as the beneficiary of her life-insurance policy. In addition you will receive a portion of her savings account. She also bequeathed all the furniture and appliances in her home to you.''

"What?'' Bubba and Sis croaked simultaneously, then stared at her, frog-eyed.

Of all the duties Amanda performed as a CPA, this was positively the best. "You heard me correctly. Nettie has been extremely generous with you. Although it will be at least a month before all the paperwork is completed, I will be delivering a check for seventy-five grand."

Bubba staggered, then plopped on the sofa before he fell down. His eyes bugged and his stubbled jaw opened and closed like a mailbox. The news had the same startling effect on Sis. Her mouth hung open. She tried to speak, but no words poured forth.

"Surprise!" Amanda said, chuckling. "And no, this is not a trick-or-treat prank. This is for real."

"Ohmigosh, omigosh. O-mi-gosh!" Sis yipped when she recovered her powers of speech. "We're rich, Bubba! Can you believe it?"

Rich was a relative term, Amanda mused. But to a down-on-their-luck couple who barely made ends met, she supposed Bubba and Sis considered that they had struck it rich.

"Do you know what this means, Bubba?" Sis wheezed. "We can buy our dream house!"

"Yeah, our very own double-wide trailer!"

Amanda silently giggled. Only the Hixes, who lived a hand-to-mouth existence, would consider a double-wide trailer the house of their dreams. But hey, to each his own.

"And maybe we can upgrade your clunker truck for something more reliable," Sis said through her stream of overjoyed tears. "Oh, Bubba, this is so wonderful!"

Amanda swallowed the sentimental lump that clogged her throat when Bubba and Sis barreled forward to hug the stuffing out of each other. They kissed and hugged and sang high praises to dear Aunt Nettie for two solid minutes.

"Feel free to stop by Nettie's place to pick out the furniture and appliances, towels, bedding, food, and anything else you want," Amanda said. "You get first pick of everything except the heirloom antiques that are bequeathed to your mother.''

Clearly overwhelmed, Bubba sank down in the chair with Sis cuddled on his lap. Amanda heard the wood creak beneath their hefty bodies and she tensed, wondering if the rickety stick of furniture would give way. The couple continued to stare at Amanda in a daze.

"However," she continued, "you don't have to haul off the furniture if you don't want to. According to Nettie's will, you are welcome to live in the homestead, rent free. Eventually the property will become yours.'' Amanda smiled at the stunned looks frozen on Bubba's and Sis's faces. "Your choice. Take the furniture and bring it here or leave it where it is and move in.''

"A real house? On a real foundation?'' Sis squeaked in disbelief. "Aunt Nettie let us have her house?''

Amanda nodded her orange-tinted head. "That's right.''

"Wow," Bubba said softly. "Wow . . .''

Amanda gave the Hixes a moment to recover from the shock of Nettie's generosity, then probed for information for her investigation.

"This may sound like a strange question, Sis, but do you recall Nettie mentioning a man from her past?'' Amanda asked.

Sis frowned, bemused. "A man?'' she repeated.

Amanda smiled nonchalantly. "A close friend that she saw socially on occasion, maybe?''

"You mean like Pad?''

Pad? What the hell kind of name was that? Amanda wondered.

"Sorry to interrupt here, 'Manda, but I need to get back to the service station so Thaddeus can take his lunch break.'' Bubba set Sis aside and stood up. He hurried over to pump Amanda's hand gratefully. "Can't thank you enough for delivering the good news. And next time somebody pulls into the station, spreading that story about Nettie's ghost—''

"What story?" Amanda cut in.

"Folks are saying that they have sighted a wraith float-ing around Pumpkin Hollow, flitting between Nettie's house, the barn, and the sheds," Bubba reported. "People driving past the farm insist they've seen eerie lights and flitting shadows every night since Nettie died."

Aha! So the little black book had yet to be found, Amanda deduced. The killer was using a Halloween hoax as a smoke screen, because he/she wanted to get hold of that journal and had yet to find it. Amanda still had a sporting chance of finding it first.

Bubba hoisted B. J. up and planted a kiss on his rosy cheek. "Gotta run, son. Now you behave yourself, hear? Help your mama pick up all these toys you've scattered around and we'll play ball when I get home from work, okay?"

Beeje nodded his tangled blond head.

When Bubba lumbered out the door, Amanda turned back to Sis. "I think there was a man in Nettie's life," she said carefully. "Or at least there used to be." *And that man may be your real father!* "Do you know anything about him? Have you heard your mom or uncle mention him? Did Nettie mention him, perhaps?"

Sis settled herself in the chair and absently toyed with the long, straight strands of hair that draped over her shoulder. "I remember Aunt Nettie talking to a man she called Pad on the phone while I was at her house for visits when I was a kid. I don't know who he was. Once I asked Mom about him and she told me not to mention his name again to anybody, ever. I was just a kid at the time and I couldn't figure out why we weren't to mention Aunt Nettie's friend."

Definitely a married man, Amanda decided. Why else would the family want to keep the sordid affair hush-hush?

"So you never actually met Pad?" Amanda prodded.

"Not exactly," Sis said. "Once, when I was about

eight, a man came to the house while I was staying overnight with Aunt Nettie. She met him at the door, then
stepped onto the porch. She told me to entertain myself
for a few minutes while she visited with her guest.''

Amanda sat up a little straighter on the sagging sofa.
''Do you recall what he looked like?''

Sis shrugged her shoulders. ''That was eighteen years
ago. All I remember was that he had reddish brown hair
and drove a fancy car. I think he was sort of tall, but I
suppose when you are eight years old everybody looks
tall to you.''

Damn, an eighteen-year-old description wasn't much
to go on. Amanda had to figure out who this ''Pad''
person was. Not only could he be Sis's biological father,
but he could have figured very significantly into Nettie's
death.

''I heard Uncle Odell mention Pad once when he
stopped by during one of my visits with Aunt Nettie,''
Sis recalled. ''Nettie about strangled Uncle Odell; then
she said that if he had any gumption he would be there
to make things right. I have no idea what that meant, but
Uncle Odell must have, because he glared at me and Aunt
Nettie, then stormed out the door.''

That was an odd statement, Amanda mused as she
struggled to rise from the dilapidated divan. Had Nettie
been referring to the traffic fatality? Or was it something
else?

''Well, I'd better get back to the office.''

''Thanks for delivering the exciting news, 'Manda.''
Sis teared up again. ''I wish Aunt Nettie were here so I
could thank her properly for her generosity. I don't know
why she was so good to me through the years, but she
was like a mother to me.''

Small wonder why! thought Amanda.

After B. J. hugged her knees and blabbered incessantly,
Amanda exited the trailer house. Pad? Was that short for
Paddy? Was it a nickname for Patrick? she asked herself

as she zipped down the gravel road, headed for town. Could Patrick be a first or last name? Hell, it could even be a middle name, for all she knew. Could it be short for Fitzpatrick? Kilpatrick? Kirkpatrick? Patrick Something-or-other? Something Patrick-or-other?

Although the possibilities were endless Amanda was determined to dig for the answer. She whizzed back to her office to check the files of her clients in her database. When she turned up no promising leads, she pored over the phone books from Vamoose, Pronto, and Adios. Mr. Mysterious had to be—or had once been—a resident of one of these three rural communities, she assured herself.

Grabbing a decaffeinated cola—Thorn insisted that she stay off caffeine—Amanda propped up her feet and took a grand tour through the phone books. It was a time-consuming chore.

NINE

"I've got the info you wanted from New Horizons," Jenny said as she breezed into the accounting office.

Amanda slumped in her chair. "Good, let's hear it."

"Nettie Jarvis was definitely on the waiting list to move into a condo at the retirement village by the lake," Jenny reported. "She made a partial down payment, which will be returned to your office as soon as we present the administrators with a death certificate. The representative handling Nettie's file said Nettie promised another installment within a few weeks."

Uh-oh, that sounded as if Nettie was expecting an influx of cash. Blackmail money, perhaps? Had the first installment to the retirement center been made with a blackmail payment as well? For sure and certain, Nettie's bank statements didn't reflect the withdrawal of a sizable check these past few months.

"How much money did Nettie pay the retirement village?" Amanda questioned.

"Five grand," Jenny reported.

The phone rang and Amanda answered promptly.

"Is Nick there?" came a quavering, frail voice.

"No, this is Hazard Accounting."

"I know, but the police dispatcher told me Nicky was on his way over to pick you up for lunch. This is Elvina Keef. I thought of something else about my traffic accident and I wanted to tell the chief."

Amanda smiled in amusement. According to Thorn, Elvina was driving him bonkers with calls about her accident. Amanda figured the lonely old woman was relishing the excitement. It gave her an excuse to talk to someone.

"Why don't you relay your information through me, Elvina. I'll pass it along to Thorn the minute he arrives."

"You're sure you won't forget to tell him?"

"Scout's honor," Amanda promised.

"You won't leave anything out?"

"Not a single word."

"Well, okay, if you're sure. Maybe you should write this down, just in case. I'll wait for you to get your pen and paper before I start."

Amanda grabbed a notepad. "Fire away, Elvina."

"I remembered there were pumpkins in the bed of the dark-colored truck," Elvina said.

Amanda jerked to attention. "Pumpkins?"

"I just remembered that this morning while I was cooking pumpkin pulp to make bread and pies for the bazaar. There was a tall antenna on top of the truck, too, as I recall. You know, like one of those newfangled two-way radio antennas the chief has on his squad car.

"I want the chief to track down that hit-and-run maniac who blows little old ladies off the road. There is a forty-five-mile-an-hour speed limit on gravel roads, and that Evil Knievel character must have been doing eighty!"

Amanda frowned, trying to recall where Elvina Keef lived in relation to Pumpkin Hollow. Could this speeding, dark-colored pickup, carrying a load of pumpkins, adorned with a tall aluminum antenna, have been zipping away from the crime scene?

"Elvina, do you recall the time of your accident?" Amanda asked.

"Certainly. It was about ten o'clock Monday morning. There was some fog in the low-lying areas on the road. Dust rising from the gravel formed brown clouds that made it difficult to see. I was driving along, minding my own business, on my way to the store to pick up the ingredients for my pumpkin bread and pies. Then whammo! This truck comes roaring over the hill and down the dale like a tornado. Ran me right off the road! I nearly had a heart attack while trying to veer toward the ditch to prevent a crash."

"I'm so relieved that you weren't injured," Amanda consoled the old woman.

"Shook me up, I can tell you for sure."

"Perfectly understandable."

"And what with all these sightings of Nettie's ghost, I sure haven't been able to sleep well at night!"

"Who mentioned those sightings?" Amanda asked.

"Oda Jean Samuels mentioned that she saw a weird-looking silhouette hovering around Pumpkin Hollow when she was on her way home from Bible study class at church," Elvina reported. "But she isn't the only one who has seen eerie specters and lights floating around Nettie's farm. There are four other women in our Morning Watch Club—"

"Morning Watch Club?" Amanda cut in curiously.

"Yes," Elvina went on, "we take turns calling each other every morning to make sure the rest of us are feeling okay."

"That's an excellent policy," Amanda commented. "Now, you were saying something about more ghost sightings?"

"Yes, well, three of the six members of our club have seen a strange figure prowling around Nettie's place this week. Maybelle Harp mentioned that the windows in the house had taken on an eerie glow."

Amanda suspected the eerie glow was the result of a flashlight that had been covered with colored cellophane. Somebody around Vamoose was determined to create the effect of a restless spirit floating around a haunted house.

"Now, Amanda, are you sure you got my full statement about my traffic accident down on paper?" Elvina harped. "You didn't leave anything out, did you?"

"Not one word. You can take it to the bank," Amanda confirmed. "Thorn will receive your full report."

When Elvina finally hung up, after chitchatting for ten minutes about the upcoming festivities, Amanda made a mental note to inspect every vehicle lined up along the streets during the pumpkin parade. If she could spot the vehicle used to make a fast getaway from the scene of Nettie's *accident*, she might be able to pinpoint the killer who practically plowed over Elvina Keef.

The phone jingled again and Amanda picked up.

"This is Arthella Carson, Nettie's home—health care nurse," came the businesslike voice.

"Yes?"

"The head nurse informed me that I was to send any outstanding bills to you, since you are handling Nettie's estate."

"That's right."

"Well," Arthella said, "I just wanted you to know that I plan to overlook what little Nettie owed me for extra medication and supplies that I picked up for her. She was a dear woman whose companionship meant a great deal to me."

Amanda frowned. Arthella sounded as if she were reading a script. Either that or the woman simply had so little personality that it was reflected in her monotone voice. A health nurse who was short on personality probably did appreciate a feisty old woman like Nettie, Amanda speculated.

"I'm glad you called, Arthella. According to Nettie's will, her caregivers are to receive a cash bonus for putting up with her. When the paperwork is completed, I will send your check in care of the home-health care office."

"Really? Nettie did that?" Arthella sounded stunned. "Well, that is so sweet of her."

"She was very generous," Amanda agreed. "I will also be sending Eileen Franklin a check. Will you tell her about Nettie's bequest?"

"Sure, I'd be glad to do it," Arthella said. "Well, I'll let you go. I have to visit another patient—"

"I have a couple of questions I need to ask," Amanda cut in quickly. "I wondered which days and what time you usually arrived to check on Nettie."

"Why? Is there a problem?" Arthella asked cautiously.

The nurse's wary tone of voice incited Amanda's suspicions. "Why would you think there is a problem?" she questioned the question.

"No reason."

The reply came too quickly, to Amanda's way of thinking. Hmmm, she mused pensively.

"I would like to know when you last saw Nettie," Amanda pressed. "Had she suffered any allergic reactions within the past few months?"

"Yes, Nettie's asthma had been acting up this fall. I had to increase her oxygen ratio, because her health was declining."

Arthella's voice had evened out again, Amanda noted. The nurse sounded very professional.

"I visited Nettie on Monday, Wednesday, and Friday afternoons," Arthella went on to say. "I usually arrived at her home about one o'clock. She was the first patient I saw after lunch."

Although Amanda couldn't imagine what Arthella might have to gain from bumping off one of her home-health care patients, Amanda had no intention of scratching the nurse's name off the list of suspects. Just because Arthella made her house calls on Monday afternoon didn't mean the nurse hadn't sneaked up on Nettie unaware that morning.

"Thank you for answering my questions, Arthella," Amanda said.

"Always glad to be of help," the nurse replied.

"Oh, one more question. What kind of vehicle do you drive while you are visiting outpatients?"

"What?"

Amanda thought her question was perfectly clear. Therefore she did not repeat it. She simply waited for Arthella to respond.

"I drive an old Ford sedan. The older-model cars seem to hold up better on the gravel roads. Why?"

"I won't detain you any longer, Arthella," Amanda said, ignoring the question. " 'Bye now. Have a good day."

Amanda hung up the phone, then glanced up to see Thorn approaching the office. When he strode through the door, Amanda grabbed her oversize purse and left for lunch. The moment they headed across the street to dine at the Last Chance Café, Amanda relayed the information from Elvina.

"I think Elvina's maniac driver could be our killer," she said in conclusion.

Thorn nodded grimly. "You are . . . er . . . probably . . . right."

It was always difficult for Thorn to admit Amanda was right. She patted him on the arm. "Thank you, Thorn."

"Velma stopped by headquarters this morning to deliver your costume for the parade and costume street dance," Thorn said as he held open the restaurant door for her.

"Oh, great," Amanda muttered. "Is it as bad as I expected?"

"Worse." Thorn grinned when Amanda groaned aloud. "The fabric is fluorescent orange, with lights sewn in the underside. You're going to glow in the dark, Haz."

"Nothing like being conspicuous," she said as she eased into Thorn's favorite corner booth. "Not that I don't stick out all over already."

With her briefcase full of printouts and three phone books on her lap, Amanda lounged in her La-Z-Boy recliner at home. At Thorn's insistence, she was spending the afternoon at home, continuing her search for the name of Mr. Mysterious.

Amanda stared at the client list until her eyes crossed, trying to figure out who "Pad" might be. She had still turned up no probable lead, after poring over the phone books twice. To be sure, there were dozens of Pats, Patricks, Kilpatricks, and such, but trying to make a logical connection to the names was like taking a shot in the dark.

Damn it, who was this "Pad" character? Did he own a dark-colored truck with a tall radio antenna? According to Sis Hix, the man from Nettie's past drove flashy cars. Did he also own a pickup truck? Hell's bells, why were all the facts Amanda had gleaned from various sources so difficult to put together?

When Bruno put up a ruckus on the front porch, Amanda set aside the phone books and waddled to the window. A pickup—dark-colored—backed up the hill and sped away. With the sun glinting off the tinted windows, and dust flying, Amanda couldn't get a positive ID or a license tag number.

An uneasy sensation trickled down her spine. Had the killer planned to search her home, looking for the missing journal? Obviously the owner of the truck wasn't expecting her to be at home this afternoon.

Amanda grabbed her keys and headed for the door. She was going to have another look-see around Nettie's farm. That journal had to be out there somewhere.

Calling to Bruno, Amanda piled into her fire-engine-red truck. Bruno hopped in and then plunked down on the passenger seat. If anyone tried to disturb her while she searched Nettie's house, Bruno would come to her defense. The dog was fiercely protective of her.

As Amanda veered into Nettie's driveway, she noted that a vehicle had recently driven between the pumpkin patch and the barn. Amanda stopped her truck and hiked over to the flattened grass. The tracks halted inside a dirt-floor shed.

Definitely wide tires, the kind found on pickups, she mused as she studied the impression in the dirt.

A ladder was propped against the barn, and the overhead door to the old hayloft was slightly ajar. Someone had searched the upper level of the barn. *The big dummy!* Did he/she think old Nettie could climb up there to stash her journal?

Wheeling around, Amanda waddled toward the house. That book had to be somewhere in Nettie's house, Amanda convinced herself. The old spinster hadn't gotten around well enough in her declining years to hide her journal in an out-of-the-way place.

Amanda didn't have much time to search, but she wanted to give the house a thorough going-over before Bubba and Sis Hix moved in, or toted off furniture and appliances—whichever. She attacked her search mission with fiendish haste, even though she could silently hear Thorn nagging her because she was supposed to be taking it easy before attending the evening activities.

She rummaged through the drawer beneath the stove, hoping to find the book beneath the pots and pans. She checked the oven and the freezer, then looked behind and under the microwave. She looked inside plastic containers that were tucked in far corners of the cabinets, then felt around inside the washer and dryer.

Muttering, Amanda toddled into the extra bedroom to search between the mattress and box springs once more for good measure. She even pulled pictures off the walls to check for a concealed safe.

All her efforts turned up nothing, zilch, nada!

Amanda returned to the living room and plunked down in the electric-lift recliner that was covered with towels. This had to be Nettie's favorite chair, Amanda presumed as she made herself comfortable. Sitting in the spot where Nettie spent a great deal of her time, Amanda scanned the room. She stared at the sofa and the matching antique end tables.

"Okay, Nettie, where did you hide the damned thing?" Amanda grumbled.

Suddenly Bruno barked his head off, signaling the arrival of an unexpected visitor. Alarmed, Amanda punched the button beneath the armrest of the recliner. The footrest hummed as it lowered to the floor, then tilted forward to gently eject Amanda from the chair. She hurried to the door to check on Bruno.

She saw the Border collie beat a path around the corner of the house; then he ducked under the barbed-wire fence. Bruno charged toward a copse of cedar trees that lined the meandering creek.

The dog *could* have been chasing a cat or rabbit, Amanda reminded herself.

Then again, Bruno could have been chasing a murderer who wanted Amanda to back off.

Amanda hoofed it—as fast as a nine-months-pregnant woman could hoof it—into the south bedroom to follow Bruno's romp through the tall grass and weeds. In the distance Amanda made out the silhouette of a pickup parked in a stand of cottonwood trees. Someone was definitely trying to spy on her—at the very least. Luckily, the ever-faithful Bruno refused to let anyone near her.

As a precautionary measure, Amanda locked all the doors and windows and grabbed the biggest butcher knife in Nettie's kitchen. She returned to Nettie's favorite chair and plopped down. Damn, her back and legs were killing her. Sighing tiredly, Amanda pushed the button that tilted the chair back and the footrest upward.

Now this was the kind of chair Amanda needed—one that did all the work with the push of a button. She wiggled and squirmed into a comfortable position, then made another careful appraisal of the living room.

If she were a decrepit older woman, where would she keep a tell-all journal that was filled with juicy blackmail information?

Amanda glanced at the antiquated coffee cup, filled with pens and pencils, that sat on the end table beside the electrified recliner. It was a sure bet that this was where Nettie sat while writing letters and paying bills. . . . And pouring her memoirs into her journal, perhaps?

Impulsively, Amanda dug both hands between the padded arms and the seat cushion. She came up with nothing but lint and cracker crumbs. When she twisted sideways to dig deeper into the workings of the automated chair she saw it.

There, Velcroed to the underside of the mechanical footrest, was a gallon-size Ziploc bag. Only when the chair was in the full-recline position was the bag visible.

"Bingo!" Amanda said as she squirmed awkwardly around her oversize tummy to retrieve the bag. Grunting and straining, she unzipped the bag to fish out the journal.

While Bruno barked and howled in the distance, Amanda pressed the button to bring the recliner to an upright position. She stood up and tucked the journal into the elastic panel on her maternity jeans.

Amanda glanced at her watch. Damn, she was running out of time. Thorn would be home for an early supper so he could help her climb into her ridiculous-looking giant pumpkin costume. She wouldn't have a chance to pore over the book until after the pumpkin parade.

When she toddled outside, Bruno was still down at the creek, barking his head off. She couldn't see her fearless guard dog for all the grass and underbrush, but he was growling and snarling. He really could sound ferocious when he wanted to.

Amanda whistled for the dog while she plodded toward her truck.

Still no Bruno.

She slid onto the seat and honked the horn. A moment later Bruno raced toward her, his tongue dangling from his mouth.

"Good boy," she praised the panting dog as he bounded onto the seat.

A smug smile pursed her lips as she pointed the pickup toward home. Nettie's supposed ghost could prowl around the farm, feeding superstitious Halloween tales and searching for the journal, but Amanda had possession of it. She would soon have all her answers. Though she would burn the midnight oil to discover who Nettie had blackmailed—so she could make the payments on her condo at New Horizon Retirement Village—it would be worth the lack of sleep, Amanda assured herself.

However, thought Amanda, she couldn't tell Thorn that she had found the journal. If she did, he would confiscate it from her, claim it contained possible evidence. Then she would get mad at him for interfering in her private investigation. In essence, she was doing Thorn a favor by *not* telling him right away, she rationalized. She was saving Thorn from upsetting her, and he was trying very hard not to upset her in her "fragile condition."

Later, she decided. She would tell Thorn later . . . when it was time for him to know.

TEN

"Thorn!"

Nick bolted upright, dropped the square hay bale he had lifted onto the top of the fence rail to feed the sheep, then wheeled around and bounded off like a jackrabbit.

"Thorn!"

Nick raced uphill at a dead run to reach the house. This was it, he told himself. Hazard's sharp, impatient voice clanged like a gong. Her labor had begun! D day had finally arrived!

"Let me change my shirt and I'll be back outside in a flash to take you to the hospital. Call Doc Simms," he said as he leaped onto the porch and made a grab for the doorknob.

"Thorn, stop!" Hazard shook her orange-tinted head in dismay. "I am not in labor. You have got to stop having these panic attacks every time I step outside to call you to supper. I'm pretty sure that we'll both know when the time comes. But *this* is not the time."

Nick's shoulders slumped. His breath seesawed in and out of his chest. This past week he had geared himself up so he would be mentally prepared the moment Hazard gave the nod to transport her to the hospital. Since then, he had raced to the rescue the instant she raised her voice. All these false starts were making him look like an idiot.

Hazard was right: he had to calm down and get a grip. If he panicked when D day actually arrived he might alarm and upset her. Upsetting Hazard, he had learned, was not a good thing. She clouded up and rained tears all over him each time he upset her. The worst part was never knowing what might set her off. Talk about walking on eggs!

"After we have supper I would like for you to help me get into that dumb pumpkin costume. It looks to be a two-man job," she said.

Nick leaned over to give Hazard a big, juicy smack on the lips. "Sorry about getting carried away again, sweetie pie."

"Second time this week," she didn't fail to point out.

"Yeah, but I'm practicing these trial runs so I can be here for you at a moment's notice. Whenever you need me, in whatever capacity you need me, you can count on me to be there for you."

Hazard teared up instantly. "Oh, Thorn, you big, sweet, adorable lug, don't make me cry."

Well, hell, he had unintentionally done it again. Nick curled his arm around her expansive waist and escorted her inside.

"Everything is going to be just fine," he cooed. "Tonight is going to be loads of fun. We'll get you into your costume in no time at all and then drive into town to join in the festivities."

"Thorn?" she whispered through a stream of tears.

"What, honey-bunch?"

"I tried to cook. I burned supper again."

Nick inwardly cringed, but he managed to manufacture a smile. "Good, *burned* is just the way I like it."

She tossed him a watery smile, then pointed toward the cremated remains of fried chicken.

What on earth had possessed her to cook something so complicated when she could barely manage creamed tuna on toast? Nick wondered. Must be some sort of nesting instinct that affected pregnant women, he decided. Hazard was trying to provide food for her family, but it was never going to happen. Long ago, Nick had accepted the fact that Hazard was a disaster in the kitchen.

"I'll get the bread and butter," Nick volunteered as they veered into the dining room.

"I'll get the cranberry juice," she said.

"No, you sit down and I'll get it." Nick helped Hazard into her chair, then strode to the kitchen.

When he returned, he sat down, determined to get Hazard's mind off the culinary catastrophe. "I came across an interesting fact during my drive home this evening," Nick said as he peeled the crusty skin from his drumstick. "I ID'd the truck Elvina Keef described to me in bits and pieces this week."

Hazard's head snapped up, her gaze intense. "The dark-colored one with a tall antenna on top?"

Nick dipped his head. "That's the one. It was parked behind Rumley Grocery. I thought we would pose a few questions to Melvin and Ginger at the parade tonight."

"Nettie must have hit up the Rumleys for more rent money, since she was planning to buy a condo at New Horizon. Her insistence might have put the Rumleys in a financial bind."

"Are you sure Nettie was moving to the retirement village?"

"Yes, according to the representative for New Horizon, Nettie put down five grand as the first installment of a down payment. Her name is on the waiting list for the first available living space. The second installment was due next week. I still have no idea where that five grand came from."

"I stopped to have a chat with Odell Jarvis this afternoon," Nick informed her.

"Turn up anything interesting, other than the fact that the man is a jerk?" she asked, then sipped her cranberry juice.

"Only that Odell sweats profusely when grilled with rapid-fire questions. I asked him if he saw Nettie the morning she died, and he demanded to know if he was a suspect in her death."

"Did he admit to seeing his older sister?" Hazard questioned.

Nick shook his dark head. "Denied any contact with Nettie during the past few days prior to her demise."

"From what Sis Hix told me, Nettie and Odell never saw eye to eye on much of anything. I think Nettie liked to rule the Jarvis roost, being the oldest and all."

Nick could relate to that. His older brother had the same tendency. Sometimes Rich's attempt to run the show, as a teenager and young adult, annoyed the hell out of Nick.

"Sis also told me that a man named Pad showed up during one of her visits to Nettie's. Sis claims that Nettie occasionally talked to this Pad person on the phone."

"Pad?" Nick frowned. "Who is that?"

Hazard shrugged as she buttered her bread. "That's what we have to find out. Sis doesn't recall much about the man, except that he drove a flashy car, had reddish brown hair, and seemed sort of tall to an eight-year-old kid. Sis mentioned Pad to Faye once and was told never to speak the name again. I'm wondering if this Pad person might be Sis's real father."

"We'll put Faye Jarvis-Mithlo on our list of people to interview after the parade." Nick carried the empty plates to the kitchen sink. "Come on, Haz, let's get you into your costume; then you can put on your makeup before we hit the road."

* * *

Amanda scrunched up her face to alleviate the itching sensation. She had slathered liquid eyeliner to make the black triangles around her eyes, nose, and mouth so she would look like a jack-o'-lantern in her fluorescent orange costume. It was difficult to move freely with the large metal hoop that was sewn into the yards of fabric.

Getting into the cab of Thorn's black farm truck had been a tight squeeze, but Amanda refused to sit in the truck bed during the drive into town. The rhinestone tiara Velma sent home with Thorn encircled her pumpkin-colored head. The damned crown had to weigh ten pounds, if it weighed an ounce. It was going to give her a queen-size headache, Amanda predicted.

"Now remember to pay attention while you're standing on top of that float," Thorn lectured her for the umpteenth time. "That float is going to bounce when it crosses the railroad track. I don't want you to cartwheel onto the street.

"And don't let all those kids who will be dressed up like ghosts and goblins, who will be sitting on the hay bales beside you, knock you off balance, either. You know how kids are when they start clowning around and showing off."

"Not to worry, Thorn—if the goblins misbehave I'll thump them on the head and put the curse of the Great Pumpkin on the little devils," Amanda insisted.

Thorn took his eyes off the crowded road to fix her with a steely stare. "This isn't funny, Haz. You could get hurt."

"Okay, okay. I'll watch what I'm doing," she promised, just to shut him up.

Thorn stopped the truck in front of the school, where the decorated floats were lined up for the parade. With the greatest care for the costume—and her person—Thorn extricated her from the cab of the truck. It took five minutes.

"Good! You're here!" *Smack, chomp.* "You look great, hon!"

Amanda teetered around to see Velma lumbering toward her, smiling with excitement.

"I brought the batteries for your lights."

"Swell," Amanda mumbled.

She stood perfectly still while Velma plugged in the batteries to the string of orange lights that had been stitched on the underside of her pumpkin costume. Bystanders oohed and aahed in delight when Amanda glowed like an Indian summer moon.

"May I present this year's Pumpkin Queen," Beverly Hill announced loudly.

Everybody applauded and Amanda forced a smile. She looked ridiculous, felt ridiculous. She tried to get into the spirit of the season and reminded herself that she needed to be a good sport about the whole damn thing.

It helped—a smidgen.

Thorn gave her a boost onto the float, then cautioned the rambunctious goblins not to knock the Great Pumpkin off her perch. The goblins and ghouls snapped to attention when Thorn's authoritative cop voice filled the cool evening air.

Rocky Hill, Bev's older brother, waved his bulky arms in expansive gestures to gain the attention of the Pumpkin Queen and her attendants. "Listen up, y'all. I'll be driving this here float. When we reach the railroad tracks, the seven-thirty special express train will roll past and blow its horn, signaling the beginning of the parade. When we cross the tracks, steady yourselves for the rough bumps. Nobody is allowed to climb off this float until we lead this long procession to the south end of town. Is everybody clear on that?"

Dozens of ghosts bobbed their heads.

"Good. Now make sure you wave to the crowd lining

the street." Rocky stared sternly at the goblins. "And if anybody starts hurling eggs at bystanders, like last year, then none of you get a free pass to the haunted house. No tricks, or else no treats. Got it?"

"Got it," the ghouls said in unison.

Amanda took her position in front of the haystack. A papier-mâché black cat was perched above her right shoulder; a scarecrow stood to her left. She scanned the school parking lot to see the string of floats that had been created by the sophomore, junior, and senior high school classes, in addition to floats designed by various businesses in Vamoose, Pronto, and Adios.

Amanda frowned when she saw the high school homecoming king and queen perched on their elevated platform, surrounded by a glowing orange archway. The royalty was decked out in formal wear, looking young, vibrant, and attractive.

They made Amanda feel more ridiculous than she already felt.

Thatcher's Oil and Gas, Rumley Grocery, Watts Mechanic Shop, and the Last Chance Café had designed their floats to advertise their services. The darkness glowed with hundreds of orange, purple, and yellow lights.

Amanda caught sight of Faye Jarvis-Mithlo and Odell Jarvis. They stood aside, glaring up at her. Obviously her investigation had made her the archenemy of the surviving Jarvis siblings. They stared at Amanda as if they wanted to boil her and make a pie out of her.

Well, tough, Amanda was not going to be intimidated by a family harboring deadly secrets. When she had time to read Nettie's journal, *she* was going to be the pie in *their* face! *So there!*

"Everybody ready?" Rocky Hill called out.

"Be careful, Hazard!" Thorn hollered as he took his position on the left side of the float.

Amanda glanced down to note that Deputy Sykes had been pressed into service and had taken his place on the right side of the float. Thorn and his misguided protective instincts, Amanda thought with a sigh. You'd think she was the president of the U.S. of A., and Thorn and Sykes were her Secret Service bodyguards!

Poor, dear Thorn, Amanda mused. The man really was stressing out this week. The additional strain of this investigation was working on him, too. Amanda definitely needed to figure out who bumped off Nettie so Thorn could relax. . . .

Amanda was jolted from her pensive musings when the float lurched forward. She grabbed the scarecrow for support. In the distance she could hear the seven-thirty special express clattering down the tracks. The train rumbled toward them, tooted twice, then blew through Vamoose.

As the parade procession made slow progress, Amanda steadied herself for the bumps on the railroad tracks. The float teetered sideways, and the goblins swayed and tumbled at her feet, then righted themselves. Amanda noticed that Thorn expelled a huge sigh of relief when she didn't swan-dive off the float and *kersplat* on the street.

The businesses on Main Street were lit up like Christmas, in honor of the annual October Festival of the Pumpkin. Although Hazard Accounting decorations were impressive and eye-catching, what with orange lights streaming up the peak of the roof, dangling like curtains from the eaves, and encircling the decorated windows, Thatcher's Oil and Gas had a display that was out of this world! Thaddeus and Gertrude had really knocked themselves out with their decorations.

Amanda stared enviously at the mechanical, glow-in-the-dark ghosts that paraded over the carport that covered the gas pumps. The glass garage doors were a sheet of twinkling orange lights. Glowing jack-o'-lanterns lined the circular driveway. Even the gas pumps had been decorated to look like pumpkin soldiers guarding the ghoulish castle.

She glanced sideways to note that Cleatus and Cecil Watts had strung lights up the guide wires to their towering flagpole. There, spotlighted in the darkness, was a gigantic orange flag with a smiling jack-o'-lantern. Every car and truck waiting to be serviced at the auto-repair shop was draped with lights, and scarecrows sat behind each steering wheel.

The haunted house, which had been bequeathed to the city of Vamoose two years earlier by the widow Plum, also boasted hundreds of winking lights. Electrified candles, with orange bulbs, sat in each upstairs and downstairs window. An orange neon-lit sign had been attached to the roof, and it beamed eerily in the darkness.

Velma's Beauty Boutique was no less spectacular with its effigies of ghouls and goblins that were positioned on the lawn and the wooden deck.

Pretty damned impressive, Amanda mused as she waved to the crowd. This was small-town America at its finest. Everyone had pitched in to set the mood of the Halloween season, enjoy the festivities, and donate time and money to the volunteer firefighters.

Amanda swallowed the sentimental lump in her throat, refusing to get teary-eyed and cause the black eyeliner that surrounded her eyes, nose, and mouth to run like black rivers.

When the float ground to a halt at the south end of town, Thorn was there to help Amanda down. "You okay, honey?" he asked. "That rough ride didn't jar anything loose, did it?"

"No, Thorn, I didn't experience so much as a twinge," she assured him. "However, Odell and Faye were giving me the evil eye when I passed them by. Good thing looks don't kill."

"They must think this investigation is going to rattle

the skeletons in their closets," Thorn said as he rearranged the yards of glowing orange fabric of Amanda's costume.

Amanda had no doubt about that. She also suspected that several closet doors in Vamoose would be flung open wide when she had time to sit down and read Nettie's tell-all journal.

Amanda and Thorn hiked past the decorated businesses and shops, then stopped to watch youngsters bobbing for apples and playing Halloween hopscotch. The sidewalk had been chalked with squares of pumpkins, black cats, and goblins. Several children were playing jump rope with neon-lit cords that flashed in the darkness. The parking lot of the Last Chance Café was lined with children waiting to have a Polaroid picture taken with the Pumpkin Queen.

"Meet me at the haunted house after you finish up your picture session," Thorn requested. "I go on duty as ticket-taker in ten minutes." With a wave and a smile, Thorn made a beeline for the house that glowed eerily in the distance.

ELEVEN

When Thorn strode off, Amanda waddled over to the haystack decorated with jack-o'-lanterns. A few toddlers squealed in fright, refusing to have their picture snapped with the glowing pumpkin. But B. J. Hix, who wasn't afraid of the devil himself, bounded up to grab Amanda's hand and flash her a wide smile.

"Hey, Beeje, how ya doin'?" Amanda asked.

B. J. jabbered in that language only his parents could translate, smiled for the picture, then bounded back to Sis and Bubba.

When the last pic had been flicked, Amanda made her way down the street toward the haunted house, where Thorn was helping Commissioner Harjo take tickets. Odell and Faye suddenly appeared beside Amanda.

"We want a few words with you, Hazard," Odell said to her in a growl.

"Yeah," Faye seconded snidely.

"Getting a little antsy, are you?" Amanda asked, undaunted.

"I don't like you and Thorn poking around, asking me questions," Odell said, and scowled.

"And I don't like you grilling Sis, either," Faye put in.

"We know you have Thorn wrapped around your finger. When you decide there's foul play involved in an accident, whether there actually is or not, you get Thorn all riled up. There was no foul play with Nettie," Odell insisted adamantly.

Amanda stopped short, her costume shifting and glowing around her. "Ha! You are not dealing with the village idiot here," she assured them.

The Jarvis siblings looked her up and down, then smirked at her costume.

Amanda ignored the unspoken insult. "I know perfectly well that Nettie planned to move to New Horizon Retirement Village. She needed money for her down payments and for monthly expenses."

Faye and Odell looked stunned. Amanda wasn't sure if they were surprised by the news or shocked that she knew of Nettie's plans. "Nettie needed extra cash, and she was privy to information that enabled her to twist a few arms if she wanted to. She had the goods on the two of you. Did she ask for cash to keep silent about what she knew about you?"

Faye's and Odell's mouths gaped. "You know?" they chirped in chorus.

Amanda nodded and smiled craftily. She didn't know for certain what she knew, but she wanted Faye and Odell to think she had information that could get them in trouble.

"I wasn't anywhere near Nettie's house when she collapsed," Odell was quick to say—and very loudly.

"That theory of objecting loudly, in order to be more readily believed, doesn't cut it with me," Amanda told him flat-out. "I know for a fact that you live in the red, Odell. You can't wait to get your itchy fingers on your inheritance."

She glanced at the stricken look on Faye's face. "Same goes for you, sister. And don't think I can't guess what happened to the child support you have been collecting all these years for Sis."

The comment turned Faye's features the color of yogurt. She staggered, as if she had sustained a physical blow.

"That's right, sister." Amanda pressed her advantage. "I know exactly what went on. Your son Roy reaped the benefits of that hush-hush agreement. But Nettie made everything right by leaving Sis with a substantial inheritance, and Sis deserves every penny she's going to get."

Odell swallowed visibly and snaked out a hand to support his wobbling sister. "Don't overestimate your importance, Pumpkin Queen. What happened all those years ago is strictly confidential. You'll put yourself at risk if you start flapping your jaws. You can't prove a damned thing, not about that, or the other incident I mentioned during our first interview. It is still your word against ours."

"Are you threatening me?" Amanda demanded.

"Take it however you want, Hazard, but the past damned well better remain in the past where it belongs . . . or else. . . ."

"Or else I can expect to have a nasty accident like Nettie? Just try it, buster, and Thorn will be all over you like a bad case of chicken pox. He is fiercely overprotective right now. One squawk from me and he will be here before you can say trick-or-treat."

Faye and Odell glanced toward the haunted house that sat in the near distance. As if on cue, Thorn glanced up to monitor Amanda's activities.

"What do you want from us?" Faye said resentfully.

"I want to know who Candice Randolph is, for starters. Her name appears on a birth certificate containing the same birth date and stats as Sis's."

Faye and Odell simultaneously stepped back, as if buffeted by gale-force winds.

"Good God!" Odell wheezed.

"My Lord!" Faye bleated.

"I also want to know who Pad is," Amanda demanded while she had the Jarvis siblings completely off balance.

Faye's hand flew to her mouth and she teetered unsteadily on her feet. Odell staggered, trying to keep his sister upright.

"Now then," Amanda said cheerily. "Shall we try it from the top again? Odell, where were you the morning Nettie collapsed?"

Odell stared at his white-faced sister. "I was with Faye."

"You told me you were feeding hay to your cattle. Now you claim you were with Faye? You are contradicting your statement."

"No, I'm not," Odell insisted, smiling smugly. "I fed hay; *then* I picked up Faye."

Amanda's narrowed gaze bore down on Faye. "Is that the story you're sticking with, Faye?"

The woman bobbed her head, but didn't speak—probably couldn't find her tongue, if the thunderstruck look on her face was anything to go by.

"What were you two doing that morning?" Amanda fired the question like a patriot missile.

"Doing?" Faye peeped.

"We—"Odell tried to cut in.

"I'm talking to Faye. Clam up, Odell," Amanda ordered brusquely.

"We . . . uh . . ." Faye stuttered shakily, "were . . . er . . . on our way to Pronto to visit Roy."

"Yeah, right," Amanda said, and snorted. She glanced around. "Where is boy Roy, by the way? I'm sure he's here somewhere. Why don't I just look him up and ask him if he can corroborate your flimsy story?"

When Amanda lurched around, her costume shifting like a sail in the wind, Odell grabbed her arm.

"Okay, so maybe we didn't visit Roy in Pronto."

"I didn't think so."

"We took flowers to our parents' graves that morning," he said in a rush. "It was their wedding anniversary."

"How touching." Amanda didn't believe him for a minute. She stepped forward and stuck her face in Odell's. "I'll track down Willis Mithlo and see if he can give me a straight answer," she threatened.

"No!" Faye squealed like a stuck pig. "Leave Willis out of this!"

Amanda pivoted to confront Faye. "Why? Because he is the guilty party who, left to his own devices Monday morning, drove out to silence poor old Nettie, while you and Odell were at the cemetery?"

Faye and Odell were really starting to squirm. Amanda stared them down. "Tell me who Pad is."

Obviously reeling from the one-two verbal punches, Faye folded up and fainted dead away. Odell barely caught her before she clanked her noggin on the sidewalk.

"Damn you, Hazard," Odell said with a snarl as he clutched his sister. "You are really asking for trouble."

"Yo!" Amanda flapped her arms to gain the attention of the fire chief, who was approaching from the south. "All the holiday festivities caused Faye too much excitement. Could you lend a hand, Delmar?"

Delmar Sparks, with his faithful Dalmatian dog at his heels, raced forward to help Odell lower Faye to the ground. He checked her pulse, then lifted her limp legs above her head to send blood rushing back to her brain.

Amanda positioned herself above Faye so she would be the first thing the older woman saw when she roused. Sure enough, Faye's eyes fluttered open; then she gasped and passed out again.

"Tell Faye I'll see her at tomorrow's pumpkin bazaar," Amanda told Odell before she turned and waddled away.

"You'll see us tomorrow, at the very latest," Odell said in a hiss through clenched teeth.

Amanda raised a brow. That sounded like another threat

to her. Odell was very good at them, she noted. Had he threatened Nettie and made good on his threat? Amanda wouldn't be surprised.

High rollers like Odell Jarvis were driven to protect their projected images of importance. She suspected Odell had a great fear of public humiliation. She had a pretty good idea how he had handled the traffic accident that took Jim Foster's life. She couldn't help but wonder how Odell had kept the gossip down when he went through his divorce. No doubt the divorce leveled a tremendous blow to his pride and reputation. Paying child support all those years must have put a kink in his wallet, too.

Had Nettie given Odell money through the years and then demanded repayment when she decided to move to New Horizon Retirement Village? Had Odell, to protect his image and failing finances, disposed of his own sister?

Amanda wasn't sure what Odell and Faye were capable of, how desperate they were to keep their secrets. But she knew she didn't like either of them. Faye and Odell were too full of themselves for Amanda's taste.

Not for the first time, Amanda found herself sympathizing with poor, departed Nettie. From what Amanda had learned, Nettie's siblings had given her nothing but grief!

Amanda couldn't believe her good fortune. She had walked only half a block, past creatively decorated homes, to reach the haunted house—and happened onto Melvin Rumley. The tall, lanky grocery store owner was smiling contentedly—until he spotted the giant glowing Pumpkin Queen. Immediately Melvin wheeled like a soldier on parade and tried to beat a hasty retreat.

"Hold it, Melvin. I would like to talk to you," Amanda called loudly enough to gain the attention of other passersby. Melvin couldn't scurry off without the residents of Vamoose wondering why he was trying to avoid her.

Amanda watched Melvin's thin-bladed shoulders slump

in defeat as he reluctantly pivoted to face her. "Nice decorations on your store," she complimented, so he would take his guard down.

He eyed her warily. "Thanks." Melvin glanced every-where except at her. "Well, I better be going. Ginger is waiting for me to take her place at the apple-bobbing contest. We are supplying the apples, you know."

"Very generous of you," she acknowledged.

"We do what we can."

Amanda decided to hit him with both barrels at once, rather than beating around more bushes. "I'm surprised you had time to gather the water barrels and folding chairs for the contest while you were shadowing me this afternoon."

Melvin flung back his narrow shoulders. His cavernous eyes nearly popped from his head. "I did no such thing!" he denied vehemently.

Amanda wasn't buying it. "Of course you did," she insisted. "My dog chased you up a tree while I was at Nettie's. You couldn't climb down to scuttle back to your truck, which was parked in the grove of cottonwoods, until I called off my guard dog. And furthermore, you ran poor old Elvina Keef off the road the morning you fled from the crime scene at Pumpkin Hollow."

Melvin clutched his chest as if he expected to have the big one. "I never!" he said in a gasp.

Amanda decided she was becoming the leading cause of fainting spells and heart seizures in Vamoose. *Well, too damned bad.* She wasn't going to pussyfoot around with folks who might possibly have disposed of Nettie Jarvis. The spinster, after all, was the one who got the bad end of this deal!

"Don't try to feed me that boloney, Mel," she snapped. "Elvina gave Thorn and me a description of your truck."

"I didn't—"

"Liar, liar, pants on fire," she sassed him, amazed at her childish retort. "*You* may be in a state of denial, Mel, but *I* have the facts, and I can ID your truck because I saw it near my house this afternoon and again on the access road to Nettie's pasture. Stop this nonsense and save both of us a lot of time.''

"Well, damn," Melvin muttered. He glanced cautiously around, then lowered his voice. "Okay, so I did whiz by Elvina. The old woman drives like a snail, and I was in a hurry. I didn't know she was paying so little attention that she would panic when I passed her on the gravel road. It's not my fault she veered toward the ditch. I gave her plenty of road space.''

"So why were you racing away from Nettie's farm?" Amanda questioned as she steered Melvin away from the crowded sidewalk.

"I had to get back to the store," he muttered.

Amanda could feel the tension rippling through him. Holding on to his arm was like administering a lie-detector test. He was strung as tight as fence wire. She halted beneath a sprawling maple tree that was decorated with rubber, glow-in-the-dark spiders and filmy white webs. Now that she was out of earshot from the festivalgoers she could grill him relentlessly.

"Why were you hurrying away from Nettie's that morning?" she fired at him, refusing to release his rigid arm.

"I already told you. I was due back at the store," he maintained.

"Why did you kill Nettie?" she asked.

"I didn't!" His heart rate skyrocketed. Amanda could see the veins popping from his neck and his forehead.

"You took care of Nettie so she wouldn't raise your rent," Amanda blasted away at him. "Then you loaded pumpkins in your truck and hauled ass, but Elvina got in your way. With the low-lying fog and flying dust you didn't think she could ID your truck, so you just kept going. Then you pulled in behind the grocery store and unloaded the pumpkins as if nothing had happened. I'm sure if I question your wife she can verify that you were away from the market Monday morning, at the precise time of Nettie's death.''

"Don't you dare bring Ginger into this," Melvin said in a growl.

Why, Amanda wondered, were Faye Mithlo and Melvin Rumley so determined to protect their spouses?

"If you don't want me to interrogate Ginger, then answer my question," Amanda bartered.

Melvin leaned back against the tree trunk and shook Amanda's hand loose from his wrist. "Okay, here's the deal," he confided, then glanced cautiously over his shoulder. "Ginger sent me out to Pumpkin Hollow to pick out some pumpkins. When I . . ." He paused, glanced around again, making certain he wasn't overheard, then continued quietly. "When I arrived Nettie was sprawled in the pumpkin patch. I panicked. I didn't know who knew Nettie had demanded more rent money from us, but I . . ."

His voice dried up as he focused on something over Amanda's left shoulder. She watched Melvin gulp hard; then she pivoted to see who—or what—had demanded his attention. All she could see was the silhouettes of passersby coming to and from the haunted house. Amanda wondered if Melvin, with his height advantage, spotted someone who alarmed him.

"Anyway," he hurried on, his breath coming in panted spurts, as if he were running laps, "I just picked up some pumpkins like Ginger told me to do and hurried back to the store. I didn't want to answer any questions about Nettie. I didn't want to get involved."

His gaze kept darting around like a steel marble in a pinball machine. The man was getting spooked.

He was also lying. Amanda was sure of it.

"Did you kill Nettie in the house, then carry her outside?"

Melvin's face blanched. "No!" he croaked. "No!"

Amanda gave him a long, assessing look, then said,

"But you know who did, is that it? You're afraid to say, afraid we're being watched?"

"No! I don't know a damn thing, except that I took the pumpkins without paying for them. I did nothing, saw nothing, heard nothing!"

Amanda stared Melvin down. She still didn't believe him. He was definitely hiding something. But what? Amanda wasn't sure. She presumed Melvin had either committed the crime and refused to admit it, or he knew who had done the dastardly deed and he was afraid to speak out.

But why would he be afraid? she wondered. He had to know she would go straight to Thorn and have the suspect arrested immediately.

Amanda put that promise to voice, but Melvin shook his head adamantly. "Don't know who did it. Don't know if anybody did anything," he said before he pushed away from the tree and fled quickly down the street.

Amanda watched him scamper away and frowned ponderously. Who was Melvin protecting. And why?

Mulling over those questions, Amanda waddled toward the haunted house. Commissioner Harjo was lining up a group of children for the spooky tour, and Thorn was sitting on the porch, taking tickets. He waved the instant he spotted Amanda. She smiled in greeting as he stood up and stepped into full view of the porch light. . . .

Then, from out of nowhere, without the slightest warning, a red brick sailed through the air . . . and caught Thorn upside the head!

TWELVE

"Thorn!" Amanda howled as he staggered dazedly, then flipped backward over the lattice railing. He collapsed in a lifeless heap.

"Oh, God!" Amanda wailed as she rushed clumsily forward. "Harjo, help. Help!"

Harjo plunged through the front door, serenaded by the special sound effects of demented howls and horrified screams.

"Somebody threw a brick at Thorn." Amanda's shaky arm shot toward the shrubs. "It came from over there!"

Harjo leaped over the lattice railing in a single bound and shot off like a blazing bullet. Amanda, hampered by her costume, tried to squat down beside Thorn—and couldn't.

"Thorn? Can you hear me?" she yelled at him.

Nothing, not even a groan.

Amanda spied a stream of blood dribbling down the side of Thorn's face. Nausea coiled inside her, and she grabbed the railing for support.

"Somebody help!" she whimpered.

Harjo was back in two shakes. "No one is there," he said, completely out of breath. "I'll get Thorn—argh!"

Harjo groaned when he tried to hoist Thorn's limp body. He glanced over his shoulder to see Buzz Sawyer, the local carpenter, and Philip Fawcett, the local plumber, rushing toward him. "Help me carry the chief into the house."

Amanda fought down nausea and rising hysterics and cursed her flighty emotions. When Buzz, Philip, and Harjo toted Thorn into the haunted house, she toddled in their wake, ordering herself to get a firm grip. This was no time to fall apart.

"Move aside, y'all." *Snap, pop.* "Coming through with the first-aid kit!" Velma trumpeted. "What happened?"

"Someone konked Thorn with a brick," Amanda said on a sob.

"Ornery teenagers," Velma muttered as she swabbed the bleeding wound. "We planned all these activities to promote good, clean fun for the festival and some idiotic hooligan decides to pull a stunt like this. Probably some spiteful brat who was aggravated with Nicky for giving him a traffic ticket. Darn kids!" *Crackle, chomp.*

Kids? Amanda wasn't prepared to write off this incident as a teenage prank. A sudden, sinking feeling filled the pit of her stomach. She remembered the haunted look on Melvin Rumley's cadaver-thin face when she mentioned his wife.

Had Nettie's killer threatened to harm Ginger Rumley if Melvin didn't keep his trap shut? Had the killer sent Amanda a warning by targeting Thorn?

Furious, Amanda whirled around. Nobody messed with her man and got away with it!

She forged through the crowd that had gathered at the front door to check on their beloved chief of police. She tramped around the side of the house, noting that one of the bricks that formed a border for the flower garden was missing. She stared every which way, wondering if the killer was still lurking in the darkness.

He/she didn't dare approach Amanda, she reasoned. Not when she was lit up like a Christmas tree. If the hugely pregnant Pumpkin Queen sustained injury, the whole town would be up in arms.

"I know you're out there, you cowardly little weasel," Amanda said in a snarl to the darkness at large. "Go ahead and search for that little black book and inspire a few more ghost stories for the season. But I'll find it before you do." She refused to make the blundering mistake of alerting the killer that she already had the journal in her possession. "When I find that book, I'll know who you are and you will be behind bars. When you mess with Thorn, pal, you mess with me. I'll make you damn sorry you did, too—"

Amanda nearly leaped out of her glowing pumpkin costume when a strong hand clamped around her wrist. She wrestled for freedom as she whirled toward her attacker. The frantic breath she had been holding came out in a whoosh when she realized Harjo had come searching for her. Amanda slumped against him in relief.

"Hazard, you are hysterical, yelling down the night like that," he said.

"Am not," she blubbered through the sudden tears that smeared her cheeks, ruining her jack-o'-lantern face.

"Thorn has regained consciousness and he is bellowing your name," Harjo reported. "Five men are trying to hold him down. You wanna come in the house and get that fire-breathing dragon of yours under control before he hurts somebody? He has convinced himself that you have been kidnapped while he was knocked out. He refuses to believe that you are alive and well until he sees you with his own eyes."

Amanda waddled toward the house, sniffing back those blasted tears.

"Here, wipe your face." Harjo thrust his handkerchief at her.

Hurriedly Amanda dabbed at her ruined makeup and took deep breaths to regain her composure. Before she set foot on the first step she heard Thorn snarling, growling, and demanding to be turned loose. Even injured and bleeding, Thorn was desperate to save her.

My hero, Amanda thought as Harjo shepherded her across the porch and into the haunted house. She was absolutely crazy about Thorn, even if his protective instincts were way out of whack.

Nick blinked when he saw two glowing pumpkins hovering in the doorway. He blinked again, trying to clear his double vision, but it didn't help. His head hurt like a son of a bitch, and his stomach pitched. He ceased fighting the five men who were pressing him down on the couch.

"Hazard, you okay?" he demanded.

"I'm fine. And you?"

Someone—Nick couldn't see well enough to know who it was—pried open his left eye and shined a penlight in his face.

"Concussion is my diagnosis," Delmar Sparks, the fire chief, said. "Did anybody round up Doc Simms?"

"He's on his way," somebody else called from the front porch.

Concussion? thought Nick. *Great, just great.* This was no time for him to be out of commission. Hazard was due to deliver any day. What kind of devoted, caring husband was he going to make if he couldn't drive his own wife to the hospital? He'd have to call an ambulance.

"Clear a path, y'all," Velma bugled. "The doctor is coming through."

Nick knew the instant Dr. Simms entered the room, because the physician's Reebok tennis shoes squeaked on the wooden floor.

"Well, what do we have here, Nick, m'boy?"

"A headache the size of the North American continent," Nick grumbled. "Fix it, Doc, and make it snappy."

Dr. Simms chuckled as he squatted down beside Nick. "Sorry, no can do. I can work wonders, but not miracles. You're going to have to take it easy for a few days."

That was not what Nick wanted to hear, damn it to hell! He squinted into the bright light aimed at his face. "Is Deputy Sykes here?"

"You bet, Chief."

Nick's glower branded Benny Sykes as a traitor—when he realized his own deputy was one of the men who had held him down. "You will have to pull double duty tomorrow until we can get a temporary cop from the sheriff's office to fill in for me."

"Fill in for you. Right, Chief," Benny repeated. "I've got it covered. I'll take care of everything while you rest. Don't worry about a thing."

"Here you go, Doc, everything to bandage Nicky properly," Velma said as she elbowed her way through the surrounding onlookers.

Nick winced and grimaced when the physician cleaned and stitched the cut and wrapped gauze around his head. "How long do I have to stay off the police beat?"

"Give it three days. If you suffer no lasting side effects of nausea and headaches you can start back on a half-day schedule."

"Tomorrow is the pumpkin bazaar and street dance," Nick mumbled.

"Maybe for everybody else in Vamoose, but not for you, Chief," the white-haired physician said, then turned toward Hazard. "Are you going to drive Nick home?"

"Of course I am," she said. "Just give me a minute to remove this costume."

Nick was forced to lie on the couch until Hazard emerged from one of the bedrooms.

"Okay, we're all set," Hazard announced.

"Give me the keys to the truck, Hazard," Harjo requested. "I'll bring it around to the curb so the chief won't have far to walk."

When Harjo jogged off, Nick was allowed to sit up—just to see if he could. The room—complete with flickering lights, dangling rubber snakes, and plastic rats—whirred around him like the spin cycle of a washing machine. His stomach flip-flopped.

Nick didn't feel so good, and he was afraid he was about to lose his unappetizing supper in front of this captivated audience.

"Okay," he bleated. "Excitement's over. Let's clear out of this place so the tours can resume."

"Tours, right," Benny Sykes parroted. "Clear the area, please. We're going to move the chief to his truck."

Vamoosians spilled out the front door to give Nick breathing room. He rose slowly to his feet, then steadied himself when his knees threatened to fold up like accordions.

"Make sure you take three days of bed rest, Chief," Dr. Simms lectured as he guided Nick toward the door. "Begin with a semiliquid diet. Once your stomach settles, you can try solid food."

Oh, goody, thought Nick. Hazard couldn't serve him leftovers of cremated fried chicken. Surely she couldn't find a way to burn soup broth, too.

"Listen up, everybody," Deputy Sykes called out, taking command of the field. "We will have to tighten security for the costume street dance tomorrow night. I'm going to deputize a few good men—"

"And women," Velma piped up. "No discrimination, Benny."

"And women," he added quickly. "We want to make sure no one else becomes the victim of a harmful prank."

Nick rolled his eyes as Deputy Sykes strode off, his thin chest thrust out, the heel of his hand resting on the butt of his police-issued pistol. His lovable, gung-ho deputy kept suffering delusions of working for NYPD.

"Truck's here," Hazard announced as she grabbed his arm. "Ready, Thorn?"

Nick, assisted by several helping hands, descended the steps. The sparkling lights took another dizzying spin around his head as he wobbled along the sidewalk. He closed his eyes before he became nauseated, and allowed himself to be led to the truck.

"What the hell hit me?" Nick asked as Hazard tucked him into the passenger side of his truck.

"A brick."

"Damn kids," he said, and scowled.

Hazard said nothing. She scooted beneath the steering wheel and drove away.

Amanda glanced in the rearview mirror, noting the headlights that had been following her since she passed the sign on the outskirts of town that read: IF YOU LIKE IT COUNTRY-STYLE, THEN VAMOOSE. She refused to tell Thorn about her suspicions that a teenage prankster was not responsible for his concussion. Thorn would worry and fret if he thought Nettie's killer was stalking them. Amanda told herself that if worse came to worst she would grab the pistol in Thorn's holster to protect them. He wouldn't have to try to rise to the occasion while battling his concussion.

When Amanda drove across the lawn and stopped beside the front porch, the other vehicle followed her to the driveway. Amanda breathed an inward sigh of relief when Sam Harjo's muscular physique appeared in the beams of her headlights.

"Thought you might need help getting the Lone Ranger to bed," Harjo said as he opened the passenger door.

"Thanks, Harjo, you're a real pal," Thorn said as he slid gingerly off the seat to accept Harjo's offered support.

"Bad as I hate to do this, I'm asking you to escort Hazard through all the festival activities tomorrow." He shot a bleary-eyed glance in Amanda's direction. "And make sure her investigation doesn't lead her into trouble."

"Sure thing, Thorn," Harjo promised.

"And don't start with your independent protests, Hazard," Thorn said, glancing glassy-eyed at her. "Humor me, please. I am not a well man right now."

Amanda knew the full extent of Thorn's protectiveness. Her husband had just asked his former male rival to serve as her temporary protector. It was so touching. The dear, sweet man put his concern for her welfare above his own unwarranted jealousy. Despite everything, Thorn respected Harjo's capabilities and his moral fiber. Thorn knew who he could count on when the chips were down.

When Amanda and Harjo had Thorn resting comfortably in bed, she followed the commish to the front door. "Thanks for all the help."

"Anytime, Hazard. You know I would do anything for you and that big clown you married. I'll pick you up at ten o'clock in the morning and we'll sample our way through the food booths; then I'll bring you home to check on the Lone Ranger."

"I'll be ready." Amanda didn't want to sound impatient, but she wanted Harjo to leave so she could fish out Nettie's journal and begin reading.

Harjo frowned in concern when Amanda shifted from one foot to the other. "You okay, Hazard? Tonight's incident didn't stress you to the point of going into premature labor, did it?"

"No, I'm just swell, or should I say *swelled*." She graced him with a bright smile.

"No twinges? No sudden pains?" he prodded.

"Damn, you're getting as bad as Thorn. Go home and stop worrying. I'm fine."

"Okay, on one condition," Harjo negotiated.

"What's that?"

"I would like to be this baby's godfather."

"That's sweet of you, Harjo. I hope you don't mind sharing that honor with Thorn's brother. Rich also has his heart set on becoming a godfather."

"I can handle that." He smiled down at her. "Well, g'night, Hazard."

When the door eased shut, Amanda shoved the dead bolt into place and closed the drapes. She didn't want anyone sneaking around to spy on her when she dragged out the journal and began searching for suspects and motive.

After checking on Thorn and finding him asleep, Amanda rummaged through the dirty-clothes hamper in the master bedroom to retrieve the little black book. She swung by the kitchen to pour herself a tall glass of milk and grab a box of vanilla wafers.

As a precautionary measure, Amanda brought her guard dog inside so he could provide protection, if needed.

Amanda plunked down in her La-Z-Boy recliner, then crammed a few wafers in her mouth. Now then, she mused as she settled comfortably in her chair, it was time to get down to business. She knew this tell-all journal was the key that could unlock the motive that had prompted Nettie's killer to strike.

THIRTEEN

The moment Amanda opened the journal several pieces of paper fell on her lap—or rather, what little lap she had in her rounded condition. She unfolded the first paper and blinked in surprise. She held in her hand a signed IOU from Odell to Nettie for ten thousand dollars.

So I was right on the mark, Amanda mused. Odell had been so determined to keep up appearances as a successful rancher and businessman that he had begged money from his spinster sister. He would have been ruined if Nettie called in his debt to pay her down payment to the retirement village.

The second IOU was signed and dated by Mickey Poag, the farmer who rented Nettie's land. Mickey was three thousand dollars in debt to his landlady. *Hmmm.* That certainly provided motive for him to bump her off. According to the figures in Mickey's tax file, he didn't have enough spare money for a rent hike, much less a hefty IOU.

The third IOU was signed and dated by Melvin Rumley. He owed Nettie five grand.

The fourth IOU, for two grand, was signed by Faye Mithlo.

Amanda frowned. Until this moment, she had been operating on the assumption that Nettie had blackmailed certain individuals to raise money for her down payments to New Horizon Retirement Village. Perhaps the truth was that Nettie had simply called in her debts and somebody had decided to cancel this one-woman collection agency.

That, Amanda decided, was the most reasonable explanation. Nettie only wanted what she was owed. Nothing illegal about that.

Amanda scanned the last IOU. The name Candice Randolph was scrawled at the bottom. She owed Nettie four grand.

Well, damn. Amanda had presumed that Candice Randolph was Nettie's alias, which she had used on Sis's birth certificate. What the hell was going on here? Where was this Candice Randolph person? How did she fit into the scheme of things?

Amanda picked up the journal and began reading. It wasn't long before she realized that Vamoose had been a regular Peyton Place in the old days. There were all sorts of references to secretive affairs between folks who were now on Medicare, receiving social security benefits.

For sure and certain, Nettie had been the social switchboard through which hush-hush information passed in this community. As barber and beautician, she was privy to scads of juicy tidbits of gossip that had been logged in her personal journal.

Amanda snorted in disgust when she discovered that one of the pompous pillars of the Ladies' Garden Society, and a vocal leader of the local Unitarian church, had fooled around with her husband's janitor while said husband made overnight business trips. The pretentious old bat, Francis Hilliard, projected an image of being very nearly as perfect as Mary Poppins.

Amanda smirked as she read the detailed account that Nettie had written about Francis's affair. And Amanda had thought President Clinton and Monica Lewinsky's affair had been kinky. *Whew!* She had learned more than she wanted to know about Francis and Will Pendergast's sexual practices!

She read on, discovering that one of the local ranchers, Ben Sharp—who was now housebound with health problems—had once made a habit of visiting the wives of three local farmers while their husbands were hauling trailer loads of cattle to the stockyards. Ben, of course, knew when and how long the husbands of his lovers would be gone, because *he* had generously volunteered to help the other men sort and load cattle in the trailers! *Sheesh!* Talk about sneaky and underhanded.

Amanda tried to picture the decrepit Ben Sharp as a ladies' man in his wilder days, hitting on the gray-haired old women Amanda had met at the beauty salon.

Nettie had named names and recorded dates of incidents she obviously heard about during her career as a barber/beautician. Amanda realized that Nettie could have blackmailed dozens of people whose closets were rattling with skeletons. In fact, any number of relatives from the aforementioned families could have snuffed Nettie out in order to protect the sordid truth about their parents.

Good grief, the list of possible suspects who had motive kept expanding with each page Amanda turned!

Somehow or other, she had to solve this case PDQ. Thorn would stew about her handling this investigation without him, but it had to be done. Although it wasn't Thorn's nature to lie in bed and allow someone else to handle his duties and responsibilities, Amanda knew she had to bear down on this perplexing mystery. Thorn had enough to worry about, what with his concussion and her rapidly approaching labor day, without getting involved with wrapping up the Dead in the Pumpkin Patch case.

Amanda resettled herself in her recliner, tossed Bruno

a vanilla wafer, stuffed a few more cookies into her mouth, and resumed reading. "Holy cow!" she chirped a few minutes later.

Nettie's journal entries and commentary had blown another of Amanda's conjectures right out of the water. According to Nettie, the true parentage of Sis Mithlo-Hix was *not* who Amanda had assumed! It turned out that Odell Jarvis had knocked up a young woman named Candice Randolph, who had wanted an abortion rather than delivering the baby.

Candice, however, had agreed to a cash settlement—paid by Nettie—to keep her trap shut about Odell's indiscretion, and to deliver the child and allow Faye and Willis Mithlo to raise it. Candice had agreed to three thousand dollars in hush money if Nettie paid the expenses for her to move to Texas during the last four telling months of her pregnancy.

Furthermore, Candice had the gall to ask Nettie for a loan to make a fresh start. But the woman had dropped out of sight a few months later and never paid Nettie back.

Well, no wonder Nettie was pissed off at her irresponsible, two-timing brother! Odell was a total jerk. But Nettie, the eldest of the Jarvis family, had financially compensated Sis Mithlo-Hix for her biological father's neglect. She had also provided the affection that had been missing in Sis's life.

Apparently Candice-the-leech hadn't been satisfied with the cash settlement she had received. According to Nettie's account, Candice had placed a long-distance call to Odell's wife after Sis was born and settled in Faye Mithlo's home. The damning phone call had instigated Odell's divorce and left him paying child support to his ex-wife for years to come.

Amanda recalled the comment Sis had overheard years earlier between Nettie and Odell. Nettie had said that if Odell had any gumption he would have been there, instead of her, to make things right. Now the comment made sense to Amanda. Nettie had been scolding Odell for refusing to take an active role in the emotional and financial support of his illegitimate daughter. Nettie had been footing Odell's bills for years!

Amanda also remembered the conversation she'd had with Odell and Faye. Amanda had spouted off her speculations and the Jarvis siblings had gaped at her, then said, "You know about that?" She hadn't known, of course—until now. Odell and Faye had been referring to the identity of Odell's illegitimate child.

Had Odell signed the IOU to pay off his ex-wife and provide financial support for his children? Or had he needed fast money after he lost, big-time, in the stock market? Amanda wouldn't know for sure until she grilled Odell thoroughly on all sides of his weasely hide.

Odell, irresponsible, insufferable asshole that he was, cheated on his wife and left his older sister to make the arrangements to conceal the evidence of his adultery, to finance his young lover, and to show fond affection for his illegitimate daughter.

But how had Nettie arranged to have that birth certificate forged? There was no mention of that detail in the journal. Could that incident have played a significant role in Nettie's death? When Nettie had begun hitting up folks who owed her debts the domino effect could have occurred.

Suspects were crawling out of the woodwork!

Exhausted though Amanda was, and in desperate need of sleep, she refused to set aside the journal when she saw "Pad" mentioned. Never once had Nettie referred to her lover as anyone other than Pad. Nettie did, however, mention that Pad had promised to divorce his wife when he was financially able, so they could marry.

Amanda snorted at that. Nettie must have been so fond of Pad that she refused to believe the man was simply making all the right noises to keep stringing her along so she would continue their secretive affair. Anyone but a blind fool in love could see that lover-boy Pad didn't want to screw up the good deal he had going.

Reading this tell-all journal assured Amanda that Nettie Jarvis had spent her life being used by a dishonest lover, and by a spoiled, selfish brother and swindling sister, not to mention by a raft of welshing tenants who squatted on her city and country property. Everyone in Nettie's social and family circle was indebted to her, and she had barely gotten by the past few years. Talk about unfair, Amanda fumed.

On impulse, Amanda picked up the phone and dialed.

" 'Lo," Rich Thorn mumbled sleepily.

"Rich, it's Hazard."

"Did you have the baby? Which is it, boy or girl? Where's Nick? Why isn't he the one calling me? You're supposed to be resting."

"I did not have the baby," Amanda informed her groggy brother-in-law. "As for your brother, he is in bed with a concussion. Doc Simms ordered Thorn to take it easy for at least three days, maybe longer."

"What!" Rich howled, coming awake in a flash. "When and how did that happen?"

"He caught a brick in the side of the head at the haunted house tonight," Amanda reported.

"Halloween pranksters?" he guessed.

"I don't think so. I believe the incident is connected to the case I'm working." Amanda took a deep breath and plunged on. "Rich, I need to ask a favor."

"Anything for my favorite sister-in-law, even if it is one-thirty in the morning and I have to leave at six o'clock to work on a special case for OSBI."

"Sorry, I didn't realize it was so late. I need some information for my investigation. I need facts on Candice Randolph."

"Is that the name of the mother on the duplicate birth certificate that you asked me to check on the other day?"

"That's the same one," Amanda confirmed. "I need to know who and where she is now. I also want you to get some background information on Arthella Carson and Eileen Franklin, who are home-health care nurses at Vamoose County Hospital. Please verify the days during the week that Arthella was scheduled to visit Nettie Jarvis. Also, check the name of the doctor who signed both of those duplicated birth certificates. I need to cover a lot of territory ASAP."

"Anything else, Hazard?" Rich asked.

"Yes, plug the names Melvin Rumley, Odell Jarvis, and Mickey Poag into your fancy-shmancy intelligence-network computer and see what you come up with," Amanda requested. "I don't want to leave any stones un-turned. I have to hurry this investigation along."

"I'll put our agency's computer wizard on it tonight," Rich promised.

"Thanks, Rich."

"No problem. Take care of my baby brother for me, Hazard."

"Consider it done."

Amanda hung up the phone and set aside the journal. She had deciphered Nettie's scrawled handwriting until her vision blurred. Groaning wearily, she shut off the lights and crawled into bed beside Thorn. She promised herself that when she found Nettie's murderer she would wallop him/her upside the head for leaving poor, dear Thorn to suffer—not to mention the deserved retribution for the dastardly crime committed against Nettie Jarvis!

Sluggish and tired though Amanda was the next morning, she rolled from bed, showered, and dressed. She checked on Thorn half a dozen times, but he roused for only a minute at a time before drifting back to sleep. Amanda skipped breakfast, knowing she was going to sample every dessert and coffee cake that could be created with pumpkins when she arrived at the bazaar.

When the doorbell clanged, Amanda waddled over to see Sam Harjo, dressed in Western wear and boots, standing on the porch.

"How's the Lone Ranger doing this morning?" Harjo asked as he stepped inside.

"Go see for yourself while I grab my purse," Amanda offered.

Harjo moseyed toward the master bedroom to check on Thorn, then returned two minutes later, grinning.

Amanda raised her brow. "You find his befuddled condition amusing?"

Harjo shook his head. "Nope, not one bit. However, I do find it amusing that Thorn managed to rouse himself long enough to spout commands at me before he drifted off again."

"Commands?" Amanda prompted.

Harjo held up his forefinger. " 'Number one, make sure you keep constant watch on Hazard,' " he quoted Thorn. " 'Number two, don't let her consume too many calories of fat at the bazaar and see that she has the recommended daily dose of protein for lunch. Number three, remember that she is still my wife.' "

Amanda smiled fondly. "That is Thorn through and through. Addle-witted though he is, because of his concussion, his one-track mind is still capable of functioning."

"I wonder if he will ever get over the fact that I chased after you during that on-again-off-again engagement of yours," Harjo said.

"Eventually," Amanda replied. "If he didn't like and respect you so darn much it would be easier for him, you know. He could deal with that much better if you were a card-carrying jerk."

"Yeah, well, I have the same problem with him," Harjo admitted as he escorted Amanda out the door. "But I'm learning to settle for having you and the Lone Ranger as my best friends.''

''Oh, Harjo, you are such a swell guy.''

When Amanda sniffed and dabbed at her eyes with her sleeve, Harjo patted her shoulder. ''Don't start with the tears, Hazard. I don't handle them any better than Thorn does. So . . . what d'ya say we go eat our way through the pumpkin bazaar.''

Amanda nodded, blotted her weepy eyes, and pasted on a smile. She walked away, cursing these annoying mood swings that could take her from temper to tears in the length of time it took to sneeze.

Nick propped himself upright in bed when the doorbell chimed incessantly. It had been two hours since Hazard had spoon-fed him breakfast, helped him to and from the bathroom, then assisted him into a pair of nylon running shorts so he wouldn't be staggering around in his briefs, in case he felt good enough to sit up in the living room recliners.

The doorbell clanged again.

''Okay! I'm coming!'' Nick yelled, then clutched his head when the sound ricocheted off his skull.

Despite his Godzilla-size headache, Nick scooted onto the edge of the bed, braced his hand on the wall, and wobbled from the room. On his way through the living room he held on to various pieces of furniture to make it to the door without falling flat on his face.

An unidentified female, who looked to be about fifty, dressed in green scrubs, wearing a stethoscope around her neck, stood on the porch.

''Nick Thorn, I presume,'' the woman said.

''Yeah?''

''My name is Eileen Franklin. Dr. Simms sent me over to check on you this morning. I'm a nurse from the home-health care unit.''

"Franklin?" Nick frowned pensively. "Aren't you the one who took care of Nettie?"

The nurse stepped inside and motioned Nick to the nearest chair. "Yes, I provided care for Nettie. I was especially fond of her, and I was sorry to hear she succumbed to a severe asthmatic attack. She has battled health problems for years, but she always kept her spirits up."

Efficiently, she laid the stethoscope to Nick's bare chest, then to his back. "Still suffering from nausea?" she asked.

"A little."

"Headache?"

"Hellish," he admitted.

She gently tipped back his head to check the dilation of his pupils. "Dr. Simms will be relieved to know your condition has improved. You should be fine in a few days. Now then, let me change the dressing on your head."

The nurse unwrapped the gauze and studied the wound. "It seems to be healing normally. We can dispense with the bandage and let the fresh air at it."

Nick hoisted himself to his feet when she took his arm. The room swam, but then settled back into place as the nurse shepherded him down the hall.

"I'm sorry I had to make you get out of bed. I thought your wife would be here to care for you."

"She has a heavy schedule today," he mumbled as the nurse ushered him into the bedroom.

"Do you have something here to eat for lunch?"

"Yeah, a friend dropped off a casserole this morning," Nick replied as he wobbled on jellied knees.

Thank goodness Jenny Long-Zinkerman had taken pity on him and detoured on her way to the pumpkin bazaar to drop off one of her mouthwatering casseroles.

"That's good," the nurse said. "I won't have to wonder if you will be receiving proper nourishment." She lowered Nick to the bed, then covered him with the quilt. "I'm going to take your blood pressure, then give you medication to ease your headache, just as Dr. Simms prescribed.''

Nick was definitely ready to say yes to drugs. Those fiendish little carpenters who were using miniature jackhammers on his skull hadn't let up since he had roused to consciousness last night.

The nurse pulled a hypodermic needle from her leather bag, swabbed his arm with antiseptic, then poked him a good one. Nick told himself the sharp pain from the injection was nowhere near as bad as his headache, but the shot still hurt like hell.

''Now just settle back and rest, Nick. Hopefully, your headache will ease up by the time you wake to have lunch. Can I get you a glass of water before I leave?''

''Yeah, that would be nice,'' he mumbled.

The medication worked immediately, Nick noted. He felt relaxed, felt as if he were sinking into the mattress. He murmured drowsily when the nurse patted him on the arm. Through a hazy blur he saw her exit the room to fetch a glass of water, but he wasn't awake when the nurse returned. The sedative put him out like a light.

Nick didn't hear the phone ring or the answering machine take a message an hour later. He was drifting in never-never land, oblivious to his horrendous headache and queasy stomach.

FOURTEEN

Amanda gazed at the colorful tents that formed a square on the city fairgrounds. The smell of pumpkin pastries wafted on the autumn breeze. Amanda took a deep whiff of the aromatic air and smiled in anticipation. She was going to gorge herself on pumpkin bread, pumpkin cake, pumpkin pie, and pumpkin delight.

"This is exactly what heaven should smell like," Amanda said as she and Harjo ambled toward the bazaar.

"Your olfactory senses must be in full-scale riot," Harjo said, and chuckled. "My idea of the scent of heaven is charcoal-broiled steaks."

"You and Thorn," Amanda said, and snorted. "You steak-and-potato men are missing the finer delicacies in the world. Desserts should be a major food group, far as I'm concerned."

"Yoo-hoo!"

Amanda glanced up to see Velma Hertzog scurrying toward her.

"Is Nicky going to be all right?"

Amanda kept walking toward the pumpkin-pie booth.

Velma fell into step beside her. Harjo brought up the rear. "Thorn is as white as the sheet he is sleeping under," Amanda reported. "But you know how tough he is. He will have this concussion licked in no time."

"Well"—*chomp, crack*—"I'd like to get my hands on the juvenile delinquent who clobbered Nicky. There he was, volunteering his time at the haunted house to raise money for the fire department, and wham! Some whippersnapper wallops him. Ungrateful brat!"

Amanda refused to confide her suspicions to Velma, who had the fastest mouth in town. Amanda didn't want to cause a panic by making her speculations about Nettie's death public knowledge.

"Have you seen Odell and Faye this morning?" Amanda asked.

"Let me see." *Crackle, crunch.* "I think I saw Faye and her brother at the pumpkin-pastry booth a few minutes ago."

"Faye's husband isn't with them?" Amanda questioned.

"No, Willis is helping set up the stage and speakers for tonight's band. Why?"

Amanda shrugged nonchalantly. "No particular reason. I guess Odell and Faye are spending time consoling each other after Nettie's accident." She turned to Harjo. "Maybe you should help set up the stage, since Thorn isn't here to do it."

Harjo raised a thick brow. "Are you trying to get rid of me, Haz?"

Yes, she was. She wanted to confront Odell and Faye with her newfound knowledge. "Of course not. But you really don't have to follow me around."

"Thorn said I did. He made me promise," Harjo informed her.

"Well, Thorn has a concussion. He doesn't know what he's saying," Amanda insisted. "That was just his misguided protective instincts making a reflexive knee-jerk reaction. I doubt he'll even remember telling you that.''

Harjo studied her for a long, pensive moment. "Well, if you're sure you'll be okay, I'll go lend a helping hand.''

"I'll be fine." Amanda smiled confidently. "What could possibly go wrong? I'll be in the middle of a crowd of friends and neighbors." She shooed the commish on his way. "I'll meet you back here in an hour.''

When Harjo strode away, Amanda waddled toward the pastry booth to see Odell and Faye chowing down on goodies while speaking privately to one another.

"Good morning," Amanda said cheerily. "Enjoying the treats?''

Odell and Faye crawdadded backward as Amanda approached.

Amanda drew them out of earshot from the crowd, then cut to the chase. "I know Odell is Sis's father and that you two owed Nettie several thousand dollars." She stared Faye down. "And you are guilty of extortion for siphoning the money Nettie gave you to provide for Sis and using it to spoil your boy Roy.''

When Faye wobbled and her eyes rolled back in her head, Amanda grabbed her arm and gave her a jarring shake. "Don't pull that crap again today, Faye. I'll still be right here, in your face, when you come to. Now why did the two of you decide to bump off your own sister? So you wouldn't have to pay those IOUs?''

"We did no such thing," Odell spit at her, his face the color of toothpaste.

"Spare me the theatrical denials, Odell. I read the journal. I know what an irresponsible jerk you are and what a weasel your little sister is. Nettie possessed all the kindness and decency in the Jarvis family. She saved your bacon numerous times, all in the name of family loyalty and reputation. Neither of you was worth her efforts. You just kept using her, didn't you?''

"We are not having this conversation," Faye snapped, her pointed chin thrusting upward.

"Sure we are. As executor of Nettie's estate I want those IOUs paid immediately."

The Jarvis siblings gaped at her.

Odell was the first one to find his tongue. "We don't have that kind of money lying around."

"Well, tough. Start selling off your cars and pickup trucks, whatever it takes to pay the long-overdue debt to your sister. The money is going to be divided according to Nettie's last wishes. If you don't have the debt paid by the end of next week I will see you in court, along with Poag and Rumley. Am I clear?"

Outgunned, Odell and Faye shut their mouths and nodded mutely.

"Good. Now y'all have a nice day," Amanda said before she lurched around and tramped off.

When Amanda spotted Melvin Rumley moseying toward the pumpkin-bread booth, she made a beeline toward him. "You owe Nettie's estate five grand," she said without preamble. "It is payable in my office within one week. If you do not comply I will not hesitate to take legal action."

"You found her journal?" Melvin tweeted, his face turning a fascinating shade of purple. "Oh, God."

"Darn right I found it. Beat you to it, didn't I, Mel?"

The grocery store owner squirmed beneath Amanda's intense scrutiny.

"You might as well tell me what your IOU was for and save me the time of reading it in her journal. I only hit the high spots last night, but I plan to be more thorough this evening."

When Melvin stood there, his thin face frozen in fear—at least that was what it looked like to Amanda—she verbally prodded him. "Well? Why did Nettie lend you money?"

Melvin swallowed and his Adam's apple bobbed repeatedly. "For inventory. When we first opened the store, we couldn't pay both the rent and inventory invoices. I asked Nettie if she would foot the bill so we could make a go of the store. We barely had a penny to our name at the time, and our kids were youngsters. We just sort of put off paying Nettie back, until she demanded the cash for her down payment at the retirement village."

"Well, it is not going to go on any longer," Amanda assured him tartly. "You spent years without paying interest on that goodwill loan. The very least you can do is pay Nettie's estate. If not, I will file a lawsuit against you. When word gets out that you took advantage of a generous old woman, your business will go right down the toilet."

"You really shouldn't have read that journal," Melvin said grimly. "I promise it will come back to haunt you. It has already." He stared at her meaningfully. "I think you know what I mean, after what happened to the chief last night."

So Melvin assumed, as she did, that the killer had made a show of force in an attempt to prevent Melvin from telling what he knew. No doubt Amanda had stepped on some very dangerous toes. The killer had retaliated, and now Amanda was pretty sure that the killer was *not* Melvin Rumley. He seemed too much of a wimp to commit the vile act. No, she thought, Melvin had simply ended up at the wrong place at a bad time. He had been threatened and he was terrified of the consequences.

"Let me tell you something, Melvin," Amanda said, staring him squarely in the eye. "If we all quivered beneath threats of evil forces at work, the good ol' U. S. of A. would crumble apart on its foundation. You are withholding information because you are afraid Ginger will come to harm. Isn't that right?"

He did not confirm or deny it, but Amanda could tell by the way his cavernous eyes widened that she had hit an exposed nerve. Melvin Rumley was running scared, no question about it.

"You are being intimidated and threatened, but the time will come when Nettie's killer will decide he can't risk letting you live, because you know too much. I have the feeling that you know who killed Nettie, but you are mistaken if you think your silence will protect Ginger. And furthermore, you won't do Ginger any good if you wind up in the same condition as Nettie. All you will be doing is taking the secret to *your* grave, Melvin. Believe me, you and Ginger will both suffer if you don't confide what you know. Like it or not, I am your only hope."

Melvin glanced every which way, as if he sensed he was being shadowed. "I can't talk about this now," he said shakily. "I have to think this through."

"You'd better think fast, Mel. This case needs to be resolved quickly or someone else might get hurt. That someone will be you," she didn't fail to point out to him.

After a moment he seemed to have come to a decision. "Okay," he said quietly. "I'll meet you tonight at the costume street dance. I'll be behind the stage during the band's performance. I'll tell you what you want to know. And don't you dare breathe a word of this to anyone, not even Thorn. Do you promise?"

"Promise," Amanda said without hesitation. "What time?"

"Seven o'clock."

"What costume will you be wearing?" Amanda wanted to know.

"Ginger made a devil's costume for me. Bright red, with horns and a tail. I won't be hard to spot."

Amanda favored him with her most intimidating stare. "Be there."

Melvin spun around and scurried off, still glancing right and left as he went. The man was so twitchy that he was flinching at his own shadow.

Well, thought Amanda as she reached for a sample of

pumpkin bread. She was finally making some headway in this case. To celebrate, she grabbed two more samples of pumpkin bread. Her taste buds stood up and applauded.

When Amanda spotted Mickey Poag hovering around the pumpkin-pie booth she toddled toward him. He was standing with a cluster of men, but that didn't stop Amanda from locking on to her target.

"Hey, Amanda," Abe Hendershot greeted her. "How are you feeling?"

Amanda smiled brightly. "Good." Her back ached something fierce, her feet were swollen, and the dull pressure deep in her tummy was uncomfortable. But, hey, she was nine months pregnant. This was as good as it got.

"Is the chief feeling better?" Abe asked in concern. "He sure had a rough night, didn't he?"

Amanda bobbed her orange-tinted head and stared directly at Mickey Poag, who was making a spectacular attempt to ignore her. "He's had better days," she reported. "Hopefully he will be up and around in a few days."

"We certainly hope so," the gray-haired man standing beside Mickey put in. "Thorn is one whale of a police chief." The man extended his hand. "I don't believe we have been introduced. My name is Claude Padden."

Padden? *Padden!* As in Nettie's Pad? The mysterious lover?

Amanda discreetly surveyed the older man who was dressed in neatly pressed slacks and a shirt. His thinning gray hair and brows gave him a distinguished look. He appeared harmless, but Amanda quickly reminded herself that looks could be extremely deceiving.

"I'm running for mayor of Vamoose," Claude informed her. "I hope you will encourage our city council to give me their stamp of approval." He flashed her another crowd-pleasing smile.

"Hey, Claude, quit politicking."

Amanda glanced sideways to see another senior citizen smiling charmingly at her. She didn't recognize this man, either.

The senior citizen, sporting a colorful Western shirt, Justin Roper boots, and starched blue jeans, offered Amanda his hand. He had a strong grip, Amanda noted.

"I am also running for mayor," he informed her. "Don't endorse Claude. Endorse me. I'm Phil Darnell, and it's a pleasure to meet you."

"I will want to hear your qualifications and platforms regarding improving the conditions in Vamoose, before I make my decision," Amanda told the mayoral candidates.

"An intelligent woman," Claude complimented. "Of course, who in Vamoose isn't aware of that? After all, you have solved six cleverly arranged murders—"

"Seven," Amanda corrected.

"Even more impressive," Phil put in. "Maybe *you* should run for mayor."

"I don't think so." Amanda turned her attention to the noticeably quiet Mickey Poag. "My accounting business is very taxing."

"Taxing?" Claude laughed heartily. "Clever pun, Amanda."

"Thank you." She smiled graciously. "If you will excuse me, I need to speak with one of my clients for a moment. I hate to mix business with pleasure, but I am working on a short clock these days." She patted her tummy and tossed out another smile. "I expect to be extremely busy very soon."

Mickey Poag had no choice but to follow Amanda to one of the vacated folding tables that had been set up in the improvised "plaza" that was surrounded with canvas food booths.

"Now what?" Mickey muttered as he plunked down in a chair.

Amanda took a load off her feet and did not mince words with the stocky, dour-looking rancher. "You owe Nettie's estate three grand in back rent."

His eyes popped. His jaw swung on its hinges. He couldn't find his tongue.

"You have one week to deliver a cashier's check to my office. If you thought bumping off Nettie would clear your debt, then think again, Poag. I'm handling the estate, and no one is going to welsh on his debts."

"How'd you—?"

"Doesn't matter how," she interrupted, then glanced at her watch. Amanda needed to return home to check on Thorn and feed him the casserole that her secretary had whipped up. "You might as well know, here and now, that strong-arm tactics won't work with me. Matters will be less complicated if you simply admit what you've done."

Mickey's eyes narrowed menacingly. "You don't have any evidence, if you are implying what I think you are implying, Hazard."

"Don't I?" she challenged. "We'll see about that. In the meantime I suggest you sell some cattle and write me a check. Otherwise you and I are destined to meet in court. And don't kid yourself into thinking you'll win, Mickey. I've got the goods on you."

He glowered meat cleavers at her. "You should have kept your nose out of this, Hazard. If you weren't a woman, and pregnant to boot, I'd like to kick your ass. Damn, but you are really asking for trouble."

"So are you, Poag," she countered. "You mess with Thorn and me and you will lose, because you are guilty of wrongdoing and we both know it. Pay up, Poag, or you will be served Christmas dinner in the slammer."

Amanda surged to her feet, glanced at her watch, then turned her back on Poag. She saw Harjo's gaze sweeping the crowd in search of her. "Over here!" she shouted, then flapped her arms to gain his attention.

"Ready to go, Hazard?" Harjo asked.

"You bet."

While Harjo walked beside her, he glanced back at the man who was still staring murderously at Amanda. "Did you say something to upset Mickey Poag? He looks as if he is about to explode."

"Does he?" she asked in feigned innocence. "Maybe he is simply suffering the gastrointestinal effects of sampling too many pumpkin pies."

Harjo stared down at her. "Uh-huh, sure he is. Just admit it, Hazard. You pushed his buttons to see if you could get a rise out of one of your suspects."

"Fine, I admit it," Amanda said as she tramped away.

"Have any luck with him?"

"Enough," Amanda hedged.

Amanda lumbered into the house, then stopped in her tracks. There was an unfamiliar scent in the air.

"Something wrong, Hazard?" the commish asked.

"Yes, and I'm not sure what," she said, sniffing the air.

"Are your feminine instincts pelting you again?"

"Maybe it's just my overactive imagination," she replied. "Why don't you check on Thorn while I put Jenny's casserole in the microwave. We'll have lunch in a jiffy."

When Harjo strode down the hall Amanda noticed that the answering machine was winking at her. She punched play on her way to retrieve the casserole from the fridge.

"Nick? Amanda? Are you there? It's Rich. Pick up. . . . Well, hell. I'll call you back later."

Beep.

"Hi, doll. It's Mother. Where are you? Did you have

the baby yet? If you did and that husband of yours didn't call to let me know I'm going to bean him on the head!''

Beep.

Amanda was certain Mother would be pleased to hear that someone had already beaned Thorn's head.

''Hey, half-pint.''

Amanda smiled at the sound of her paternal grandfather's voice. Pops, as she affectionately called him, had a knack for cheering her up.

''Have you had that little squirt yet? Can't wait to see the tyke. Just hope it doesn't turn out to look like your mother. Poor kid.''

Beep.

Amanda smiled again. Pops and Mother got along like two bulls in a pasture full of heifers. Battles were always breaking out.

''Nick? Amanda? Where the hell are you?''

It was Rich's voice again. Amanda stuffed the chicken casserole in the microwave.

''Okay, I don't like to leave the kind of info I have for you on an answering machine. Call my cell phone number the second you get this message.''

Beep.

An uneasy sensation skittered down Amanda's backbone. She snatched up the phone and dialed the number, but an urgent voice echoed down the hall.

''Hazard! Get in here quick!'' Harjo shouted.

Amanda dropped the phone and plowed down the hall. *Oh, my God! What had happened to Thorn? He wasn't—?*

Don't panic, Haz. Stay calm. You might induce labor if you don't keep yourself under control. The longer you can hold out, the better; that's what Doc Simms says.

Amanda skidded clumsily to a halt at the bedroom door. She gasped in dismay when she saw Thorn's rubbery neck lolling up and down on Harjo's arm, while the commish tried to sit him upright.

''I can't get him to wake up,'' Harjo said, looking

alarmed. "Geez, he's really out of it, Haz. I can't even prop him up on the pillows without him slumping sideways."

The unfamiliar scent in the air! Warning bells clanged in Amanda's brain. Someone had entered the house. A female, judging by the lingering scent of perfume. It wasn't Jenny's, her secretary. Amanda was familiar with the fragrance Jenny wore. Good Lord, who had entered the house, and what the blazes had happened to Thorn?

FIFTEEN

"Can you get Thorn in the shower?" Amanda asked as she toddled forward. "Maybe we can rouse him with cold water."

"I'll have to drag him. He's too damn big to carry."

Harjo grabbed the sheet beneath Thorn's limp body and gave a mighty tug. Muscles popped out on Harjo's forearms as he pulled Thorn to the floor. Amanda cradled his head and cushioned the anticipated blow. The poor, dear man didn't need his melon cracked again this soon, Amanda reminded herself.

Slowly but surely Harjo pulled Thorn across the carpet to the private bath, then stepped into the shower and tugged again. Once he had Thorn sprawled on the tile floor, Harjo turned on the faucets full blast.

Amanda felt her stomach drop to her ankles when she noticed the red spot on Thorn's arm. Injection! Yikes, who had shot Thorn with a hypodermic?

"Take care of Thorn. I'll call his brother," Amanda said before she hurried over to grab the phone beside the bed.

Her hand shook as she dialed. She told herself not to get hysterical. This wasn't the time to crack up.

"Hello?"

"Rich? It's Amanda. Give me that info and make it snappy. I have a situation here and I don't have much time." Amanda cast a worried glance toward the bathroom.

"What's wrong, Hazard?"

"I think somebody came in here while I was gone and gave Thorn a shot with a hypodermic syringe. He might have had an adverse reaction."

"What!" Rich yowled.

"Harjo and I are trying to bring him around. What did you find out?"

"Candice Randolph dropped out of sight twenty-five years ago," Rich reported. "She hasn't turned up since and is presumed dead."

"How is that possible?" Amanda darted another glance toward the bathroom and crossed her fingers, hoping Thorn would come to. "Is Candice in the Witness Protection Program or something?"

"No, she simply stopped renewing her driver's license, and her social security number hasn't shown up on any documents in twenty-five years. And get this, Hazard— that Carson woman you asked me to check on has been dead for thirty years. Died in an auto accident. Buried in Pronto cemetery."

"That can't be right."

"That's what I figured, so I dug a little deeper. I found out that someone posing as Arthella Carson wrote to the Bureau of Vital Statistics to request a duplicate of her *supposedly* missing birth certificate. Then three months later, a member of the Carson family . . . Hold on a sec. Let me check this out to make sure I have it right."

Amanda tapped her foot impatiently while Rich did whatever OSBI agents did when they booted up detailed information from their sophisticated computer system.

"Okay, here it is. A woman named *Jane* Carson wrote to request a copy of her sister's death certificate. Then later, *Arthella* wrote to the social security office to request a duplicate of her *supposedly* missing card."

"Holy cow! Are you thinking what I'm thinking, Rich?" Amanda wheezed.

"Probably. We have seen this kind of scam a few times recently, but this one evidently took place twenty-five years ago. A person drops out of sight and is presumed dead after seven years. Suddenly a dead person comes back to life with all the vital and necessary credentials, but he turns up at a distant locale where no one is familiar with the name."

Amanda's mind reeled with possibilities that could apply to this case.

"I cross-checked both Arthella Carson's and Candice Randolph's birth certificates. And guess what?" Rich said.

Amanda was in no mood for guessing games. "I give up. What?"

"Candice Randolph is the same age—give or take a few months—as Arthella Carson. I suspect this Candice character wandered through the cemetery to find someone near her age, then sent off for the necessary documents so she could change identities."

"And this kind of thing happened because the intelligence agency didn't have sophisticated computer technology to cross-check such oddities twenty-five years ago?" she presumed.

"Exactly. The various bureaus previously had difficulty cross-checking each other on cases like this. Even today the scam can slip past us unless somebody calls in and brings it to our attention. I swear, Hazard, there are some real weirdos out there who take that cliché about 'getting a life' real seriously. I'm beginning to wonder if Arthella Carson is actually Candice Randolph."

"Oh, shit!" Amanda gasped. "There is another nurse

you'd better check out, too. Find out if Eileen Franklin is really who she says she is. She might turn out to be the real Candice Randolph. Rich, call Vamoose County Hospital and tell them we're bringing Thorn to the emergency door immediately.''

''What!'' he bellowed. ''Is he taking a turn for the worse? What the hell is going on there?''

''As I said, when I got home a few minutes ago, Thorn was out cold. There was a strange scent in the house. After what you just told me I doubt that he is suffering an unexpected reaction to the medication he was given.'' Amanda gulped hard. ''I think that maniac woman, Randolph, Carson, or Franklin—whoever she really is—purposely shot something into Thorn's veins to keep him knocked out.''

''Oh, my God,'' Rich chirped.

''And don't you dare tell your mom that I wasn't here when it happened,'' Amanda added hastily. ''Your mom doesn't like me much anyway. I don't want to give her more weapons and ammunition to blast away at me.''

''Got it, Hazard. Do you want me to call an ambulance?''

''No, Harjo is here. He's got Thorn in the shower, trying to rouse him. We'll load him in the truck and haul him to the hospital. It will save us valuable time.''

''I hope you solve this case, pronto,'' Rich muttered. ''My baby brother can't take much more abuse without a breather. I'll be there as soon as I can to stand guard over Nick. I'll be packing hardware!''

Amanda clicked off the handheld phone, tossed it on the bed, and rushed to the bathroom. To her relief Thorn had gained a small degree of coordination, but he was still oblivious to what was going on around him.

''We're taking him to the hospital,'' Amanda announced as she grabbed a towel.

''Okay, consider it done, doll face, but do not go into

labor on me," Harjo ordered sternly. "One crisis at a time, agreed?"

Amanda breathed in several quarts of air and ordered her heart rate and blood pressure to settle down.

Calm. Stay calm. Relax. Thorn is going to be fine when he's under Doc Simms's excellent care. Just get Thorn to the hospital and everything will be okay.

Amanda repeated the consoling spiel while Harjo dragged Thorn onto the front porch, then raced toward Amanda's truck.

Harjo drove the fire-engine-red pickup across the lawn and stopped beside the porch. "We'll have to put the Lone Ranger in the pickup bed," Harjo said as he unhooked the tailgate. "I'll sit in the back with him while you drive. You can do this, can't you, Hazard? You aren't going to fall apart on me?"

"I can do this," she said.

With great effort, Harjo jockeyed Thorn's limp body into the pickup bed, then hopped up to cover him with blankets. "We're ready to roll," he said, panting. "Don't kick up dust if you can help it. You can speed up when we reach the paved highway."

Amanda struggled to climb beneath the steering wheel, then flicked on the emergency lights. All the while that she drove to the county hospital, located an equal distance between Vamoose, Pronto, and Adios, she silently vowed to locate the treacherous Candice Randolph, alias Arthella Carson or Eileen Franklin. The woman had somehow managed to change her appearance to such extremes that the Jarvis siblings hadn't recognized her.

Of course, they probably hadn't seen the woman since Sis was born. But Candice had obviously kept track of the Jarvis family and had taken up a profession that allowed her to get close to Nettie this past year.

Why? Amanda asked herself. Nettie had paid for Candice's hospital bills and loaned her money. What was Candice after? Why had she turned her vengeance on

Thorn? Was Candice, alias Arthella or Eileen, the person who had launched the brick at Thorn's head last night? Was Amanda dealing with two separate wackos or just one?

Amanda didn't have a clue what was going on, but she knew Thorn had become the target of retaliation against her. She was being sent another warning. If she didn't back away from this investigation, Thorn was going to get hurt—just as Melvin Rumley feared his wife Ginger would suffer consequences.

She zoomed toward the hospital, wondering if Thorn's condition was also meant as a distraction to keep Amanda from concentrating on solving this case. No wonder Melvin Rumley was quaking in his boots, leaping at the sight of his own shadow. That fruit cake of a woman could walk up and stab Ginger with a hypo before she knew what hit her. Candice/Arthella/Eileen had the ways, means, and knowledge to induce a coma or death. . . .

"Don't go there, Hazard," she told herself. "Don't think the worst."

Praying nonstop, Amanda veered into the hospital parking lot to see Doc Simms waiting with a gurney. The medical assistants had Thorn loaded up and wheeled away before Amanda could crawl from the pickup.

When Amanda toddled into the hospital Doc Simms fired questions that she couldn't answer. She didn't have a clue what had been shot into Thorn's veins, didn't know what time Thorn had received the injection.

To her frustration, Doc Simms booked Amanda into a room and ordered her to lie down and relax while he tended Thorn. For what seemed like hours Amanda stared at the ceiling, trying to figure out what demented scheme might occupy Arthella/Candice/Eileen's twisted mind. What did the woman hope to gain, other than a distraction and a vivid warning to back off? What was in Nettie's journal that the lunatic didn't want known? It must be something crucial, Amanda decided, because that maniac female had gone to extremes to protect her secrets.

Could it have been Arthella/Candice/Eileen who launched the brick at Thorn's head, then stabbed him with a hypo? Was there a conspiracy going on here? Or was Amanda trying to tie two separate incidents together when they were not truly related? She had to think this through, she told herself. This was no time to leap to ill-founded conclusions, not when Thorn had become the target of two attacks.

A deep twinge grabbed Amanda's attention and made her break out in a cold sweat. "Not now, not yet," she grumbled. "Revive Thorn, solve the case, *then* have the baby."

Amanda repeated the preferred order of events to herself when another uncomfortable pain stabbed her lower back. Geez, what else could possibly go wrong?

She decided she'd better get her act together and figure that out before disaster struck again.

Nick roused to consciousness to hear the buzz of fluorescent lights. Familiar faces hovered above him in an unfamiliar room. "Where the hell am I?" he wheezed. God, his throat felt like sandpaper!

"In the hospital." Doc Simms patted his arm. "You've had a rough morning, Chief."

"Where's Hazard? Is she all right?" Nick tried to bolt upright, but several arms shot out to anchor him to the bed. He experienced a feeling of déjà vu when he was forcefully held down.

"Calm down, kemosabe," Harjo ordered. "Hazard is here."

"Yeah? Well, I don't see her fuzzy face and orange-tinted hair in my range of vision. Where the hell are you, Hazard?"

Feet shuffled; then Hazard's blurred image appeared

beside the physician. "Oh, Thorn! I'm so sorry I did this to you!" she wailed loudly enough to blast his eardrums. Apparently he wasn't the only one who got his ears cracked, because several people groaned in discomfort.

"What did you do to me?" he asked, befuddled.

When Hazard burst into tears, Doc Simms escorted her into the hall.

"What the hell is going on?" Nick demanded, then frowned when he recognized his brother's hazy image. "Rich? Is that you? What are you doing here?"

Rich sank down in the chair beside the bed and stared grimly at his waxen-faced brother. "I came to see if you are okay. Do you feel up to telling us what happened?"

Nick gathered his thoughts, then presented the report of Eileen Franklin's visit, at Doc Simms's request, to check on his condition. Then he reported that Eileen had given him something to help him rest comfortably. "I don't remember anything after that. I got so sleepy I couldn't keep my eyes open."

"Are you certain it was Eileen Franklin who came to see you?" Rich questioned.

"That's who she said she was," Nick replied. "But then, I didn't know her from Adam. Why do you ask?"

Rich pivoted toward Harjo. "Ask Dr. Simms to come back in here, will you? We need to verify who gave Nick that shot."

Harjo strode off, then returned a few moments later with the physician.

"Nick, describe the nurse who paid you a house call," Rich requested.

"Mid-fifties," Nick said. "Wearing green scrubs. She had short red hair and blue eyes."

Dr. Simms frowned. "We only have one redhead on our staff, and she is in her thirties. That doesn't sound like Eileen Franklin or Arthella Carson."

"Could you get them to come in here for an ID?" Rich asked.

"Sorry," Dr. Simms said. "They are off duty right now. It may take a while to get in touch with them, but I will certainly try."

When the physician wheeled around and scurried off to the nurses' station, Rich stared at Nick for a long, ponderous moment.

"What the hell is going on?" Nick demanded.

"That is what we are trying to find out," Rich grumbled. "Until we get a positive ID on your supposed nurse, we aren't sure what went down. But something weird is going on in Vamoose. For starters, the nurse known as Arthella Carson does not exist. She died twenty-five years ago. As for Eileen Franklin, the OSBI computer guru is checking her out as we speak."

Nick stared owlishly at his brother. "Are you telling me that Franklin and Carson might be in cahoots? You think one or both of them tried to dispose of me?"

"I'm not sure what to make of this yet. All we know is that someone, unauthorized by Dr. Simms, showed up at your house to stab you with her hypo. The doctor doesn't know exactly what she gave you, so he had to pump your stomach and give you an intravenous universal antidote to clean out your system. If you feel as if you've had a visit from Dracula it's no small wonder. They've drawn blood for several tests to figure out what happened. Doc's best guess is that you took a strong dose of morphine or a similar substance that reduced you to a vegetative state."

"Well, hell. What'd she do that for?" Nick asked. "Did I put the woman in jail for a crime she committed years ago and she decided to come back to retaliate?"

"No," Harjo interjected. "We think this might have been a retaliation against *you*, in an effort to distract and threaten Hazard." His arm shot out to restrain Nick when he tried to lever onto his elbows. "No, don't even think about getting up. Hazard and I saved your life by getting you to the hospital in time, and she is okay. Well, as okay as she can be in this phase of drastic mood swings and gushing tears,'' he amended.

That was an understatement, Nick mused. These days Hazard could go off like a launched rocket with very little provocation.

"Hazard called me last night," Rich reported. "She told me that you caught a brick in the head; then she asked me to check out some of her suspects in this case. One of them was Candice Randolph. Another was Arthella Carson. We are wondering if they are one and the same. The verdict is still out on Eileen Franklin and her involvement in this case."

Nick's dulled mind reeled. Rich was talking faster than Nick could assimilate information. "I don't get it."

Rich went into a lengthy spiel about what his computer search had turned up. "And so Hazard believes Candice, alias Arthella or Eileen, is somehow connected to Nettie's death, but she hasn't figured out how or why. Hazard is puzzled about Eileen's involvement, and she also mentioned something about a man named Pad. She isn't certain how he fits into this, either. He may be mixed up with Candice.

"My educated guess is that Candice Randolph— whichever name she is using as an alias now—will follow the same MO and disappear the same way she did twenty-five years ago. Then she will probably turn up somewhere else with a new identity. I'm hoping to track her down with the APB I sent out. This time around we will be checking for discrepancies with the various federal bureaus. I plan to throw the book at her for knocking you out with her hypo."

"As for you, Lone Ranger," Harjo said as he levered down to rest a hip on the opposite side of the bed, "you are restricted to absolute bed rest for the day, maybe longer. So don't kick up a fuss or Doc Simms will sedate you to keep you quiet."

"Damn it to hell," Nick muttered sourly. "Now I'm

going to have to ask you for another favor, Harjo. You've got to keep track of Hazard. You know what she's like when she's in her investigative mode. Like a hound on the scent at a dead run.''

''I know, but the Pumpkin Queen, glowing with orange lights while attending the costume street dance to give her speech at the Festival of the Pumpkin ceremony, should be easy to keep up with. I'll never let her out of my sight. You have my word.''

''And I will be on guard duty at the hospital to ensure that no one who isn't fully authorized by Doc Simms gets near you,'' Rich put in.

Nick sighed tiredly. ''I want to talk to Hazard before she heads off to the baby shower.''

Rich and Harjo left the room and Hazard entered. Despite his blurred vision, Nick noted that she was still in a highly emotional state. She was pacing the floor and wringing her hands. Her orange-tinted head tipped up and down, then right and left.

Nick smiled to himself, wondering if Hazard was beginning to understand the hell he went through every time one of her unofficial investigations turned sour and he sweated bullets until he rescued her from impending disaster.

''Thorn?'' She squeezed his hand, then sniffled. ''Are you okay? Really okay? Give it to me straight.''

''I'll be fine,'' he was quick to assure her. ''But I will *not* be fine if I'm worried sick about you.''

She bobbed her frizzy orange-colored head. ''I will be careful, but I gotta tell ya, Thorn, I am going to take apart that ruthless woman—Carson or Franklin, whoever she is pretending to be—with my bare hands for venting her anger for me on you.''

''No,'' he said firmly, ''you are not. The woman is obviously a psycho. It's no wonder the Jarvis family wanted to take Sis away from Candice Randolph and let Faye Mithlo raise her. The woman is dangerous. I do not want you anywhere near her. Harjo agreed to be your bodyguard until I'm back on my feet. I am also going to ask Rich to call our undercover agent friends—''

"The ones you used on the Dead in the Dirt case?"

"Those are the ones," he confirmed. "They will be at the street dance, keeping tabs on you and trying to track down the real Candice Randolph."

He drew Hazard down onto the edge of the bed and forced her to stare him squarely in the eye—though she was more or less a blur to him. "No daring heroics, Haz. Promise me."

"Okay, Thorn."

"You swear on a stack of Bibles?" he persisted.

"Yes, a whole stack of them."

"You swear on the wedding ring I gave you at our ceremony?"

"All right, already, Thorn, don't get carried away," she muttered in annoyance. "I said I would be careful, didn't I?"

"No," he corrected. "You promised no daring heroics. There is a difference. I do not want you to place yourself in any situation that endangers you. I do not want you tearing off on an avenging crusade in my honor and putting yourself and our baby in harm's way. If you get hurt in the pursuit of truth, justice, and the good ol' American way, I may as well put a gun to my head and end it all. Life without you would be no life at all."

"Oh, Thorn," she whimpered, then blubbered in tears.

"Now promise me," he insisted.

"Fine, but I still want that maniac female shot, stabbed, poisoned, and hung out to dry," she said spitefully.

Nick grinned at her forceful tone. "You're crazy about me, aren't you, Haz?"

"Absolutely nuts," she assured him. "Now then, you have your guard dog watching over you and I have mine, so we are both going to be okey-dokey." She patted his cheek. "I have to freshen up before I attend the baby shower. Considering all the guests Velma and Bev invited, we will be raking in tons of baby gifts. I'll have Harjo help me haul all the loot home.''

"Be careful," he cautioned for the last time.

"Get your rest, Thorn," she said, kissed him squarely on the mouth, then waddled out the door.

Nick settled more comfortably on the bed and closed his eyes. He was going to rest—fast. This was a very bad time for him to be laid up in the hospital, suffering from a concussion and an overdose injection of who knew what! Although Hazard gave her word that she would try to stay out of harm's way, Nick knew she suffered from tunnel vision when she was bearing down on an investigation. Hazard was relentless, unswerving. Her overactive sense of justice never let up.

Sighing, Nick pulled the sheet to his chin and sent a few prayers winging heavenward. Hazard's guardian angel had darn well better be working overtime!

SIXTEEN

Amanda inwardly groaned when she walked into the school cafeteria to see the cake and decorations Velma and Bev had used for the baby shower. The cake Maggie Whittlemeyer baked for the occasion was shaped like a baby sitting upright in its diaper. Diaper pins were pressed into the icing. A pacifier was stuck in the mouth made of pink icing. Yellow icing, resembling curly blond hair, capped the cake-baby's head.

Life-size photos of Thorn and Amanda were stuck to the cinder-block walls. There were at least a dozen goofy pictures of the soon-to-be parents from age one week to three years.

Glossy pink and blue streamers were draped from the ceiling and cascaded down the wall directly behind the refreshment table, which was teeming with pink punch, assorted nut bowls, and the baby cake.

Velma, carrying napkins and plates, lumbered from the kitchen. "Well?" *Chomp, smack.* "What d'ya think, hon?"

"Like, Aunt Velma and I just love this sort of stuff," Bev enthused.

"You've outdone yourselves," Amanda said tactfully.

"How's Nicky feeling this morning?" *Pop, snap.*

Amanda decided not to confide the latest disaster that had befallen Thorn. "He is resting comfortably and he is disappointed that he will be unable to attend this come-and-go shower."

Velma grinned broadly as she glanced through the glass door that granted a view of the parking lot. "Nicky sent Sammy Harjo to take care of you, I see. Can't believe Nicky and Sammy turned out to be such good buddies after they were such fierce rivals before your marriage."

Amanda didn't want to get into the changing dynamics of the triangular relationship between herself, Tom Selleck's look-alike, and the younger version of Clint Eastwood. However, she felt inclined to say, "We're like the Three Musketeers these days. Very best of friends."

"Like, that is so sweet," Bev murmured. "Maybe one of these days Aunt Velma and I can find the perfect match for Sammy. But the woman will have to be somebody extraspecial."

Amanda knew Sam Harjo could get his own dates without the help of these two matchmakers, but she kept the comment to herself.

"Did you invite the Rumleys to the shower?" Amanda asked as she helped Velma arrange the pink and blue napkins.

"Yeah." *Crackle, crunch.* "But I doubt if Melvin will show up. Men don't go in for this sort of thing." Velma frowned pensively. "Don't know what's gotten into Mel this week. He's been as jumpy as a grasshopper. Always glancing around as if a ghost is following him and has him spooked. Trudy, the waitress at the Last Chance Café, said he has been drinking about a gallon of coffee a day. Way too much caffeine." Velma shook her copper-red head in dismay. ''That stuff will give you the shakes if you don't watch out.''

The man was definitely stressing out over what he knew about Nettie's demise, Amanda speculated.

''I met the two mayoral candidates this morning,'' Amanda commented casually. ''I don't know either of them very well. What's the scoop on Claude Padden and Phil Darnell?''

As expected, Velma was willing and eager to impart gossip, and Amanda was eager to figure out if one of the mayoral hopefuls was Nettie's mysterious ''Pad.''

''Well''—*chomp, chomp*—''both men have been in Vamoose forever. Grew up here, raised their families here. They're well-respected pillars of society and all that. One's a retired lawyer and the other a retired doctor who turned his family practice over to Doc Simms a few years back.''

Retired doctor? *Hmmm.* That was interesting. A physician would have come in handy when Odell needed to have his illegitimate daughter's birth certificate altered. Of course, the attorney could have helped out with that little detail, too, Amanda suspected. The doctor, or lawyer, might have been coerced into assisting, *if* he was Nettie's secret lover.

Very interesting indeed, thought Amanda.

''Like, Mama says Claude Padden used to be a real wheeler-dealer attorney in his prime. He liked to take controversial cases that gave him additional publicity.'' Bev scooped up a few assorted nuts, picked out the cashews, and popped them into her mouth.

Amanda cringed when Bev tossed the rejected nuts back into the bowl.

''Is Claude Padden married?'' Amanda inquired.

''Oh, my, yes.'' *Crunch, smack.* Velma stepped back to appraise the refreshment table, like an artist assessing a masterpiece. ''Claude married into one of the top-drawer families from Adios. Inherited hundreds of acres of fertile farmland and gushing royalties from oil production. That's the good news for Claude. The bad news is that his wife is a bona fide bitch.''

Amanda swallowed a smile. "Oh?"

"Yeah, oh." When Velma wrinkled her nose her heavy coat of makeup cracked on her forehead. "Don't know how Claude puts up with the woman. Talk about particular! Hazel Padden has to have the very best of everything. Most expensive house in the county, a flashy car. Best lawn and garden. Most exclusive designer clothes. She wouldn't be caught dead in a T-shirt and jeans, and she doesn't like to rub shoulders with anyone below her lofty station in life. She doesn't think I'm good enough to do her hair. She drives to the city and pays big bucks for some highfalutin stylist.''

"Like, I heard Hazel is attending the costume street dance tonight, dressed as a royal queen." Bev giggled. "Surprise, surprise. Hazel will probably drag out all her diamond and pearl jewelry to flaunt at us peons."

"What about Phil Darnell? Is he married?" Amanda asked.

"He was," Velma replied as she lumbered around the cafeteria, resituating the folding chairs. "Sylvia passed on about a year ago. I swear she and Hazel used to compete for best dressed at every social gathering. Bless Sylvia's heart, she suffered from the prima donna syndrome, same as Hazel.''

Velma fluffed the wrinkled tablecloth, then continued. "In fact, if I have my gossip straight, Claude used to date Sylvia in high school. Don't quote me on that, though. That came down through the long, winding grapevine. That's been years and years ago.''

So Hazel and Sylvia had been competing for Claude Padden's affection. He must have been quite the ladies' man in his heyday.

"How does Phil feel about his wife's old high school

sweetheart?'' Amanda inquired. ''Any hard feelings between them?''

Velma shrugged her shoulders. ''Don't rightly know. Phil doesn't appear to be bothered by it, not that I ever noticed. He came from money and he could have had any woman he wanted. Sylvia inherited her share of money, so it just seemed natural that they get together, I guess.'' *Pop, crunch.* ''The Paddens and Darnells played their own version of keeping up with the Joneses for decades. It doesn't surprise me in the least that Phil and Claude are campaigning for the same political office. They're probably into one-upmanship.''

Given what Velma said, Amanda was pretty sure one of the mayoral hopefuls was Nettie's secret lover. No doubt Pad hadn't wanted to sacrifice his lifestyle, reputation, and prestige to marry Nettie. Pad probably became even more cautious after Odell's affair with Candice Randolph. Watching Odell's marriage dissolve must have made Pad realize that the same thing might happen to him when word got around town.

Amanda was itching to interview the mysterious Pad to see if he could shed some light on this cloudy case. She would also like to get Odell Jarvis alone and see if she could verbally twist his arm and convince him to tell her what he knew about Candice Randolph.

If that wacko nurse, packing a loaded syringe, went on the rampage, Odell might not live long enough to tell everything he knew!

Amanda wasn't allowed to ponder this perplexing case, because a flood of Vamoosians poured through the door, bearing gifts and wearing cheerful smiles. She noted that her appointed bodyguard decided to enter the cafeteria when the crowd thickened considerably.

Harjo explained to the curious crowd that Thorn, overprotective as he was of his wife these days, insisted on having his wife looked after, just in case the baby decided to make an early debut. The throng of women cooed over

Thorn's charming concern and gladly accepted Harjo's male presence. The eligible females in the cafeteria openly flirted with Harjo when they passed through the reception line to offer their gifts to Amanda.

After two hours of smiling, Amanda swore her face would crack. Her back was killing her, her feet swelled up, and twinges nagged at her. Finally the showergoers trailed off and there was nothing left of the cake-baby except crumbs. With Harjo's help, Amanda loaded the gifts in the bed of her pickup truck.

"Man, you and the Lone Ranger really raked in the goods," Harjo commented as he chauffeured Amanda home. "There's enough disposable diapers in the back to keep you stocked for months. And toys? Sheesh! The kid won't be old enough to play with half of that stuff until he's four."

Amanda glanced over her shoulder to survey the heaping loads of baby supplies. It was a good thing Thorn had added the new master bedroom, equipped with walk-in closets and private bath, to their house. Even with the additional room, Amanda wasn't sure there was enough space in the house to stash all this paraphernalia.

"Getting anxious, Hazard?" Harjo asked as he veered onto the gravel road.

"Definitely. I would like to solve this case pronto."

Harjo chuckled. "I was talking about the baby."

"Oh, of course you were. To tell you the truth—and don't breathe a word of this to Thorn or I'll have your head on a silver platter—I don't know what kind of mother I'm going to make."

"The very same kind as the wife, friend, and accountant you are now, I predict," Harjo said. "Highly efficient and probably as overprotective of the baby as Thorn is of you."

Amanda groaned aloud. If she went as far overboard as Thorn probably would, their children would be smothered with too much concern and gasping for independence and freedom. She made a mental note to give her kids a little breathing space and make sure Thorn did the same.

"Hey, don't panic, Haz," Harjo said when he noticed the frown on her face. "You and Thorn will do just fine. Great parents. Model parents. Model kids, the whole nine yards. If you are worrying about that already, then don't."

Amanda took several deep, relaxing breaths, using the trip to Thorn Farm as a rest period. Harjo didn't say a word, just kept his eyes on the road and his hands on the wheel. She appreciated his silence, because she wanted to focus her brain power on the information she had gathered the past week, then sort it all out and track down Candice Randolph, alias Arthella Carson or Eileen Franklin, before the maniac and her hypodermic needle struck again.

Although targeting Thorn was a blatant warning to back off, Amanda simply did not have it in her to do that. Her fierce sense of justice and her crusade for the truth would not allow it. She had to find out why Nettie ended up dead in the pumpkin patch and see that the guilty culprit paid for the crime.

All the while that Harjo and Amanda toted baby gifts into the nursery to stack in empty corners, Amanda kept pondering what she had learned about Odell, Faye, Melvin, Mickey, Pad, and Candice. Was Candice the one who had disposed of Nettie, or had she simply panicked when that tell-all journal turned up missing? Was the woman simply trying to conceal her past and her illegal means of assuming a new identity?

The facts refused to settle neatly into place. Amanda couldn't figure out what was pertinent information and what was confusing clutter. All she knew was that Melvin Rumley seemed genuinely terrified that something might happen to his wife. Amanda couldn't swear Mel would confide in her this evening, despite his promise. She was anxious to find out if Mel had seen Arthella Carson or

Eileen Franklin at the crime scene. Or had someone else gotten the best of poor Nettie?

Well, tonight should be the turning point in this investigation, Amanda told herself. Tonight she would rendezvous with the devil in red. Hopefully he would confirm her suspicions that *he* knew who killed Nettie.

While Harjo camped out on the couch in the living room, watching the World Series, Amanda ambled to the bedroom. She rummaged through the dirty-clothes hamper to retrieve the journal she had stashed there for safekeeping. . . .

Amanda frowned when she came up empty-handed. She was sure she had crammed the journal in the hamper before she toddled off to bed the previous night.

An uneasy feeling grabbed hold of her as she glanced around the spacious room. Her gaze landed on the dresser drawer that wasn't completely shut. Amanda marched across the bedroom to pull open the drawer. Sure enough, Thorn's underwear, neatly stacked there on laundry day, was in disarray. Someone had searched this room for the journal!

Candice Randolph, alias Arthella Carson or Eileen Franklin, certainly had had the opportunity after she drugged Thorn. . . .

Amanda muttered several colorful obscenities. No doubt Candice, posing as a health care nurse, had waited until Amanda left the house, then preyed on Thorn this morning. Candice wanted to search for the journal, and she didn't want Thorn to see her do it. But why was Candice so determined to get her hands on that journal? Because of the previous scandal? If she had changed her name twenty-five years ago, what difference would it make to her? Was it because she wanted to blackmail someone whose name was listed in that little black book? That would certainly ensure living expenses until she resurrected some other defenseless soul from a cemetery and assumed another identity.

Scowling, Amanda plunked down on the king-size bed to take a load off her swollen feet.

Think, Hazard. Put yourself in that mentally deranged woman's place and figure out what her next move might be.

Amanda sank back on the pillow and stared off into space in profound concentration. If she were Candice Randolph, who might possibly have bumped off Nettie and had been seen by Melvin Rumley—who arrived to buy more time before he had to pay off his three-thousand-dollar IOU, and to pick up a truckload of pumpkins— she would want to ensure Melvin's silence.

No doubt that was what Candice had done, *assuming* she was the one who disposed of Nettie. She could have threatened to do Ginger Rumley bodily harm if Melvin didn't keep his trap shut. But Candice, obviously a mistress of disguises, altered appearances, and identities, might have seen Amanda grilling Melvin near the haunted house. Candice might have decided to distract Amanda by targeting Thorn with a brick, then a hypodermic needle.

If her hypothesis was correct, Candice planned to target Melvin—the one person who could positively identify her and place her at the crime scene at the time of Nettie's death. With Mel silenced permanently, Candice could send her blackmail notes to those folks listed in the journal and she would be financially stable for years to come. The woman could perform another of her vanishing acts, and it could take Rich Thorn and the OSBI years to track her down.

This hypothesis and conclusion, of course, was based on the speculation that Candice Randolph was the murderess. However, Amanda could not forget the venomous glower Mickey Poag had leveled at her when she had grilled him this morning. The man had been positively furious and looked as if he wanted to vent physical abuse on her.

The thought prompted Amanda to reach for the phone to dial her brother-in-law's cellular number.

"Rich Thorn here," he answered after the first ring.

"Rich, Hazard here. How's Thorn doing?"

"He was pitching a fit because the doctor wouldn't sign his release, but then he drifted off to sleep a few minutes ago. He's been catnapping since you left."

"With all the excitement this morning I forgot to get the scoop on the other individuals I asked you to check out."

"Yeah, it slipped my mind, too," he mumbled.

Amanda heard the crackling sound of paper being unfolded.

"I've got it right here, Hazard. Rumley is clean as a whistle, not so much as a speeding ticket in the last ten years. Odell Jarvis has a couple of ancient DUIs and DWIs and two recent speeding tickets. Eileen Franklin is who she says she is. Her record is clean. Dr. Simms found a photo to show Nick. Eileen was not the woman who gave Nick that hypo. It turns out that it was Arthella Carson posing as Eileen Franklin."

"What about Mickey Poag?"

"Well, that's another story. Seems Poag has a prison record. He served time twenty-five years ago for assault and battery in Texas."

Amanda gulped. Those alarm bells were clamoring again. "Texas? Assault and battery? Rich, do you recall whether those duplicate birth certificates you checked out for me came from Oklahoma or Texas?"

"I'll have to call you back on that one, Hazard," Rich murmured. "The agency's computer guru found the correlation for me. He was cross-checking all over the place when he came up with that."

"I need to know if Sis Mithlo-Hix's birth took place in Texas."

"Mmm, I see which way you're drifting here, Hazard. I'll let you know what I come up with."

"Work fast, Rich. I have to be at the ceremony that

takes place before the costume dance this evening, you know.''

"Gotcha. This is a rush. Later, Hazard."

Amanda replaced the phone, her thoughts whirling like the vortex of a cyclone. Poag? Randolph? Texas? True, it was a big state, but still . . . Assault and battery? Odell Jarvis?

When her thoughts finally circled back to her rendezvous with Melvin Rumley, an uneasy premonition bombarded her. On impulse, Amanda scooped up the phone and dialed the mom-and-pop grocery store. She felt the need to warn Melvin to watch his back until their meeting at seven o'clock. The phone rang a dozen times, but no one answered.

Amanda glanced at her watch. Damn, the Rumleys must have closed up early so they could dress for the costume street dance. At least Amanda *hoped* that was why the Rumleys had not answered the phone.

Following her instincts, Amanda called the police dispatcher. Janie-Ethel picked up on the second ring.

"Vamoose Police Department."

"Hi, it's Amanda."

"Did you have the baby? Is Thorn okay? Deputy Sykes said the chief took a hard blow to the head last night."

Amanda sighed. If she had been asked once this week if she'd had the baby, she had been asked a hundred times. "No baby yet," she reported. "Thorn is recuperating. I need to contact Deputy Sykes. Will you ask him to call me at home, ASAP?"

"Sure thing, Amanda. He should be checking in with me in a few minutes."

Amanda replaced the receiver and waited. Seven minutes later, Benny Sykes returned her call.

"What's up, Hazard?" Benny asked. "No baby yet, huh? Thorn is doing better, right?"

Obviously Janie-Ethel had relayed the information to Benny. "Everything is peachy keen." She hoped. "Listen, Benny, I would like for you to run by Rumley's Market—"

"Having another one of those weird cravings again, are you?" Benny snickered. "The chief says you have the strangest urges for food at the most unpredictable moments. He says that cranberry juice kick you've been on lately is nauseating him. He absolutely hates the stuff."

"He does? He never mentioned it to me."

"Oops, maybe I shouldn't have said that."

Amanda made a mental note to give up the cranberry craving, since Thorn felt obliged to drink what she drank. She would stick to milk and orange juice.

"I just wanted you to check on Melvin for me," she told Benny. "He has been nervous and upset lately. I'm concerned about him. When I saw him this morning he didn't look well."

"Didn't look well. Right," Benny repeated. "Okay, Amanda. If it will make you feel better, I'll cruise over to the store. I'll do a ten-thirty-nine and ten-forty-nine at your request."

Amanda didn't bother asking Benny to translate the police jargon he loved to spout off. She wanted him to get his butt in gear and check to see if Ginger and Melvin were all right.

"Thanks, Benny. I have to leave pretty soon, so call me back as quickly as you can."

"Ten-four, over and out."

When she hung up, Harjo tapped lightly on the bedroom door, then poked his head inside. "It's time to get you into your pumpkin costume," he reminded her.

Amanda blinked in surprise when Harjo sauntered into the room wearing his Zorro costume. "My, you look dashing," she complimented.

Harjo bowed gallantly, retrieved his plastic sword, then swished it in front of her a few times for effect. "Thank you, madam. I am at your service."

"Good." Amanda pushed herself to her elbows, then

shoved herself onto the side of the bed. "It takes about fifteen minutes to get that dumb pumpkin suit arranged, what with all those flickering lights stitched to the underside and all those yards of fabric sewn to the metal hoop."

"Well, then, let's get at it, Haz. You have to give a speech at the opening ceremony and then introduce the entertainers. It wouldn't do for the Pumpkin Queen to be late."

Ignoring the deep pressure in her tummy and the nerve-tingling twinge, Amanda wrestled her way into her giant pumpkin costume, then arranged the scads of orange fabric around her.

"Let me check your batteries," Harjo offered as he reached beneath the hem of her costume. "And don't tell Thorn I did this. He would probably take it the wrong way, jealous as he is."

Amanda expected Harjo was right. His sticking his hand under her dress, no matter how harmless the reason, would set Thorn off like a stick of lighted dynamite. Amanda waited for Harjo to flick the switch. She lit right up. The batteries, it seemed, were in good working order.

She wasn't so sure about herself. She felt kind of odd, twitchy, jittery. She wondered if the nerve-racking events of the past two days and this perplexing case were getting to her.

Although Amanda wanted to hang around the house to see if Deputy Sykes and her brother-in-law called her back, she was running short on time. When Harjo got her loaded in the truck, there was no time to spare.

During the drive to Vamoose, Amanda mentally prepared her speech to thank the good citizens for participating in the festivities and contributing to the Volunteer Fire Department. Amanda preferred speaking with detailed notes at her fingertips, but she could occasionally handle impromptus, though they offended her fierce sense of preliminary preparation and meticulous organization.

Considering what a hectic week it had been, Amanda knew she would just have to wing it.

A fleeting thought skipped through her mind, making her smile to her herself. She wondered how her sense of organization was going to hold up when she became a mother. Her need for order would probably be shot all to hell.

SEVENTEEN

Amanda was impressed by the turnout for the costume street dance. Everyone from Vamoose, Pronto, and Adios was in costume. There were walking bananas, a giant tomato, ghosts, ghouls, princesses, an entire family of aliens, pint-size cartoon characters, a couple of Elvis Presley sightings, and a Little Bo Peep with her sheep.

Velma the gum-chewing beautician was dressed in an Energizer Bunny costume. Beverly Hill was decked out as Cleopatra. Her costume glittered and sparkled beneath the streetlights. Her incandescent half-moon golden eye shadow glowed in the dark. Thaddeus Thatcher and his wife Gertrude came as Adam and Eve. Plastic leaves covered their vital parts. The Watts brothers were dressed as Groucho and Harpo Marx.

Amanda also noted several President Clintons and Monica Lewinskys in the milling crowd, along with three sumo wrestlers and half a dozen vampires.

The high school athletic booster club had set up refreshment booths on both sides of Main Street. Tables of left-over pumpkin bread, pie, cake, and pastry were being sold to the public, along with colas.

Amanda wished Thorn could have been on hand to enjoy the festivities. Poor baby, laid up in the hospital, with his big brother standing guard over him.

With Zorro's assistance, Amanda climbed onto the stage to be officially crowned Pumpkin Queen, then gave her brief speech. Applause clattered around her as Billie Jane Baxter, Vamoose's native daughter and country music star, belted out the first song in her twangy voice. How Billie Jane became Nashville's sweetheart Amanda would never know, but Billie Jane and her Horseshoe Band delighted fans with her upbeat songs, her flashy turquoise and silver jewelry, and her tight costumes that bordered on indecent.

Amanda stood beside Zorro, watching the gaily adorned citizens doing the two-step beneath the streetlights.

"Wanna dance, Hazard?" Zorro asked.

Oh, what the hell, thought Amanda. Clumsy and awkward though she was, dancing beat standing around waiting for her rendezvous with Melvin. "Sure, why not."

Amanda would let the dashing Zorro perform his bodyguard duties for a few more minutes; then she would excuse herself to use the rest room. Then she would sneak behind the stage to confront Melvin. She didn't need Zorro breathing down her neck while she spoke to Melvin. Nervous as Melvin was, he wouldn't make a peep if Zorro was on hand.

Discreetly, Amanda checked her watch. It was ten minutes to seven.

"Thank you for the dance, Zorro. You dance divinely, but I need to take a bathroom break." She pointed a jack-o'-lantern-tipped finger toward Thatcher's service station, where glowing ghosts paraded above the lighted carport. She had no ill feelings about the Thatchers' taking the blue ribbon for best festive decorations. Their ingenuity was absolutely spectacular.

"I'll come with you," Zorro volunteered gallantly.

Amanda didn't need gallant. She needed her own space. "Oh, for heaven's sake. Don't get carried away with your chivalry here. There are some things I want to do myself. This is definitely one of them."

"Maybe so, but Thorn said—" he tried to object, for all the good it did him.

"Thorn is overprotective. You said so yourself," Amanda interrupted. "Go dance with the Energizer Bunny. She's standing by the refreshment table all by herself, itching to kick up her heels. I'll be back in a few minutes."

"Well . . ." Zorro said hesitantly.

"Don't upset me, Zorro. You know how fragile a pregnant woman's emotions are. If I start crying over nothing—and it would not be the first time—my face will be smeared with black eyeliner. Then I'll look like—"

Zorro held up his hand and sighed audibly. "Okay, okay. Just don't be gone long or I'll start worrying about you."

Amanda zigzagged through the dancers to reach the rest room, then ducked inside to wrestle with the restrictive costume. She pulled the batteries from her pumpkin suit so she wouldn't be as conspicuous as a walking lightbulb, then stuffed the batteries in the deep side pocket on her suit. Waddling, she darted behind the service station, then circled to the stage.

The backdrop from the stage plunged the sidewalk into total darkness. Amanda squinted into the shadows, searching for the devil she was supposed to meet.

Amanda checked her watch. It was straight-up seven. Where the hell was Melvin? She inched forward, then saw a pair of feet protruding from the metal framework below the stage.

"Oh, damn!" Amanda muttered as she scuttled through the shadows. The red-clad feet of the devil were turned toes up.

That was not a good sign.

Amanda hunkered down to check for a pulse on the devil's ankle.

There wasn't one to be found. The devil was definitely dead.

Hurriedly, Amanda fished into her pocket for the batteries to shed light on the crime scene. "Help!" she yelled at the top of her lungs. "Helllp!"

Unfortunately, Billie Jane Baxter's nasally voice and the band's electric guitars and pounding drums overrode Amanda's call for assistance.

When Amanda's pulse rate doubled in frustration she felt a deep cramp assail her. "Not now!" she muttered. "Not yet!"

She inhaled a deep, fortifying breath and battled to get herself under control. Her attempt to save Melvin Rumley from disaster had obviously failed. Her call to Benny Sykes had come too late. Poor Melvin. He had been at the wrong place at the wrong time, and poof! He had been permanently silenced.

Amanda, her orange lights flickering, waddled around the side of the stage to summon assistance.

"Zorro! Where are you!" she trumpeted.

Zorro wheeled around, then charged toward her with his cape flying behind him. To Amanda's stunned amazement, a man dressed like the Lone Ranger, wearing a white hat, mask, and packing six-shooters on his hips, also came toward her at a dead run.

Amanda's eyes narrowed in irritation. That was definitely Thorn dressed in those tight-fitting pants that accentuated his lean hips and muscled thighs and a chest-hugging shirt that showcased his broad shoulders, pectorals, and washboard belly. The Lone Ranger was supposed to be convalescing in the hospital. What did he think he was doing out of bed? He was going to suffer a relapse if he didn't watch out!

"Damn it, Thorn, you are not supposed to be here,"

Amanda castigated her husband in the Lone Ranger costume.

"Damn it, Hazard, you were not supposed to leave Harjo's side. You promised!" he shouted back at her.

"Oh, I must have forgotten," she said lamely.

The Lone Ranger's thick brows swooped down and disappeared behind his mask. "No," he said, and scowled. "You did not forget. You chose to thumb your nose at my concern for your welfare." He pivoted to glare at Zorro. "Some protector you turned out to be. You can't even keep track of a giant, lighted pumpkin for one damn hour!"

"Thorn, lower your voice before you give yourself another headache. It is not Zorro's fault," she defended her bodyguard. "I tricked him so I could rendezvous with Melvin Rumley, because I didn't think Mel would confide in me with Zorro looming around. I think Melvin knows . . . knew," she hastily corrected, "who bumped off Nettie."

"Well, if you went to all this trouble to lose your shadow so you could have a private rendezvous, then where the hell is Rumley?"

Amanda clung to the Lone Ranger's rigid arm for support, then gestured behind the stage. "He's over there." She swallowed shakily. "But Thorn, there's a problem."

"There usually is," he smarted off. "What is it this time?"

"Uh . . . Melvin didn't offer me information . . . because Melvin is dead."

"Well, shit," the Lone Ranger muttered as he wheeled around and stamped off.

Zorro lifted his mask and glared at Amanda for deceiving him, then whipped around, his cape fanning out like bat wings, and followed in the Lone Ranger's wake to assist in pulling the victim from beneath the stage.

When Amanda returned to the scene of the crime, the

devil was sprawled on the sidewalk and Zorro and the
Lone Ranger were hovering over him.

The Lone Ranger pulled the red mask from the victim's
colorless face, then glanced up at Amanda. "This is *not*
Melvin Rumley."

Amanda scurried closer to see Mickey Poag's face
glowing eerily in the orange lights from her costume.
"You're right. That is definitely not Melvin. What do
you suppose Mickey Poag is doing in Melvin's costume?"

"You're the one who always thinks she has all the
answers. You tell me," the Lone Ranger muttered crab-
bily.

"Zorro, would you mind scouring around under the
stage for me?" Amanda requested grimly.

"Why? What am I looking for?"

Amanda gulped. "The remains of a hypodermic needle
that was probably meant for me."

"What!" the Lone Ranger howled.

"What!" Zorro yipped.

"That is my best guess. I can't prove my speculations
until I receive a confirmation from Rich, but I think
Mickey Poag has been in cahoots with Arthella Carson
for a long time."

The Lone Ranger's and Zorro's mouths dropped open.

"How in the sweet loving hell did you come up with
that?" the Lone Ranger demanded in a strangled voice.

"This is pure conjecture, of course, but I think Arthella
already disposed of Melvin, then convinced Mickey to
wear the devil costume and lie in wait for me tonight
with a syringe in hand. I assume that Mickey's assistance
in this murder scheme was no longer required, so he was
double-crossed and conveniently taken out of the loop.
When I flicked on my costume lights to check on the
victim and yelled for help, I must have frightened off my
intended killer."

"Good God, Hazard, you could have been murdered!"

Thorn gasped for breath and sank limply to the ground. "Damn, I'm not feeling so hot."

"Of course you aren't. You are supposed to be under medical observation at the hospital. If you pass out and clank your fool head again, then you probably have it coming. Now where is your brother?"

"He is monitoring activities with the undercover agents," Thorn said weakly.

"A lot of good that hotshot agent is doing," Amanda said, and snorted.

While Thorn reclined on the sidewalk, Harjo slithered around on his belly beneath the framework of the stage. He scooped up a discarded syringe, then held it up in front of Thorn.

"Look familiar?" Harjo asked.

"Yeah, a little too familiar. I took one of those babies in the arm this morning," Thorn bleated.

"I'll go flag down Rich," Amanda volunteered. "It shouldn't be too hard for him to spot me in this getup." She wheeled around and toddled off.

It didn't take long for the undercover agents to converge on Amanda. She hadn't thought it would. No doubt Thorn had given his brother and the other agents a precise description of her costume.

"Why did you let Thorn talk you into leaving the hospital?" Amanda scolded her brother-in-law. "That was a dumb thing to do, Rich. The man has a serious concussion, for crying out loud! At this very moment he is sprawled on the sidewalk behind the stage, sporting a killer headache and a queasy stomach."

Rich, dressed in a mask and scrubs that he had obviously confiscated from the hospital staff, shifted awkwardly from one size-twelve foot to the other. "You know how Nicky is when he is afraid you are putting yourself in danger. He is impossibly persistent. He threatened to demolish the room if Doc Simms didn't grant him a leave of absence. Really, Hazard, Doc said Nicky would be okay if he took it easy."

"Well, he didn't take it easy and now he is paying for it," Amanda snapped. "And to make matters worse, I stumbled over another dead body." She stuck out her hand, palm up. "Let me borrow your cellular phone. I need to call Deputy Sykes to check on another possible victim."

Rich handed over the phone, then pivoted around to gesture across the street. "We have another victim down over there."

Amanda blinked. "You do? Who?"

"We aren't sure yet. He is just coming around."

Amanda pointed herself toward the victim, then pulled up short when she saw Phil Darnell sprawled on the grass. His head rolled from side to side, as if the mayoral hopeful was trying to get his bearings.

Amanda squatted down beside him, then whispered, "Pad?"

"Nettie?" he murmured groggily.

Aha, so this was Nettie's secret lover, the prestigious doctor who refused to divorce his wife to marry the woman who had remained true to him until the day she died.

"You should be ashamed of yourself, Phil," Amanda scolded crossly. "You led Nettie on for years, sneaking around, keeping your secret. I'd like to clobber you!"

Phil Darnell shook his head, as if coming out of a trance, then flinched when he realized it was Amanda Hazard-Thorn looming over him. "Oh, damn . . ."

"*Oh, damn* is right, Phil," she sputtered at him.

"Hazard, what the heck is going on?" Rich demanded from behind her.

"This is between Phil and me, nothing for you to concern yourself with, Rich. Why don't you and the agents go check on Thorn while Phil and I have a private conversation."

"But the man is down and I am not supposed to let you—"

"Phil is fine, aren't you, Phil?" she insisted, glaring at the peaked retired physician.

"Fine," he mumbled uneasily.

"We are both fine. Beat it, Rich. I have business to conduct here. As soon as Phil feels up to standing, I will meet you behind the stage."

Reluctantly, Rich and his agents trooped off.

"Now then, what happened to you? Did you take a shot in the hip as a warning about what might happen if you didn't fork over blackmail money?" Amanda questioned hurriedly.

Philip Arthur Darnell pushed himself into a sitting position, then raked his hand through his gray hair. "Does everyone in town know about this?"

"No, only the mother whose name was listed on the birth certificate you falsified twenty-five years ago at Nettie's request. And me, of course," she assured him. "So how much money is Arthella Carson trying to pry out of you?"

Phil crawled onto his hands and knees, then staggered to his feet to rub his hip. He glanced around to see if anyone was within hearing distance. "The first installment is to be twenty thousand," he admitted.

"You need to renegotiate," Amanda insisted. "If you are paying for tampering with the two birth certificates and for carrying on a long-standing affair, you should only be paying ten thousand."

Phil, still suffering the side effects of the hypodermic tranquilizer, stared at her, uncomprehending.

"I'm beginning to think, though I don't have enough evidence to prove it yet, that Odell Jarvis was *not* the father of the child—the one whose birth certificate Nettie asked you to falsify to save her family from embarrassment. I think Mickey Poag and his girlfriend pulled a fast one on Odell one night when he had too much to drink. They dreamed up a way to get Nettie to pay living and hospital expenses, while they went merrily on their way.''

Phil blinked like a deer caught in headlights. Amanda wondered if she was speaking too rapidly for the dazed man to keep up with her.

''Let me put this to you as simply as I can, since your brain still isn't functioning normally,'' Amanda said. ''The woman who is blackmailing you, the one who shot you with the syringe, knows you were Nettie's lover. She stole the journal from me and she must have come across your name. If you want to pay for your adultery, that is your business. However, if you want my opinion—''

''I have the feeling I'm going to get it, whether I want it or not.''

''You're right, Pad. My advice is that you call Arthella Carson's bluff. Nettie is gone, God rest her soul, and so is your wife. I wouldn't pay a red cent to that conniving, manipulative murderess. But if your reputation means more to you than Nettie's unfaltering feelings, then I feel damn sorry for you, Dr. Darnell.''

Amanda wheeled around to stalk off, but Phil's voice brought her to a lurching halt. ''I know you don't think much of me, Ms. Hazard, but for what it's worth, I never stopped loving Nettie. The fact is that we were planning to move into New Horizon Retirement Village and make a fresh new start, all aboveboard. I'm the one who paid Nettie's first down payment and talked her into renting out her homestead. She planned to let Sis and Bubba Hix live there for practically nothing.''

Phil stared very solemnly at Amanda. ''I want to see Nettie's killer behind bars just as much as you do. Probably more. There was only one Nettie . . . and I have to live with the fact that I didn't have the gumption to shed my loveless marriage and enjoy the only true happiness I found in life. Now it's too late. I'll regret my mistake until the day I die. . . .''

When his voice cracked, Amanda blinked back tears, then grimaced when another pain shot through her lower back. Damn, she didn't have time to stand here feeling sorry for Phil Darnell because he blew his one chance at happiness. She had to check on Melvin and Ginger Rumley and catch herself a killer before these blasted pains got closer together than they already were!

Decidedly uncomfortable, Amanda lumbered around the crowd of dancers to find a secluded spot so she could place a call to Deputy Sykes.

"Vamoose Police Department."

"No, Janie-Ethel. I didn't have the baby yet," Amanda said quickly. "Where is Deputy Sykes?"

"Well, you probably won't believe this—"

"Try me," Amanda cut in swiftly.

"Benny swung by the grocery store, just as you requested. He found Ginger collapsed in the produce section!"

Amanda stopped breathing for an instant. Had Arthella stabbed Ginger with a syringe, causing Melvin to go berserk?

"Ginger was out cold," Janie-Ethel went on. "Deputy Sykes called an ambulance. He was on his way outside when he heard somebody pounding on the door to the meat locker. Melvin was stuck in there, and he nearly froze to death before Benny freed him. If you hadn't called Benny, we wouldn't have checked on them until it was too late! How did you know there might be a problem?"

Amanda sighed in relief. She had gone with her hunch and saved two lives. Ignoring the dispatcher's question, Amanda asked. "Is Ginger going to be okay?"

"Doc Simms was still working on her at last report."

Amanda imagined the physician was treating Ginger in the same aggressive manner with which he had treated Thorn this morning. Hopefully Ginger hadn't been given an injection of fast-acting poison, as Mickey Poag had.

"What about Melvin?" Amanda wanted to know.

"He's suffering from hypothermia and he's hysterical. He refuses to calm down until he knows for certain that Ginger is going to survive. Deputy Sykes said the doctor was going to give Melvin a sedative if he didn't settle down soon."

"Thanks for the update, Janie-Ethel."

Amanda switched off the phone, then tucked it into the deep pocket of her pumpkin costume. She waddled toward the back of the stage, then stopped to lean back against a tree when another stabbing pain knifed through her. Oh, rats! she thought. She did not have time for this right now!

EIGHTEEN

Amanda forced herself to think past the cramping pain and concentrate on this case. She suspected that Arthella Carson had entered the grocery store, probably wearing a costume. The timing for the maniac nurse's dastardly deeds couldn't have been better, what with the Halloween festivities in full swing. Arthella might have trapped Melvin in the freezer, letting the icy temperatures do their worst, then stabbed Ginger with a hypodermic when her back was turned.

It would have been a simple matter for Arthella to swipe the devil costume and convince Mickey Poag to put it on. Once Mickey, who was probably unaware that he was Arthella's next target, was disposed of, she lurked in the shadows, waiting for Amanda to show up. Fortunately, things hadn't worked out as well as Arthella hoped. Amanda had already plugged in her lights and started yelling for assistance. Instead, the lunatic nurse must have decided to make good her threat to Phil Darnell.

If Amanda's assumptions were correct, Arthella had been trailing Melvin the past week to ensure he didn't disclose what he knew. Arthella had the poor man running scared during the day, while she frantically searched for Nettie's journal at night—inciting rumors about ghost sightings in Pumpkin Hollow.

Amanda was pretty certain that Arthella was the one who had searched Thorn Farm and absconded with the tell-all book. The fact that Phil Darnell had been targeted for blackmail—and stabbed with a syringe so he would know Arthella meant business—signified that the crazed nurse was in possession of the journal.

Finding the demented sniper, who packed a hypodermic syringe as her weapon, in this costumed crowd would be as difficult as searching for a needle in a haystack. Luckily, Rich and his undercover agents were present to lend extra hands. It was time for Amanda to scuttle behind stage and take command of this search. Arthella had to be apprehended—and quickly.

Since the pain had subsided Amanda pushed away from the tree. She froze to the spot when she felt the prick of a needle against her neck. Damn it to hell, she had lingered too long in thought. She didn't have to search for Arthella; the maniac had come to *her!*

"I shouldn't have to tell you what this hypo will do to you and your unborn kid, Hazard," came a quiet hiss behind her. "Come with me, and don't try any funny business. You'll be down and out before you know what hit you. I've got the fastest draw you've ever seen."

Amanda didn't doubt it for a minute. Arthella had struck all her victims hard and fast.

"Now move it, Pumpkin Queen."

A gloved hand clamped around her arm to drag her toward a nondescript, old-model sedan that had all the bells and whistles in its interior.

At needle point, Amanda was crammed into the backseat. Before she could right herself, her wrists were taped together and secured to the door handle.

"You will never get away with this," Amanda felt

obliged to say as she watched the woman, who was decked out in a Wicked Witch of the West costume, slide beneath the steering wheel.

"You think not?" Arthella cackled. "You would be surprised what a woman can get away with if she is clever enough."

Amanda muttered sourly as the witch—an appropriate costume for this evil madwoman, in Amanda's opinion—switched on the ignition, then shoved the sedan into gear.

Thorn was going to be furious with her, Amanda thought with a grimace. Thorn always became furious when one of her investigations went haywire and she found herself in mortal danger.

Nick rolled to his knees, willing the darkness behind the stage to stop swirling like a roulette wheel. Billie Jane Baxter's twangy voice, accompanied by screaming guitars and thumping drums, put his head and stomach on a roll. He thought he heard his brother's voice in the near distance.

"Rich?" Nick called thickly.

"Right here, bro. Hang on for a few more minutes. We're checking the body for the point of entry of the hypodermic. . . . Yep, here it is. The guy took a shot in the hip. Looks like the killer came at him unaware, considering the angle of impact."

Nick grimaced at the possibility that a lethal injection had also been meant for Hazard. *God!* If he lost that woman he didn't know what he would do with himself. . . .

Wildly, Nick scanned the shadows, squinting at the silhouettes that hovered around him. "Hazard? Where the hell is Hazard!" he bellowed.

"She went to check out the other man who was down on the opposite side of the street," Rich reported.

"What other man? Was somebody else shot with a syringe?" Nick asked bleakly.

"Yeah, a gray-haired senior citizen. I haven't seen the guy since I was just a kid, growing up in Vamoose, but I think it was Darnell."

"Phil Darnell?" Nick frowned pensively. "How did that retired physician get mixed up in this mess?"

"I don't have a clue," Rich replied. "But Hazard seemed to know what was going on. She insisted on speaking privately with Darnell; then she borrowed my cell phone to place a call to Benny Sykes."

"Why did she need to talk to Benny?" Nick asked, getting more confused by the second.

"Hazard said she needed to check on another possible victim, whoever the hell that is. Damn, this festival might turn into the scene of a mass murder if we don't find the fiend with the hypodermic syringe, PDQ!"

Nick racked his concussed brain, trying to remember if he knew who Hazard might have been concerned about. He drew a blank.

It had been that kind of day.

"Does anybody else have a mobile phone I can borrow?" Nick asked as he struggled to sit upright.

"Here you go, Chief." One of the agents strode over to hand the phone to Nick.

Nick scanned the shadows behind the stage. "Harjo? Are you still here?"

"You bet, kemosabe," Harjo called back.

"Go see if Hazard has finished making her call. I'll see if I can get in touch with Deputy Sykes and find out what the hell is going on."

"Done." Harjo strode off, his Zorro cloak fluttering in the air as he set a swift pace.

Nick dialed headquarters to speak with Janie-Ethel. She gave him the update on Melvin and Ginger Rumley. Ginger had finally regained consciousness and Melvin, who had been beside himself, finally calmed down enough for Benny Sykes to take a statement. Melvin had confided that he had been at the scene of Nettie's death and he knew who had disposed of her.

According to Benny's report, Melvin had arrived at Nettie's farm in time to see a man and woman dash behind the barn, then roar off in a battered pickup. Later Melvin had been contacted by phone and instructed to keep silent. Otherwise the price he would pay for going public with his knowledge was his wife's life. Melvin claimed he had been too terrified to come to Thorn with the information.

Melvin also reported that earlier in the afternoon a woman wearing a witch costume had arrived at the store. She had asked for several cuts of beef that Melvin stored in the meat locker. When Melvin walked into the freezer the woman locked the door behind him. Melvin hadn't had the slightest idea what had happened to his wife until Benny arrived—at Hazard's urgent request—to spring him free. When Melvin discovered that Ginger had been shot with a hypodermic and was unconscious, he had gone off the deep end and had not calmed down until he received news that his wife had survived the ordeal.

"Janie-Ethel, I want you to call the coroner and tell him we have another stiff behind the stage at the street dance," Nick requested. "I believe the killer is the same person who tried to dispose of Melvin and Ginger. Tell Benny to hightail it over here, ASAP."

"Got it, Chief. I'll send Deputy Sykes right over."

"One more thing, Janie-Ethel. Take down the number of this cell phone so we can keep in touch." Nick rattled off the number.

Nick clicked off the phone and glanced up to see Zorro towering over him. A feeling of sickening dread roiled in his stomach. "Where's Hazard?"

"Vanished," Zorro reported bleakly. "No one has seen her for a quarter of an hour."

"Damn it to hell!" Nick staggered to his feet, cursing the light-headed feeling that overcame him. "Everybody fan out to locate Hazard. Giant pumpkins don't just vanish into thin air!''

Rich and his agents scattered like a covey of quail. Zorro shot off like a cannonball, and Nick wobbled around the corner of the stage, holding on to the framework for support.

Criminey, why did this have to happen while he was still feeling dazed and nauseous? He needed to be operating at one hundred percent.

He wasn't even close.

Squinting, Nick watched the costumed dancers whirling beneath the glowing lights. Laughter undulated through the crowd. But Nick had nothing to laugh about. He had the unshakable feeling that whoever had given Mickey Poag the lethal injection had stalked and captured Hazard.

Hell's jingling bells! This was not a good time for Hazard to become embroiled in calamity. Considering the harrowing day she'd had she might go into labor and find herself at the total mercy of her would-be killer. How could Hazard devise a clever scheme to extricate herself from trouble if she was paralyzed by pain?

Nick stood there, clinging to the corner of the stage, feeling totally frustrated and utterly helpless. He was accustomed to racing to Hazard's rescue. Now he was forced to rely on others. It didn't sit well with him.

Half an eternity later the undercover agents trickled back to report no sightings of the Great Pumpkin. Then Rich and Zorro arrived, with nothing to show for their frantic efforts. They looked to Nick for a course of action, but Nick didn't have the foggiest notion where to begin his search.

His wife had disappeared without a trace, and Nick was terrified that he had seen the last of her!

Amanda shifted uncomfortably on the backseat of the sedan. When her nose began to itch, she doubled over to scratch it, though her hands were tethered to the door handle. Candice, alias Arthella, hadn't made a peep since she sped off in her sedan. Amanda knew that was not a good thing. She needed to distract this homicidal maniac by striking up a conversation—and she'd better be quick about it! There was no telling what evil thoughts were chasing each other through this woman's crazed mind.

"I assume that you became aware that Nettie Jarvis kept a journal while you were pretending to provide her with health care this past year. I wouldn't be surprised to discover that you have been sending fraudulent bills to Medicare for supposed compensation for taking care of Nettie and your other patients. You have been making a killing by sucking the home-health care program dry, haven't you?" Amanda accused as the witch circled the block to ensure that she wasn't being followed.

"Brilliant, Sherlock," the witch smarted off. "I have been making all sorts of money on the side. Then I saw Nettie jotting notes in her little black book several times and I figured money was to be made there, too. But Nettie was careful not to stash her journal away while I was in the house. I have been searching for that damn thing for six months. I got Darnell's name after he called to talk to Nettie while I was in the house. All I had to do was punch in star-six-nine on the phone and it was easy to find out who Nettie's secret friend was."

She glared at Amanda in the rearview mirror. "My plans of blackmail would have come off without a hitch if you hadn't poked your nose into my business. But then, Mickey warned me that you would be a problem. And everyone in this podunk town has been singing your praises since I returned."

"I must admit that Nettie's murder might have slipped past me if you hadn't made a crucial error that alerted me to foul play," Amanda said as calmly as she knew how.

"What error was that? I never could figure out what tipped you off."

"The house shoes," Amanda replied, determined to keep her kidnapper talking so she wouldn't have time to plot too far in advance.

"The house shoes?" the witch repeated blankly.

"Yes. You of all people should have known that Nettie always changed into her Nike tennis shoes so she would have more stability when she went outdoors, most especially when she was tramping through the vines in the pumpkin patch. That was clearly an oversight on your part," Amanda pointed out. "It didn't help that you neglected to vacuum up the black cat hairs that were left on the patchwork quilt after you suffocated Nettie with the pillow sham. That was careless, if you don't mind my saying so."

The witch spat a few foul oaths that would have burned Mother's ears. Mother was strongly opposed to cursing. Ladies, Mother always said, did not swear. Candice Randolph, alias Arthella Carson, was no lady!

"I must compliment you, however, on arranging this scam," Amanda went on, while she strained against the tape handcuffs. "I agree that you are clever and ingenious."

"Thank you," the witch said haughtily. "I have always prided myself on knowing what I wanted and how to go about getting it."

"Except for your oversight with Mickey Poag all those years ago," Amanda reminded her. "After you accidentally turned up pregnant with Mickey Poag's child, down Texas way, that really cramped your style, didn't it? And correct me if I'm wrong, but you weren't able to control Mickey as well as you thought. The blundering fool lost his temper, beat somebody up, was charged with assault and battery, and got sent to prison. That put another unexpected kink in your plans, I suspect."

"Damn, Hazard, you're smarter than I thought. How

did you come up with all that? The incident wasn't noted in Nettie's journal because the old hag knew nothing about my affair with Mickey.''

The witch cackled sardonically. "But you are dead wrong about my inability to control Mickey. Men are easy to manipulate. Their brains are located below their belt buckles.''

Amanda frowned pensively, then said, "So you are saying that you had no qualms about Mickey pounding someone flat, is that it?''

"Yeah, that is it," the witch confirmed. "But the stupid fool—''

"—didn't cooperate on your most recent scheme," Amanda inserted. "That is why you left Mickey belly-up under the stage this evening. Right?''

"Yeah, the idiot," she muttered. "He has been in a state of panic since the moment Melvin Rumley saw the two of us at Nettie's house Monday morning. Mickey wanted to bump off Melvin immediately, but I knew that would draw too much attention. I told him it was better to twist the man's arm by threatening to kill his precious wife. We could buy some time and distance between Nettie's death and Melvin's unfortunate demise. Mickey was never too long on patience or brains.

"I set it up so Mickey could give you a fatal injection tonight when you came behind the stage for your rendez-vous. But Mickey was getting cold feet and didn't want to give you the shot. He was afraid your connection with Thorn would cause him to get caught.''

"So you gave Mickey an injection while he wasn't looking and then decided to finish me off yourself," Amanda speculated.

"Worked for me. I'm very adaptable," the witch said.

"I suspect you had Mickey launch that brick at Thorn last night. Strong and stout as Mickey was, he could shot-put the brick hard enough to knock Thorn off his feet," Amanda muttered.

"Very good, Hazard," the witch complimented. "I knew we had to act quickly after you cornered Melvin Rumley last night. I wanted you and Melvin to know I meant business."

Amanda watched Candice zip around the corner and head for the highway, leaving the lights of Vamoose behind her. Another pain ripped through Amanda and she was forced to plunk back and wait for it to pass. Confound it, she did not want to deal with this agonizing back pressure and these spasmodic pains at this critical moment!

"So, tell me, Candice. You don't mind if I call you that, do you?"

"Call me whatever you want," she said with a lackadaisical shrug. "I've gone by a dozen names over the years. One is no more sentimental to me than another."

Amanda suspected as much. This lunatic didn't care what name she went by. Candice was simply out to show the world that she was smarter than everybody else. No doubt whatever had happened in Candice's childhood that squeezed out all her saving graces and good qualities still controlled her behavior. Candice Randolph was simply out to get even, to get ahead, to use whoever necessary to acquire what she wanted—money.

Amanda suspected Candice had grown up poor, scratching, clawing, and scheming to elevate herself in society. To Candice, whatever means necessary justified the end—nothing short of, and including, murder!

"So who was it that Mickey Poag beat the crap out of for *you,* then served time in prison? Was it your father?"

Amanda saw the woman tense, saw her hands clench on the steering wheel until her knuckles turned white. The answer to Amanda's question was blatantly obvious. Candice hated men, had no respect or affection for them. No doubt those bitter, resentful feelings had taken root in her childhood. "I presume dear old Daddy liked to knock you around, and you finally had enough of that.

Since you were no match for his brute strength, you found yourself a boyfriend who was big enough and strong enough to take on dear old Daddy and give him the kind of beating you were forced to endure. Am I right, Candice?''

"Damn right," Candice bit off. "The sorry bastard had it coming, I tell you for sure. Mickey beat my old man to a bloody pulp, and that is the way I want to remember the son of a bitch, exactly as he was the last time I ever saw him. And if Mickey hadn't insisted that he swing by his house to pick up a few belongings before we skipped town, the law wouldn't have caught up with him.''

"So there you were, pregnant and without a place to stay. Your boyfriend was hauled off to jail for doing your dirty work for you," Amanda speculated. "I assume you grew up in small-town Texas, and being familiar with the dynamics of rural communities, you decided to lose yourself in small-town Oklahoma, while Mickey was serving his sentence.''

"Damn, Hazard, how the hell do you come up with all this stuff?" Candice snorted in disbelief. "Do go on. I'm curious to see how accurate you are.''

Amanda watched the electric poles whiz past the window as Candice sped down the highway. She took a deep breath and told herself to stay calm. She had been in these fixes before—though she had not gone into labor at the time of her previous investigative disasters.

Keep talking, Amanda instructed herself. *Keep Candice's mind off whatever scheme she plans to execute this evening.* Execute . . . Amanda wished she had used another word. That one made her excessively nervous.

"You came to Vamoose and started asking around town about the residents. I presume you were looking for a pigeon who would be susceptible to your scam of a paternity suit," Amanda speculated. "Odell Jarvis turned out to be the perfect pigeon. He was eaten up with self-importance, he was married, drank a little too much, and he came from money. All you had to do was pretend to enjoy fooling around with him a couple of times and presto! You could claim he was the father of your child. Either he paid up or you blew the whistle on him. With a sister like Nettie, who spent her life bailing out her irresponsible brother when he got himself in a bind, the situation worked out perfectly for you. . . . How am I doing so far, Candice? Still on the right track?''

"Impressive, Hazard. What a shame to have to *waste* that brilliant mind of yours."

Amanda didn't spend much time pondering the implications of the comment. She had to keep talking. It wasn't all that difficult to hold Candice's attention. It was glaringly apparent that the woman's favorite topic of conversation was herself.

"Because of Nettie's generosity, and her desire to spare her family public humiliation, she offered to pay your expenses when you left town to deliver the baby. Nettie also insisted on raising the child within her own family. I'm sure that suited you dandy fine, since you didn't want a kid anyway. You were eager to give up the baby for adoption, and you insisted on returning to Texas to live while waiting for delivery. It gave you a chance to visit Mickey in prison and tell him about the scam you had arranged to pay expenses until he was released. I'm sure he thought Vamoose was ripe for the picking and decided to set up housekeeping when he got the nod to walk."

"Yeah, the idiotic fool," Candice muttered. "I wanted to put Vamoose miles behind us, but Mickey's duty in prison was working the farm ground to raise crops for the inmates. He got hooked on the concept of becoming a self-employed farmer. Being an ex-con, he figured it would be difficult for him to find a decent job, so he bought some broken-down machinery, repaired it, and went to see Nettie about renting her land. He also had the stupid notion that he should hang around the area to see how our kid grew up."

"But parenthood and farming weren't in your future plans," Amanda guessed. "The kid didn't mean anything to you, and you found nothing glamorous and exciting about rubbing shoulders with cattle and driving tractors for a living."

"Damn straight," Candice confirmed. "I spent my childhood doing farm chores while dear old Daddy got liquored up and took his hangovers out on me."

"So you decided to take a new identity and leave Mickey to his plowing and his child watching."

"Exactly," Candice replied as she increased her speed. "I shook the dust of Vamoose off my heels and promised Nettie I would never come back if she loaned me enough money to leave the state and make a new start. I headed for Las Vegas—"

"And lost the whole bundle?" Amanda broke in.

"Well, what do you know, Hazard, you are finally wrong about something. The fact is that I made enough money to settle in Montana for a few years. When money got short I started caring for invalids, and I saw how the home-health care nurses operated. It wasn't long before I figured out how to falsify a nursing degree."

"So you took on the identity of a departed nurse," Amanda presumed. Geez, this lunatic stopped at nothing when she wanted to change locales and identities. Amanda was afraid to ask how that nurse in Montana ended up dead.

"Yeah," Candice said unrepentantly. "When I found a nurse to impersonate, I moved to Idaho for a few years."

"So what brought you back to Vamoose?" Amanda wanted to know.

Candice shrugged nonchalantly. "Call me sentimental—"

Amanda would never call this self-absorbed, bloodthirsty con woman sentimental!

"—but I wanted to see how my kid turned out. I had just planned to pass through, but old Nettie was ripe for the picking again. That little black book of hers was worth a fortune in blackmail money. I was able to look over her shoulder one day while she was jotting notes and I saw a few familiar names and knew I could make a killing. When I found out about that fatal traffic accident that Odell was involved in, and that business about Nettie having a secret lover who falsified my kid's birth certificate, I knew I would be set for life."

"So you coerced Mickey Poag into helping you with the scheme, because you knew he was in hock to Nettie," Amanda said thoughtfully.

"Yeah, I knew I had to act quickly, because Nettie got upset when she saw me hunting for that journal. She threw a fit and threatened to have me dismissed from the health care staff."

"I expect that since Mickey had gone straight for so many years he didn't want to get involved and didn't want the scandal in his past exposed, right?"

"Right," Candice replied. "But I made sure he knew I would leave him between a rock and a hard spot if he didn't cooperate. I took care of Nettie in the house; then Mickey hauled her outside to stage the scene of the accident."

"Then you had no more use for a man who had developed a bit of a conscience over the years," Amanda said grimly.

"You didn't expect me to leave that sap alive, did you?" Candice asked, then smirked. "And if you hadn't been wearing that billowing costume and flicked on those lights behind the stage, you would already be dead and we wouldn't be having this conversation right now, Hazard."

Amanda realized that this balloonlike costume had made it difficult for Candice to get a direct hit with her hypodermic needle. If she had been wearing a close-fitting costume she would have been stuck for sure and certain.

"But I guess when it comes to disposing of you, one place is as good as another. Actually, things worked out better this way. Everybody in that podunk town will be frantically searching for you, instead of me. That distraction will buy me time to get the hell away from here." The witch smiled nastily. "It won't be long now, Hazard, and the suspense will be over."

Amanda fell silent when another nerve-tingling spasm axed through her. *Oh, brother, that one really hurt!* She was in serious trouble here!

NINETEEN

Amanda slouched on the seat and sucked in a breath as quietly as possible. She didn't dare let Candice know what bad shape she was in! Were these pains the real thing? Or just the Braxton Hicks false contractions that Thorn had mentioned when he rattled off all that prenatal information to her? Amanda sincerely wished she had paid more attention while Thorn was lecturing her. She had erroneously assumed she would have time to sit down and read up on labor and delivery. She had planned to, really she had.

Amanda felt sweat break out on her forehead and she pulled frantically at the tape that bound her wrists. Geez, not here, not now! she thought desperately.

When the spasm tapered off and the tightening sensation in her abdomen eased, Amanda forced herself to think rationally. She had to come up with a plan before the twinges became even more intense, making it impossible for her to focus on anything else.

How far apart were the darned things? Amanda wasn't sure. She'd had entirely too much on her mind all evening to time them. She had probably been in a state of denial the whole day. She hadn't realized what was happening—had tried to wish the pains away—but now it was too late.

Amanda drew a bracing breath and wrenched her hands this way and that, trying to loosen the tape handcuffs.

Amanda noticed that Candice had veered off the state highway and was headed east. Apparently Candice's destination was Nettie's abandoned farm. If Candice stashed Amanda in Pumpkin Hollow her body might not be discovered for days, weeks maybe. She had the unmistakable feeling that Candice had decided to toss her into the crumbling storm cellar behind Nettie's house and let nature take its course.

Really frantic now, Amanda twisted her hands until they were raw, until her muscles burned from the exertion of trying to free herself.

By the time Candice stamped on the brake and stopped beside Nettie's house, Amanda had managed to pull her right hand loose. When Candice put the car in park, Amanda gritted her teeth and strained against the tape. She had to get loose! She was running out of time!

"Sit tight, Hazard. I'll be back in a minute. Your wait is almost over."

Candice opened the door and stood up. Amanda yanked hard—her arm nearly came out of its socket—but she freed her left hand the split second after Candice closed the car door.

While Candice hiked off to open the rickety wooden door to the storm shelter, Amanda bolted upright, clanking her head on the roof of the car. Whimpering, she doubled over the front seat to press the button for the automatic door locks.

This was going to work; it had to! she told herself as she flung a leg over the front seat, then slithered ungracefully beneath the steering wheel. Hurriedly, she switched the wheel into a higher position to accommodate her oversize tummy. If her luck held, she could shove the idling car into reverse and lay rubber before Candice realized Amanda was making her getaway.

Wincing as another stab of pain expanded and intensified, Amanda mashed the accelerator and threw gravel. She grabbed the little black book Candice had left lying on the front seat and crammed it into her pocket. No way was anybody else going to get their grubby hands on that journal!

"Hey! Damn you!" Candice raged as she lurched around, then charged toward the car. "Come back here!"

"Yeah, right." Amanda snorted as she shot backward down the driveway.

She didn't bother to stop to throw the sedan into drive when she reached the road. She wasn't giving Candice the chance to launch herself at the car or break out a window and make a grab for her escaping captive.

"Ow!" Amanda sucked in her breath when another pain plowed through her. Sweat dribbled down her forehead and burned her eyes, impairing her vision.

Veering from one side of the road to the other, kicking up dust that made it difficult to see where she was going— backward!—Amanda attempted to keep the car between the steep ditches. One miscalculation and she could lose control and end up in the ditch. Then Candice would overtake her, and it would be all over but the shouting.

Only when she had outdistanced Candice by a quarter mile did she take time to stamp on the brake and attempt a U-turn on the gravel road. Candice was still coming on strong, shaking her fist in fury and cursing up a storm. Amanda's pulse was racing a mile a minute by the time she got the sedan turned around and progressed forward rather than backward.

Gunning the engine, Amanda whizzed away, leaving Candice to eat dust and spit gravel.

"Free at last . . . Ouch! . . . Damn, that hurts!" Amanda hissed through her teeth when another contraction pummeled her. The pressure in her lower back was making her nauseous. Tears flooded her eyes and dripped down her cheeks. Sweat poured down her spine, and her skin felt cold and clammy.

Amanda told herself to get a grip. She *was* in labor, wasn't she? False labor pains weren't supposed to feel *this* real, were they? Damnation, why hadn't she taken time to read those blasted manuals? Then she would know what was happening. But no, she thought she would have time before D day arrived. Well, this was what she got for thinking!

"Oh, shiiit!" Amanda gasped when another contraction hit her full force.

She panted rapidly and kept her hands clamped on the steering wheel. She refused to stop the car and wait for the pains to pass. Candice was not going to have the opportunity to recapture her!

Okay, okay, Hazard. Just calm down. Get hold of yourself. You can handle this. Pain or no pain, just keep driving.

If only Thorn were here, she thought as she wiped at the sweaty tendrils of hair that drooped over her eyes. Thorn would know what to do. He was more prepared for the delivery than she was. If only she could get in touch with him . . .

The cell phone! Amanda suddenly remembered she had stashed her brother-in-law's cell phone in the deep pocket of her costume. Hand shaking, she leaned onto a hip and thrust her hand into the pocket to retrieve the phone.

What was the number? Hell, she'd called it a hundred times. Why couldn't she remember it now? "Think, Hazard! You can do this. You *have* to do this! What the hell is the number?"

A dozen phone numbers buzzed through her frantic mind before she finally settled on the right one. Amanda punched in the numbers and waited for what seemed minutes before Janie-Ethel finally picked up.

"Vamoose police."

"Janie-Ethel, *now* I am having the baby!" she yelled. "Get hold of Thorn quick!"

"Okay, okay. Don't panic, Amanda. Everything is going to be fine."

"No, it isn't," Amanda yipped. "I'm having another pain—Oh, shit, that really hurts. Get Thorn here. Now!"

"Where are you?" Janie-Ethel wanted to know.

"I'm a mile from the state highway, driving a dark-colored sedan. I can't stop because there's a maniac killer on foot who is trying to catch up to me. Tell Thorn that I'll take the highway—Ow!" Pant, huff, gasp. ". . . to the hospital and he can catch up with me."

"Not a good plan, Amanda," Janie-Ethel came back. "You shouldn't drive on the highway when bombarded by labor pains. You might have a wreck. Cross the highway and go a mile west; then turn north. Stay on the gravel roads so you can pull off in case the pains get too intense."

"*Get* too intense? Hell, I can't imagine how they can get worse than they are now!" Amanda howled.

"Just relax, Amanda," Janie-Ethel cooed. "Take deep, panting breaths when the contractions hit. I'll give the chief your cell phone number so he can call you right back, okay?"

"Fine, great."

Amanda held the phone up to the dash lights to see the numbers, then repeated them to Janie-Ethel. "Now tell him to hurry!" she all but screamed before she switched off the phone.

Nick jerked upright when the mobile phone that was still clamped in his fist jingled.

"Thorn here."

"Chief, I just got a call from Amanda," Janie-Ethel said hurriedly. "She's in labor!"

"Oh, God. Ohhh, God!" Nick wailed. "Is she okay? Where the hell is she?"

"She is northbound on the gravel road one mile west of the state highway. She's driving a nondescript sedan and she says there is a lunatic on foot giving chase, so she is afraid to stop until you catch up with her."

"She's driving while she's in labor? Holy hell!" Nick wheezed.

"Here's her number. I told her you would call her right back."

Janie-Ethel gave him the number. Nick repeated it over and over while he hung up. Then, with hands trembling, he dialed the phone.

"Thorn? God, that had better be you!" Hazard howled.

When her voice hitched and she whimpered, Nick panicked. "Honey, are you okay? Is it bad?"

"No, I'm not okay, and it's terrible. This hurts like—ouch—hell! Argh. Damn you, Thorn!"

"Damn me? What did I do?" he asked, dumbfounded.

"This is all your fault. I hate you. I hate all men everywhere. Don't you dare—ow!—come near me ever again. Ouch! Hurry up and get here. I can't stand this much longer!"

The woman was hysterical, Nick realized. He waved his arms in frantic gestures, motioning Zorro to him; then Nick cupped his hand over the mouthpiece of the phone while Hazard exploded in another tirade of earsplitting oaths. If she had left out any of the common curses Nick could not imagine which one it might have been.

"Hazard is in labor. Go get my truck. It's parked behind Thatcher's service station," he told Zorro, then turned his attention back to the phone. "Yes, I heard you, Hazard. I know I'm an absolute jerk. You wouldn't be suffering through this agony if we hadn't fooled around. Yes, I should be there with you. And I will be as soon as Zorro brings my truck."

When Zorro took off at a dead run, Nick motioned to

his brother and the other OSBI agents. Hazard was still cursing him up one side and down the other for being male—the unforgivable sin for which she swore he could never atone.

"Hazard," Nick said, breaking into her ranting and raving. "Calm down for just a minute and tell me where your kidnapper is. I'm going to send Rich and the agents to pick her up."

"Near Nettie's hou—ow—se! She's wearing a witch costume. Ouch!"

"Okay, now breathe, Hazard. Just like the books said to do. Remember?"

"No, I don't know h-how," she yowled. "I-I never found time to read the d-damned books. Argh!"

Again Nick covered the mouthpiece and gave Rich directions to Pumpkin Hollow. Hazard raved on.

"I'll get a helicopter to commandeer the manhunt," Rich volunteered, then wheeled away. "Don't worry about a thing, bro. You take care of Hazard and I'll apprehend that maniac kidnapper."

"Thorn. Are you there? Hello? Ouch! Hello?"

"I'm here, sweetheart." Nick raked a shaky hand through his hair and tried to think past his throbbing headache. "Now, let's start breathing together, sugarplum. Ready?"

"Are you kidding? I can't breathe! The contractions hurt too damn much."

"Yes," he said firmly, "you can, Hazard. Breathe in." Nick sucked in a loud breath. "Now breath out slowly, deeply." He *whoosh*ed into the phone for Hazard's benefit. "Now relax and give in to the pain."

"You're so good at this that you should be having the baby," she snarled at him.

"Remain calm, honey. Zorro is here with my truck. I'm walking toward him," he said, giving her a blow-by-blow account.

"Run, Thorn, run!" she railed at him.

Nick jerked the phone from his ear when her voice broke the sound barrier and ricocheted around his sensitive skull. "Okay, I'm running." His head thrummed with each jarring stride, and for a moment Nick thought he was going to black out.

In the distance Nick heard the microphone on the stage squeal. Then Billie Jane Baxter's nasally voice called out loudly. "News flash, y'all! Hazard is on her way to the hospital to have Thorn's baby!"

Nick scowled. Obviously the police dispatcher had passed along the word, and news had spread through the crowd at the street dance like wildfire.

"Thorn!" Hazard screeched in his ear.

"I'm getting into the truck," he assured her. "Zorro flicked on the emergency lights so you can spot us when we drive up behind you. I'll be there as quick as I can, sugar."

"Do not call me, sugar, damn you! I'm about to die and you don't even care. . . ."

When Hazard broke off into a bloodcurdling wail, then snorted and hiccuped, Nick's gut clenched. He was beginning to wonder if it would be easier to suffer Hazard's contractions himself rather than listen to her howl in torment. She had no idea what this was doing to his nerves. They were snapping like strands of rope. He felt utterly helpless, and every bit as tormented as she was.

Resolutely, Nick reminded himself that the prenatal manuals stressed that a father could not allow the mother's screams to rattle him. But damn, that was easier said than done!

Zorro put the pedal to the metal and roared down the street. When he reached the highway the speedometer hovered at eighty-five. Zorro stared intently at the road through his black mask while Nick tried to console Hazard over the phone. She erupted in another string of obscenities, then cursed him to hell and back—twice.

"There she is," Zorro said as he sped down the gravel

road. "She's right up ahead with her emergency lights flashing. . . . Oh, hell, I'm wrong. That's a pickup and trailer."

As Zorro slowed down to pass, Nick noticed the local farmer had stopped to jack up his truck after blowing out a tire. It was second nature for Nick to stop to help, but Hazard's emergency took precedence tonight.

"That must be her up ahead," Zorro said a minute later. "Lordy, she is driving all over the road. Tell her to pull off."

"Hazard, pull off. We are right behind you," Nick repeated.

Before the truck rolled to a complete stop, Nick opened the passenger door and hit the ground running. Zorro pulled in front of the sedan so he could lead the way to the hospital.

"About time you got here," Hazard said, panting as she sidled from beneath the steering wheel.

Nick sank onto the seat and stared into Hazard's bloodless face—a cadaver had more color. Her orange-tinted hair was a mass of curlicues around her face, and her sweaty bangs stuck to her forehead. The tears she had shed caused the black eyeliner to smudge her cheeks and jaw. She had wiped her eyes, smearing black makeup like Indian war paint. She was holding her tummy with one hand and frantically groping for his arm with the other.

Nick swallowed hard. Hazard looked like she had been through hell—and then some.

The instant Hazard grabbed his forearm, her nails clenched in his skin like bear claws. She squeezed hard enough to draw blood, but Nick refused to howl in pain.

Hazard was howling loud enough for both of them.

"We aren't . . . oh, geez! . . . going to make . . . it," Hazard said through clenched teeth.

"Of course we are," Nick said with a confidence he didn't feel. He was a nervous wreck, sporting a super-duper-deluxe headache that exploded through his skull each time Hazard wailed in pain.

He shoved the sedan into gear, checked the rearview mirror, then laid rubber.

"No more babies, Thorn," Hazard said as she squeezed his forearm in two. "This is it. I'm never going to do this again, *ever,* so don't even ask!"

He told himself that Hazard's declaration was pain-generated. "Maybe when this is all over—"

"No!" she refused, then yapped when a contraction ripped through her. "If you want more kids, then you'll have to figure out a way to have them yourself. Promise me, Thorn . . . ohhh, geeezzz . . ."

"Okay, I promise," he said hurriedly. "Whatever you say, Haz."

Nick forced himself to pay attention to his driving, but Hazard's death grip on his arm had cut off the circulation and he was very conscious of her pain—and his.

When the lights surrounding the hospital came into view, Nick sighed in relief. "Almost there, darlin'. Just hang on. It won't be much longer."

"Hurry the hell up!" she shrieked, then flopped back against the seat.

Nick knew he was not going to survive this. His heart rate and blood pressure were going through the roof. He was hyperventilating. By the time he ground the car to a halt in front of the emergency entrance, he could barely draw breath.

Commissioner Harjo, still dressed in his Zorro costume, yanked open the passenger door, then froze to the spot when he saw the condition Hazard was in. "Oh, my God! What happened to her?"

"I'm having a baby, you idiot," she said in a snarl to Zorro. "What the hell do you think happened to me?

Now get me the hell out of this car—ooowww!—and be damned quick about it!''

Zorro swooped down to scoop her up. She whacked him on the shoulder, then soundly cursed him for being born a male.

Nick dashed forward to open the door and found Doc Simms, wearing his scrubs and squeaky Reeboks, smiling in greeting. A nurse waited beside the physician with a wheelchair.

"Hi, Hazard. The dispatcher called to say you were on your way," Doc Simms said as Zorro carried Hazard inside, then gently placed her in the wheelchair.

Hazard frowned darkly at the physician. "What are you smiling about? You think this is—ouch!—funny?"

"Not at all, dear girl. But I have been through this hundreds of times."

"No, you haven't," she said in a growl. "You men have no idea what this is like!" Her voice ricocheted off the walls and echoed down the hall. "These contractions are off the charts!"

Nick smiled apologetically at the physician. "Sorry, Doc. When Hazard ain't happy, ain't nobody happy. And she definitely ain't happy now."

"That's quite all right. She does have a point, you know. We men have no idea what she's going through." He smiled sympathetically at Hazard. "We're going to get you to your room and hook up the electronic fetal monitor. We will be there with you every second."

Hazard latched on to Nick's hand as she was wheeled away. She practically pinched off his fingers when another contraction slammed through her.

"My goodness," Doc Simms exclaimed. His eyes widened as he picked up his pace and jogged down the hall. "You really did cut it close, didn't you, Hazard?"

"You thought I was exaggerating? I never exaggerate." She snatched in a quick breath and braced herself. "Damn, here it comes again. . . .''

Nick pried his hand loose from Hazard's and clung to the doorjamb for support. His head was pounding like a tom-tom. He had to get a grip on himself before he walked into the birthing room!

TWENTY

The cell phone in the pocket of Nick's Lone Ranger costume jingled abruptly while he clung to the door for support. He pried one hand off the doorjamb to grab the phone.

"Thorn," he said shakily.

"Nicky, it's your bro."

In the background Nick could hear the whir and thump of helicopter blades, indicating that Rich was still searching for Candice Randolph.

"What's wrong?" Nick demanded.

"Somehow or other our suspect eluded us."

"What!"

"Yeah, that's what I have been saying for the past half hour. We are using night-vision goggles and heat-seeking electronics. We have two ground units combing the area. Not only is that woman a mistress of disguises, but she is an escape artist deluxe. She must have stolen a vehicle and sped off while we were en route. Do you know who lives near Nettie's place?"

"Mickey Poag, the deceased," Nick muttered. "She

must have taken his wheat truck. If Mickey followed my practice of leaving the key in the truck, she could have confiscated the vehicle without much trouble.''

"That must be what happened," Rich replied. "Clever as that maniac appears to be, she probably ditched the truck for another vehicle the first chance she got. She is making it difficult for us to track her."

"Keep looking," Nick ordered.

"I plan to, but I wanted to update you so you can keep your ears open and your eyes peeled. No telling what that lunatic female will do and where she might turn up."

"Well, hell," Nick muttered.

"Is Hazard doing all right?" Rich asked anxiously.

"Screaming her head off and cursing me with every other breath," Nick reported.

"Understandable, considering that she's about to deliver. Call me when the baby gets here. Don't let your guard down, not even for a minute. Hear me? I don't want our suspect to sneak into the hospital and try to retaliate because Hazard spoiled her murder and blackmail operation."

Neither did Nick.

Damn, that was all he needed right now—a murderer hell-bent on revenge, Nick thought as he pocketed the phone. He had already stressed out when he couldn't locate Hazard earlier that evening. He had teetered on nervous collapse when he heard her wailing in pain over the phone. Seeing her reduced to agony, tears, and curses in the car had sent him reeling. His emotions had been sucked dry. He was holding himself together with only a few frazzled nerves. He had to compose himself, had to make a strong, supportive showing in the delivery room.

Nick dragged in a cathartic breath and pushed upright, but the sad truth was that he was whipped, and he didn't know how much energy he had in reserve.

"Thorn, you wimp! Get in here now!" Hazard yelled at him. "I don't want to do the rest of this by myself!"

Nick swallowed hard and wobbled into the room. He could endure, he told himself. He was a tough, macho cop. He had seen just about everything humanity could do to one another. He had been in and out of hot water so often in the line of duty that he had felt like a load of laundry. He had been beat up, knocked down, stomped on, and shot at. He could handle this, no sweat. . . .

He glanced at the electronic monitors that beeped and flashed. He saw the color drain from Hazard's face again, and he felt his knees fold up like lawn chairs. . . .

"Oh, hell! Nurse, call some of the orderlies. We've got a man down!"

Doc Simms's voice, coming from what sounded like a long, winding tunnel, was the last thing Nick heard before he did the unforgivable and passed out.

Nick awoke to find himself slouched in the lounge chair beside Hazard's hospital bed. Dr. Simms and his nurse were hovering over Hazard. Her pitiful moans and groans prompted Nick to shake the haze from his brain and sit up straight. He clamped his hands around the armrests of his chair when he heard a squall that overrode Hazard's long, drawn-out groan.

"Ah, here we go. The first one is a boy," Doc Simms announced.

"The *first* one?" Nick bleated.

"Oh, that's right. I forgot that you wanted this to be a surprise." Doc Simms's eyes twinkled above his mask.

Hazard, her face drenched with perspiration, her white knuckles locked on the metal bars beside the bed, glowered at him. "Surprise, Thorn." She hissed her breath through clenched teeth. "Twins. Boys. I hope the hell you're happy!"

Nick's eyes rolled back in his head. He fainted a millisecond after Doc Simms delivered the second squalling baby boy. The last thought to cross his mind, before the world turned black, was that his kids definitely had Hazard's lungs and vocal volume.

Sunlight spilled through the blinds covering the window, reminding Amanda that she'd had very little sleep the night before. Lord, she was tired. Delivering babies was exhausting work, and she didn't dare look in the mirror to see how awful she looked.

She stared across the room to see the two sleeping babies wrapped tightly in receiving blankets, wearing powder blue stocking hats. No matter how much hell she had been through, no matter how bad she looked, it was worth it.

Amanda shifted on the bed, then muttered to herself as she rearranged the hospital gown that granted little modesty. She would be glad when Thorn arrived with her suitcase so she could change into a gown that wasn't split down the back.

Amanda glanced up when the door creaked open. Thorn strode in, toting her suitcase and two bouquets of roses. She had forgiven him for fainting—after she was coherent enough to recall that poor Thorn was still recovering from a mind-boggling concussion and an injection that left him temporarily comatose.

Thorn, however, had been thoroughly embarrassed and had yet to forgive himself for drifting into la-la land while she was delivering the twins. Refusing to meet her gaze, he placed the flowers on the bedside table, then sank meekly into the same chair where the orderlies had planted him after he collapsed.

"Hazard, I'm so damn sor—"

"If you apologize one more time I am going to strangle you, Thorn," she cut in. "Now tell me how the Rumleys are doing."

"They are down the hall, recovering nicely," he mumbled, head downcast. "They will be released this afternoon." He glanced toward the third bouquet of flowers in the corner. "Who brought those to you?"

"Philip Arthur Darnell," Amanda replied. "He turned out to be Pad, in case you hadn't figured that out yet. Phil was immensely grateful that I solved Nettie's case, not only for Nettie's sake, but because he was about to become one of Candice's blackmail victims."

Amanda didn't bother mentioning that Darnell was the physician who falsified the birth certificate twenty-five years earlier. The way Amanda figured it, Darnell was suffering enough. He had waited years so he and Nettie could be together. Now she was gone and he was left wishing he'd had the courage to publicly admit his affection for her years ago.

Amanda didn't mention the fact that Odell Jarvis was also to become a blackmail victim, either. There would be time enough later to reopen that traffic accident case that left Jim Foster dead. Amanda didn't know if the statute of limitations applied to the incident, but she intended to find out. If nothing else, the truth was going to come out. And for once Odell was going to own up to his reckless, irresponsible mistakes.

"Candice told me that she saw Nettie writing in her journal when she made her house calls," Amanda continued. "But Candice never could figure out where Nettie stashed the thing. Last Monday Candice came by earlier than usual and Nettie caught her rummaging through the house in search of the journal. The feisty old woman made the crucial mistake of confronting her nurse, never once realizing that it was the same woman she had paid off twenty-five years ago. Candice left the house, but she returned a half hour later to dispose of Nettie before she blew the whistle."

"In the meantime, you spoke to Nettie," Thorn presumed. "That was why Nettie was upset, why she wanted you to take the journal. She didn't want her nurse, or anyone else, to get hold of that black book.''

Amanda nodded. ''Once Candice took possession of that tell-all journal she had an extensive list of potential blackmail victims. She planned to prey on them after she relocated.''

''I wonder what happened to that little black book?'' Thorn mused aloud.

''It's in my pocket,'' Amanda informed him. ''I confiscated it when Candice stopped the car at Nettie's farm and climbed out to open the door to the storm cellar, where she planned to stash me.''

Before Thorn pressed her for details about last night's harrowing incident—and stressed himself out again— Amanda switched topics.

''Did Rich and his agents round up Candice?'' she asked.

Thorn squirmed uneasily in his chair. ''No. She managed to lose herself between the time you escaped and the time Rich arrived to attempt to track her down.''

Amanda gaped at him in alarm. ''You mean that lunatic is still running around loose?''

'' 'Fraid so. She swiped Mickey Poag's wheat truck. Rich found it abandoned in town. Deputy Sykes reported that Abe Hendershot was plowed over by a woman in a witch costume, shortly after the costume dance shut down for the night. The witch took his truck and roared away. But not to worry. Rich and his agents are standing guard around the clock at the hospital.''

''Because he predicts Candice is coming here to take her revenge on me?'' Amanda presumed.

Thorn nodded grimly.

Then suddenly an enraged screech resounded in the hall. Amanda bolted upright as Thorn launched himself out of the chair and barreled through the doorway.

''You stay here and protect those babies!'' Thorn ordered, then disappeared from sight.

* * *

Nick burst into the hall to see his brother battling a dark-haired woman in scrubs who had slammed him up against the wall with a gurney. She was ramming the metal frame of the gurney into Rich's abdomen repeatedly. When she jerked a hypodermic needle from her pocket and lunged at Rich, who was unable to get his hands on the pistol that was tucked in the shoulder holster beneath his jacket, Nick snarled to make his presence known.

Whirling, the woman turned to hiss, cackle, and screech at Nick while making stabbing gestures with her needle.

"Be careful," Rich wheezed as he pushed the gurney away and dropped to his knees, holding the private parts of his male anatomy that had been hammered at.

Nick could tell by the lack of color in Rich's face that the punishing blows had left him weak and light-headed. But there was no time to help his brother back to his feet. The witch wielding her hypo was jabbing at him each time he came within striking distance.

"I'll teach you to mess with me, you bastard," Candice said in a snarl as she darted around the hall like the crazed maniac she was.

Nick leaped back when the needle very nearly poked him in the arm. He shadowboxed this way and that, telling himself to be patient, to wait until Crazy Candice made a tactical mistake.

"I'll send you and that nosy wife of yours to hell," Candice said with a sneer. "Those brats of yours, too!"

She yanked off her black wig and glasses and hurled them at Nick. When he instinctively ducked, she lunged. At the last possible second Nick shifted sideways to avoid being stuck with the lethal injection. He kicked out his leg to trip Candice, but she bounded back to her feet as quickly as she had fallen. Nick couldn't get the drop on her while she was waving that damned needle in his face.

"Damn you," Candice spit hatefully. "You ruined everything!" Her eyes sparkled menacingly as she raised the needle like a dagger and plowed toward Nick with a full head of steam.

Nick decided it was now or never. With a growl he dropped into a crouch and launched himself at Candice's knees. She screeched furiously as she teetered off balance. Still spitting curses, she thrust her arm downward, trying to stab Nick in the back, but he shoved her arm away.

"Watch out, bro!" Rich wheezed as he crawled forward on hands and knees.

Nick grabbed Candice's wrist when she tried to stab him a second time. When she found herself restrained she bit down on Nick's shoulder. Woman or not, Nick struck out in self-defense. He jerked back before Candice could bite a chunk out of his flesh and slammed his doubled fist into her jaw.

A dull groan escaped Candice's lips and her arm went limp. The hypo dropped to the floor, and her head clanked on the tile. Panting for breath, Nick pushed himself into a squatting position to stare at the unconscious lunatic.

"Damn, that was close," Rich croaked as he sat down gingerly. "You okay, bro?"

"Yeah. How about you?"

"I guess I'll be okay in a few minutes," Rick said. "Man, that old battle-ax knows how to hit a man where it hurts the most. She kept ramming me with that gurney until I was on the verge of passing out."

Nick extended his hand, palm up. "I hope you have a set of cuffs on you. I won't trust this lunatic until she is tethered tightly and I've frisked her for more needles."

Rich reached into his pocket for the cuffs, then dropped them in Nick's waiting hand. "Fasten her to the gurney and I'll drag her sorry butt down the hall to the exit."

Nick secured Candice to the gurney, then pulled her limp body toward the exit at the far end of the hall.

"Thanks, Nick." Rich ambled uncomfortably down

the hall and forced the semblance of a smile. "I think I can handle it from here. I'll contact the other agents, and they can help me get this fiend incarcerated."

Nick stared down at the woman who had wreaked so much havoc in Vamoose. The thought of Hazard being held in this maniac's clutches gave Nick cold chills. He was damned lucky Hazard had managed to escape when she did.

Inhaling a calming breath, Nick rearranged his clothes, which had been twisted during his scuffle; then he turned toward Hazard's room.

Thank God the worst was finally over ... or was it? he asked himself when he saw the mob of people that cluttered the hall.

Amanda slumped against her pillow and breathed a relieved sigh when Thorn returned to the room ten minutes after he had charged off. If she knew Thorn—and she knew him exceptionally well—he had made short work of Candice Randolph, who had been hissing and shrieking like a banshee.

"Is everything under control now?" Amanda asked as she appraised Thorn's appearance.

A smile spread across his handsome face, making his brown eyes sparkle. "The witch is dead meat," he reported triumphantly. "My big brother became suspicious when a woman wearing a black wig, thick glasses, and scrubs tried to transport a gurney to your end of the hall. She went berserk when he waylaid her."

"So I heard. Was Candice packing a syringe?" Amanda questioned.

"Yeah, several of them, in fact," he replied. "She tried to stab Rich with one, but I had the distinct pleasure of confiscating the hypo from her."

Amanda studied him in concern. "She didn't poke you with it, did she?"

"Nope. She tried to stab me a couple of times, but I managed to tackle her. She didn't put up much resistance after my fist accidentally connected with her jaw."

"Accidents do happen," Amanda said, grinning. "Nice work, Thorn. I knew Candice wouldn't stand a chance against you. And now that she is in custody, I will be anxious to testify against her. When we're through with Candice she will be wishing she had never tangled with us."

Thorn ambled to the bed and braced his arms on the metal railing. "I don't want to talk about the case anymore. I'm certain justice will prevail and Candice will receive the severe punishment she deserves." He paused, then added, "I want to talk about you and me."

"What about us?" Amanda asked, bemused.

"Well, this is more about you than me," he amended. "You came through this ordeal like a trouper." He stared at the air over her orange-tinted head. "But I . . . failed you when you needed me most. You didn't even have the luxury of an epidural or any type of anesthetic during delivery, because we barely made it to the hospital in time."

"Tell me about it," she said caustically. "I remember every agonizing moment with vivid clarity."

"What I am trying to say is that I can handle just about anything in the line of duty, but seeing you in pain nearly killed me." He stared solemnly at her. "Don't you know you are the center of my universe, Hazard? When you're in pain I bleed. When you're hurting I die inch by tormenting inch."

Amanda gazed at him through a blur of tears. She had hoped the days of drastic mood swings were behind her. Apparently not. "Oh, Thorn, you are the dearest, sweetest man ever to draw breath!"

She flung her arms around him and hugged the stuffing out of him.

"I'm nuts about you, Hazard," he murmured against the side of her neck. "And those two boys of ours are the best-looking kids on this planet, maybe in the whole galaxy."

"No doubt about that," she agreed as they clung to each other.

"One more thing, Haz."

"What's that, Thorn?"

"We are going to be pretty busy raising these kids of ours, don't you think?"

"I expect so."

"You may have to cut back on your unofficial investigations," he said tactfully, then added. "At least until the boys start kindergarten."

Amanda smiled to herself. "Probably won't have any new cases turn up for years."

"Hopefully not."

"So we don't have a thing to worry about, do we, Thorn?"

Thorn drew back and eyed her warily. "You aren't ever going to back off, are you, Hazard?"

She batted her baby blues at him and flashed a smile. "A woman's gotta do what a woman's gotta do, you know."

"Yeah." He sighed, resigned. "I guess she does. Just like now. Better brace yourself, Hazard. Your mother and my mom are standing outside the door, itching to get their mitts on little Jake and little Matt."

Amanda groaned. The last time Mother and Mom were together, at the wedding, they had come to blows. There was no telling how those domineering women would act now that they were grandmothers. "You are in charge of mob control, Thorn," she commanded.

He snapped to attention. "Nobody, and I mean nobody, will harm one hair on those precious babies' heads."

"They're both bald," Amanda reminded him before he opened the floodgates to let the anxious grandparents— and the majority of the population of Vamoose—view the two young Princes of Wails.

Dear Reader,

Thank you for accompanying me on my latest escapade. I will be exceptionally busy in the next year, what with caring for these two little darlings and managing the accounting office. But rest assured that if crime threatens small-town America, I will be prepared to fight for truth and justice. Nobody gets away with murder on my turf—not if I have something to say about it!

Yours truly,
Amanda Hazard-Thorn, CPA